Her breathing grew shallow...

She was light-headed, on the verge of blacking out. Could a person suffocate from fear?

"Brooke, nothing bad is going to happen to you." His fingers curled around her wrist. His touch was light. Gentle. Soothing. "I won't let anybody hurt you."

She used to be the one to reassure victims. Now the tables had turned. If only she could go back in time, she'd change the event that had changed her. But that was impossible. Now she could only hold it together until the panic subsided.

Jared stroked her hand. Up close, his jaw looked wider and his lips fuller. She wondered how they'd feel pressed against hers. Would his kisses be slow, deep, thrilling—

"What are you thinking?" he asked.

Heat flooded her cheeks. She couldn't tell him that she was thinking about kissing him. Not when her worst nightmare had come true. Not when someone was out to kill her...

Dear Reader,

Have you ever been in the wrong place at the wrong time?

That idea, pushed to its extreme, fired up my imagination and inspired me to write *Risk It All*.

Brooke Rogers has a new career as a private investigator. The past she wants to forget has left her with trust issues and nightmares, but at least she's alive. Then she unknowingly sets foot on property owned by a mafia boss and is captured. Fortunately for Brooke, FBI agent Jared Nash is working undercover nearby and his conscience won't allow him to leave the gorgeous blonde in harm's way. After he rescues her, he has no desire to let her go. She's smart and feisty but also surprisingly vulnerable, and he is attracted to her far more than he should be. Jared accepts her offer to help him search for his missing brother, partly to keep her close and safe. He can tell some past event still haunts her, and the only way to gain her trust and unleash her passion is to reveal deeply personal experiences of his own.

I hope you enjoy Jared and Brooke's story of danger and passion.

Anna Perrin

RISK IT ALL

Anna Perrin

ISBN-13: 978-0-373-27948-7

Risk It All

This edition published by arrangement with Harlequin Books S.A.

For questions and comments about the quality of this book, please contact us at CustomerService@Harlequin.com.

Printed in U.S.A.

Anna Perrin grew up reading romances and thrillers, so it's no surprise she loves creating romantic suspense stories. She is a two-time Romance Writers of America Golden Heart Award winner, has a bachelor's degree in business administration and lives west of Toronto. Her favorite pastimes are spending time with her two terrific daughters and enjoying the crazy antics of her many pets.

Books by Anna Perrin

Harlequin Romantic Suspense

Risk It All

Harlequin Intrigue

The Enforcer

Visit the Author Profile page at Harlequin.com for more titles.

To Hayley and Julie, my amazing daughters
I feel so lucky and proud to be your mom

To Patience Bloom, editor extraordinaire
Your encouragement and suggestions
are truly appreciated

Chapter 1

FBI special agent Jared Nash shut off the industrial-grade mower he'd been using on the grounds surrounding the Sidorov mansion. Sweat trickled under his sunglasses while he scanned the sprawling front yard, the dense hedges bordering the property and the quiet residential street beyond. Nothing. No overt signs of trouble at all.

He blew out a frustrated breath. Two and a half long days of staking out former Russian mob boss Dmitry Sidorov in Langeville, a small city east of Columbus, had worn on his nerves. A year ago Sidorov had left Brighton Beach, the Russian mob's unofficial headquarters in the United States, after he had barely survived a spray of bullets. Since then he'd been living a quiet life, no longer involved in anything criminal, at least according to the organized-crime branch of the FBI. But Jared's younger brother, Steve, had mentioned

Sidorov despised him right before he had gone missing. Steve's connection to the former mobster was a mystery and the only lead Jared had, so he'd gone undercover to check out Sidorov.

He hefted the mower and dumped it into the open bed of the battered Green Thumb pickup. The truck and equipment, as well as the T-shirt he wore, were courtesy of a local gardening company whose grizzled veteran owner had been more than willing to cooperate, no questions asked, with a federal agent.

Parked next to the truck, a silver Lexus sedan gleamed in the midday sun. Jared had already taken a good look at its briefcase-carrying owner and memorized the license plate so he could check up on Sidorov's visitor later.

Out of the corner of his eye, he glimpsed the hired muscle, Sergei Latschenko, pacing the length of the tennis courts. He had spoken to the guy several times and learned Latschenko had recently quit smoking. Nicotine withdrawal was making him twitchy—and potentially dangerous, because of the Glock 19 semiautomatic pistol he carried inside his leather jacket.

Steering clear of him, Jared retrieved hedge trimmers and rawhide gloves from the truck. The four-acre estate, with its exotic flower gardens and expansive lawns, required a lot of upkeep. His calves and back still ached from hours spent yesterday digging yet another freaking garden and transplanting a dozen hydrangea plants. The lawn-maintenance-worker gig meant he was free to roam the property, but it hadn't allowed him access to the mansion, which was a serious problem. If he couldn't wrangle his way inside, how could he gain more intel on Sidorov?

He'd spent a wakeful night, considering and rejecting scenarios to gain entry to the place. With Latschenko and his gun patrolling the grounds, it was too risky to head inside uninvited. The occupants of the house included Sidorov, his twenty-two-year-old daughter and his housekeeper. The latter he'd met briefly, and he'd noticed her tentative smile and kind eyes. Instinctively, he knew she would be his way in if he could gain her trust.

Early this morning, he'd seen her struggling to carry a huge terra-cotta pot from the shed, so he'd stopped unloading bags of soil from his truck and gone to help. She'd immediately taken pity on his hot, sweaty self and waved him into the mudroom, where she'd handed him a cold can of cola from the extra fridge located there. When the phone in the kitchen had rung, she'd gone off to answer it, her slippers swishing on the tile floor. He'd taken the opportunity to steal into the main-floor office and install a bug. He'd been sorely tempted to flip through the file folders on Sidorov's desk, but decided that was pushing his luck.

Upon her return to the mudroom, the housekeeper had offered him a taste of her Russian cooking after his chores were done. The timing was perfect because he'd overheard Sidorov telling Latschenko they had a meeting across town in the afternoon. After he'd sampled the housekeeper's food, he'd find a way to remain inside, check out the contents of those folders and search the house.

He walked to the perimeter of the property and began trimming a long row of hedges. A few minutes later, his sense of unease returned. He stopped and looked back at the house. In the distance, a shadow moved under Sidorov's office window. Was it a shrub shifting in the breeze or the trouble his instincts had alerted him to?

Striding across the grass, he wished he was carrying his gun instead of hedge trimmers.

Brooke Rogers had no qualms about peering into strangers' windows, but she usually got paid to do so. Today was a freebie for her sister.

Thirty minutes after their phone conversation, Savannah's words still rang in her ears. "Trevor is cheating on me, Brooke."

"What? No way," she'd answered, her gaze skimming the final sentences of the document on her laptop, unconcerned by her sister's pronouncement. Savannah, affectionately called Chicken Little by family and friends, was a pessimist who predicted dire outcomes no matter how innocuous the circumstances.

"It's true. Trevor doesn't love me anymore."

"What makes you think that?" Brooke had stifled a yawn as she'd gazed longingly at the stairs that separated her main-floor work space from the second-floor living quarters of the house she rented. She'd pulled an all-nighter and had promised herself a well-deserved nap as soon as she had emailed this report to her client.

"He's been out late three nights this week, supposedly working, but I'm sure he's being unfaithful. He'll never admit to it, so I need you to get me proof—*photographic proof*—to throw in his lying face."

Brooke had winced at her sister's shrill tone of voice. "Didn't you tell me he got promoted at the bank last month? That probably explains his long hours."

"I can't believe you're defending him. You're not usually so trusting."

Absolutely true. Two years of spying on cheating spouses and tracking down deadbeat debtors had made Brooke pretty jaded. An occupational hazard of being a private investigator, she supposed. Was her brother-in-law screwing around? He didn't seem like the type, but she'd learned motivated adulterers were astonishingly devious. She hoped her sister was wrong, because Savannah would be devastated by that kind of betrayal.

What her sister had said next proved she was on the verge of losing it. "I followed Trevor's car to a lavish house in Langeville. I fully intended to make my presence known, but then I just couldn't ring the doorbell and meet my competition in person. I need you to get a photo of him with his rich lover so I can confront him."

She should have talked Savannah out of her craziness. Heaven knew, Brooke had years of practice dealing with her emotional sibling. But would reassuring words be enough to ease her sister's mind? For a day or two, maybe. Then her doubts would return, stronger than ever.

"You know about my miscarriages, Brooke. I can't lose Trevor, too." Savannah's voice had broken, the pain real this time, not a melodramatic ploy for attention, and Brooke knew she couldn't deny her request.

"Where are you?"

"At a coffee shop in Langeville."

Slurping down coffee and stress-eating a sour-cream glazed donut, Brooke had guessed, the caffeine and sugar aggravating her anxiety. "Go home," she'd told her sister gently. "I'll come, but I won't be able to concentrate if I know you're hovering somewhere nearby."

She'd jotted down the address, then promised to call later and give a complete account of her visit.

After quickly emailing the report to her client, Brooke had left Columbus and headed to Langeville's most exclusive residential community.

Her GPS had led her to a gray stone mansion with a multitude of elaborate columns, positioned at intervals along the front, and recessed niches, showcasing statues. On the top floor, a domed solarium let in sunlight from all directions. The impressive house and grounds had her whistling under her breath, but a familiar Lexus in the driveway confirmed she was at the right place. She parked her SUV several blocks down—in case Trevor happened to glance outside—and walked back.

Normally, she'd find a vantage point and rely on the sophisticated lens on her camera to capture details of her target's illicit encounter, but she couldn't be sure she'd wind up with the evidence that would reassure Savannah. No, this time she had to get up close.

Despite serious misgivings, she squeezed through a space in the hedges, then stayed near the cover until the house was only a short distance away. If caught trespassing, she'd have a heck of a time explaining her presence, but she'd made a promise to her sister and she couldn't break that promise. Two years ago, she could have flashed her Columbus Police Department badge, saying she was following up on a complaint from a neighbor, but her career had ended after she'd been shot. She still mourned the loss when she let herself think about it, which was almost never.

She slowed her steps next to a truck loaded with yard equipment, eyeing the house uneasily. Was her brother-in-law meeting with a bank customer? That was the most logical explanation. Anybody wealthy enough to afford this impressive place could demand special treatment and get it—unless Savannah's worries were valid and her husband was giving *very special* treatment.

The odor of cut grass tingled in her nose as she hurried across the manicured lawn. Spotting a window with open drapes on the far side of the house, she squeezed between several tall bushes, her sneakers sinking down into the rich soil of the garden. Unfortunately, the property sloped in such a way that, even at five feet ten inches, she wasn't tall enough to see inside. Muttering under her breath, she hoisted herself up and braced her left elbow on the window ledge. A quick look inside… and she was exhaling in relief. No sexual frolics were going on in the bookcase-lined room. Her brother-in-law, wearing a gray suit, his steel-rimmed glasses and a serious expression making him look every inch the successful banker that he was, sat on the visitor side of a mahogany desk, leafing through papers in his briefcase. The man behind the desk appeared to be in his late fifties with a hooked beak of a nose and a square jaw.

Clinging to the wall like a gecko caused strain in muscles Brooke hadn't realized she possessed. Her ponytail stuck to her hot neck, and her armpits became damp with perspiration. She lifted her camera and peered through the viewfinder. The stranger's nose made a clean, sharp edge, so she squeezed the shutter. Next she took a picture of Trevor with his papers.

Her supporting elbow and toes screamed in protest, but she blocked out the pain. One more shot with the two men in it, and she was out of here. As if she'd willed it, the older man came around the desk to stand beside Trevor. Excellent. This last photo should get rid of Savannah's suspicions about her hubby entirely.

The man pointed a gun at Trevor's head.

Oh God.

Her elbow gave way and gravity did the rest, dragging her down to the garden below. When her butt hit the ground, the discomfort hardly registered over the shock of what she'd witnessed and the terror of expecting a gunshot to ring out.

Her heart zigzagged like a rabbit in her chest. No shot yet. She dug around in her pocket. *Crap.* She'd left her cell phone in her car. No way to call 911. She crawled along the back of the garden on her knees, determined to put distance between her and that window, then broke through the bushes, her camera clutched to her midriff.

A low, masculine voice said, "What the—?"

With a sinking feeling, she looked up. In front of her stood a strapping six-foot-plus guy wearing grass-stained jeans and a green T-shirt stretched tight over impressive muscles. Mirrored sunglasses hid his eyes, a baseball cap covered his hair, and dark stubble shadowed his jaw.

"This is private property," he said, stating the obvious. "You're trespassing."

As she got to her feet, she eyed the Green Thumb logo on his T-shirt, which matched the one on the truck in the driveway. The guy was an outside contractor with no vested interest in who came onto the property. So why was he objecting to her presence? Unless he resented her scrambling around a garden he was paid to take care of.

"You have to leave," he insisted sternly. "Now."

The name *Joe* was stitched on his shirt pocket, and one gloved fist held a pair of heavy-duty, long-handled hedge trimmers.

Joe's bossy manner set her teeth on edge, but he still deserved a warning about what was going on inside the house. The image of her brother-in-law with a gun to his head had drained every drop of moisture from her mouth, so she had to wet her lips in order to speak. "You need to leave, too. It isn't safe here."

His sunglasses stalled on her mouth for a moment, then shifted downward to the camera in her hand. "What are you doing here?" he demanded.

"That doesn't matter. What matters is that I saw a man with a gun."

His body went rigid. "Where?"

"Inside the house."

"Inside?" The location of the gun seemed to surprise him more than its existence. Then he shook his head. "How could you have seen inside the house?"

"I climbed up on the window ledge," she admitted.

"Why?"

She frowned. "I don't owe you an explanation."

"You can answer me, or you can explain yourself to the owner," Joe said. "And before you decide, you should know that Mr. Sidorov is very protective of his privacy and won't be pleased to learn you're trespassing. Especially with a camera."

"Can you forget about my camera and focus on the gun?"

He eyed her skeptically. "You're probably mistaken about what you saw."

"I'm not mistaken," she said, though she wished she was. But the sight of that gun pointed at Trevor's head was an image she would never forget, even without the photographic evidence on her camera. "Can I borrow your cell phone to call the police?"

"I don't have one with me."

"Is it in your truck?" Without waiting for an answer, she headed in that direction, and he fell into step beside her.

"No, it's not in my truck."

Seriously? Who didn't carry a cell phone these days? Or was Joe lying so as not to get involved? "Look, Joe, maybe I was trespassing, but this is a life-or-death emergency. I didn't just see a gun. It was pointed at my brother-in-law's head."

His expression turned even grimmer. "Who is your brother-in-law? Why is he here?"

"I don't know," she admitted. She wanted to scream with frustration. Her heart was still racing, her stomach sick with fear, as she waited for the report of the gun. She hadn't seen a silencer on the barrel, so she knew if the trigger was pulled, she would hear the resulting shots. The absence of any such sound so far gave her hope. Maybe the home owner—Sidorov—didn't intend to kill Trevor. But, at the very least, he'd threatened him, and she'd feel a lot better when her brother-in-law was out of range of that gun and there were cops crawling all over this place.

The whole situation felt surreal, as if things could spin out of control at any moment. She had no idea what was going on in the house, why Trevor had come in the first place. Even if he was released unharmed, a crime had still been committed, and there should be consequences. "The police need to know about this, and I can prove what I saw." She patted her camera, grateful Savannah had insisted she bring it. “Please, loan me your phone.”

Joe shook his head. “I wish I could help, but Sidorov doesn’t allow outsiders to bring cell phones onto the property. He takes his privacy seriously, and his ban on phones is intended to prevent unauthorized photos of his property and his family.”

This time she believed Joe. She’d have to return to her car, use her own phone and pray the police responded quickly. She hated the idea of leaving the premises—it felt too much as if she was abandoning Trevor—but it was the only way to get the assistance he needed. She quickened her pace, cutting a path across the expansive lawn.

Joe’s long, muscular legs had no trouble keeping up with her. He spoke in a low voice. “There’s a security guard, Latschenko, who patrols the grounds. He’s new and eager to impress his boss. He was down at the tennis courts ten minutes ago, so hopefully you’ll miss him.”

And if she didn’t miss him, she didn’t want to think what kind of trouble would ensue. “Thanks for the warning.” When Joe stopped walking, she broke stride in confusion. “Aren’t you leaving, too?”

“Nah. I need this job. Latschenko likes to talk, so I’ll try to keep him occupied while you make your getaway.” His teeth flashed white in his tanned face, and then he veered off in the opposite direction.

Despite his initial bossy manner, Joe had turned out to be a surprisingly decent guy, she thought as she broke into a run. Her sneakers pounded across the lawn toward the driveway, her breath puffing in and out in controlled bursts. Within minutes, she'd be back at her car and the police would be on the way.

A man suddenly appeared from out of the shadow of the lawn-maintenance truck, looming in front of her and blocking her escape. "Stop," he ordered, and she had no choice but to obey or plow into him.

The guy was heavyset with acne-scarred cheeks and a fierce scowl. He must be the security guard that Joe had warned her about. She'd expected him to be wearing a uniform, so she was surprised by his black leather jacket, a choice which struck her as masochistic on such a hot summer day. Was that bad-to-the-bone thug style really worth the discomfort? Or was Latschenko dressed like that to conceal a weapon?

She quickly eased her right hand—the one holding the camera—behind her back, and not a moment too soon. The guard's gaze moved over her in a thorough, head-to-toe survey that made her skin crawl as if he'd touched her. "Who are you? Show me some ID."

"I don't have any with me." She'd left her purse locked in her car, wanting to keep her hands free to take photos.

"How long have you been here?"

"Uh, only a few minutes."

He pointed a finger at her accusingly. "Put both your hands where I can see them."

The camera. She pressed it harder against her spine, wishing she could make it disappear.

He unzipped his jacket. "Hands. In front. Now."

If she'd still been a cop, he wouldn't be talking to her with such disrespect. Or if he had, she'd have told him to watch his mouth and get out of her way. Unfortunately, she was no longer in a position of authority, and his uptight facial expression and body language told her he wasn't going to back down until she had complied with his demands.

As she moved her right hand with the camera into view, Latschenko's eyes bulged in their sockets, and he reached inside his jacket. She knew, with absolute certainty, what would be in his hand when it cleared the black leather, and she was right.

He held a semiautomatic pistol pointed straight at her.

Chapter 2

Brooke stared into Latschenko's cold eyes and remembered another time, another place, when she'd found herself staring into the barrel of a gun. Would today end the same way? With bullets ripping into her flesh? With her collapsing onto the ground and blood trickling out of her like water out of a leaky garden hose?

Latschenko's gaze shifted downward to the camera, then back to her face. "Damn, I thought that was a *gun*. What the hell are you doing here, lady?"

Fear clogged her throat like a massive rock, preventing her from uttering a word, a sound or even swallowing. She knew her silence would make this confrontation even more dangerous, but her vocal cords had shut down at the first glimpse of his weapon. She knew the damage it could unleash. She knew the physical agony that came with a gunshot wound and the mental terror of wondering whether it was severe enough to result in death.

He made an impatient gesture with the weapon. "Hand over the camera."

She told herself she had no choice, that he had the power to take it from her, so there was no point resisting, but anxiety had short-circuited her brain's signals to her muscles. Her arm wouldn't budge. She was paralyzed. Helpless. Useless. A complete disgrace to the profession she had once revered.

"Yo, Latschenko."

The yard-maintenance guy was back from the tennis courts, and his calm voice was at complete odds with the tense situation. Was Joe clueless or cocky, or a mixture of both? Given her current situation, Brooke didn't care. As she watched his tall, athletic figure stroll across the manicured lawn, she experienced a wave of relief so strong her legs nearly gave out. Surely, Latschenko wouldn't shoot her in front of a witness.

Joe spoke again. "What's with the gun? Why are you scaring my girl?"

"Your girl?" Latschenko sputtered. "What are you talking about? What the hell is she doing here?"

Joe continued walking until he stood next to Brooke. The mirrored sunglasses made it impossible for her to see his eyes, to gauge what he was thinking. With a half smile, he slung one heavily muscled arm around her shoulders and gave her a squeeze that felt oddly protective. He still held the hedge trimmers, which hung down beside his jean-clad leg. Heat radiated from his body, and the warmth seeped into her, easing her fear-induced paralysis. "She noticed I'd forgotten my lunch at home and didn't want me to go hungry."

"What about the camera?" Latschenko demanded.

Brooke stole a glance at the street. How good was Latschenko with that gun? It was harder than most people thought to hit a moving target. She flexed her leg, relieved to feel the muscles respond. Maybe she should run for it—

Joe's fingers tightened on her arm, a subtle warning not to do anything rash. "I told her about the terrific gardens here," he said. "I guess she wanted to take a few pictures."

She coughed to hide her surprise. Joe was the best liar she'd ever met. Better than her, which was seriously impressive, given her success at her job often depended on her ability to dissemble. She was only screwing up today because of that damn gun.

Latschenko's scowl intensified. "She came onto the property without permission and she brought a camera."

"That's my fault," Joe said. "I forgot to tell her about the rules here. She was only being thoughtful of her man. That's not such a terrible thing, is it?"

Latschenko's gun eased downward until it was no longer aimed at her torso. "No, more women should be like that," he agreed.

What a load of chauvinistic crap, Brooke thought. Did Joe really believe what he was saying or was it part of his boyfriend ruse? She supposed she shouldn't complain, as he was doing a good job of bonding with Latschenko, and that could work in her favor. Although being passive ran contrary to her nature, she decided to stay quiet and see if Joe could talk her way out of this mess.

The guard stuck his chin out belligerently. "In spite

of her good intentions, your girlfriend's coming here is a breach of security. I'm paid to make sure only people approved by Sidorov come onto the property."

"I get that, man. Totally." Joe's voice was mild and nonconfrontational. "It was a simple misunderstanding and won't happen again. Mr. Sidorov doesn't need to know she was ever here."

"If he finds out, it could cost me my job."

Joe's lips turned down, suitably chagrined. "You shouldn't get into trouble over something meaningless like this."

"No, I shouldn't."

"She was leaving when you stopped her. Let her go. Please."

Latschenko stared at Brooke for a long moment while she tried to appear apologetic and naively innocent. It wouldn't be the first time she'd made strategic use of the misconception many people had about blond hair and a low IQ. "I'm very sorry. I didn't mean to cause a problem."

The guard's expression became less fierce, his stance less intimidating. Mostly, he looked hot and irritated. The danger had seeped out of the situation, Brooke realized. He was going to let her go. *Nice work, Joe.*

Finally Latschenko spoke. "I need to check her camera."

Oh crap. This was bad. Very bad. Those shots of Sidorov couldn't be explained away, no matter what Joe or she said.

Once again, Brooke's fake boyfriend interceded on her behalf. "That's just going to waste time," Joe objected. "The longer she stays here, the bigger the risk your boss sees her and blames you."

The guy in leather mulled over Joe's comment, and his head began to nod in agreement. Then he suddenly seemed to reconsider, his face hardening in resolve. "If the camera shots are of flowers, she can leave. If they show anything else, Sidorov will have to decide what to do with her." His outstretched palm came toward her while the gun in his other hand prevented her from bolting.

Her first impulse was to hurl her camera onto the flagstones underfoot, which would smash the viewing screen. Unfortunately, that would only delay, not solve, the problem. The memory card would still be intact, and the images on it could be downloaded onto a computer.

Latschenko lifted his gun until the barrel was level with her chest. "Give me the—"

He didn't get a chance to finish his sentence. The metal blades of Joe's hedge trimmers cut through the air and slashed down on Latschenko's outstretched hand. The guard doubled over, clutching his injured hand against his groin while his weapon dropped near his feet. His cry of outrage warned he wasn't ready to give up, and with his head down like a bull, he charged his attacker. Brooke darted around both men and kicked the gun. It skidded across the grass until it lay out of reach.

Sidestepping him, Joe swung the trimmers again. This time they connected with the side of Latschenko's head. *Thunk.* The burly man pitched onto the ground, flattening a wide patch of grass.

Brooke stared at the unmoving figure, feeling a mixture of relief and horror. A little blood matted the hair at his temple. Was he dead?

Joe pressed his fingertips to the man's neck and answered her unspoken question. "He's okay, but he'll have a helluva headache when he wakes up."

That awakening probably wouldn't happen anytime soon. Latschenko looked to be out cold. Good. He deserved to feel some pain for threatening her, as well as stirring up the terrifying memories she wanted to keep buried deep down in her psyche.

Joe grabbed her arm. Hustling her over to the Green Thumb pickup, he shoved her into the cab from the driver's side and followed her in. As the truck reversed quickly down the driveway, the lawn equipment slammed around in the open bed of the vehicle.

Her mind couldn't let go of the image of Latschenko's gun pointed at her, primed to maim or kill her. Her new line of work wasn't supposed to expose her to life-threatening situations; that was one of the reasons she'd quit being a police officer. Her near-death experience and months-long recovery wasn't something she was willing to put herself—and her family—through again. But if Joe hadn't been holding the hedge trimmers and been willing to use them, she might be the one bleeding on the grass instead of Latschenko. Or alternatively, they might have been forced into a confrontation with Sidorov. If the home owner had discovered the shot she'd taken of him holding a gun on Trevor, she had no idea how he might react. Would he have been content to confiscate her camera's memory card, then release her and Joe? Or would he have decided they were witnesses who needed to be disposed of? And what about Trevor? Would their presence have endangered him even more?

When she'd agreed to Savannah's request to check up on her husband, it had seemed straightforward and simple, even silly. Instead, it had morphed into a dangerous incident that could have ended in multiple homicides.

Brooke managed to fasten her seat belt only seconds before a trio of familiar sensations hit her: a steel band squeezing her ribs, the runaway pounding of her heart and an overwhelming urge to throw up.

She closed her eyes, swallowed repeatedly and ordered herself to calm down. Naturally, that only exacerbated the problem, and her anxiety spiked higher. The truck lurched to one side, and she grabbed on to the dashboard to steady herself. Meanwhile, she kept up an inner reassuring dialogue. *This is nothing new*, she reminded herself. *You know what to do.* Sucking air deep into her lungs, she concentrated on a slow, even count. *One...two...hold. Three...four...release. Again.*

After several repetitions, her nausea retreated, and her heart settled into a rhythm that was still quicker than usual but no longer insanely fast. She released the dashboard and concentrated on keeping her hands open and relaxed on her thighs. As the panic attack gradually faded, awareness of her rescuer crept in. She thought about Joe's unruffled demeanor throughout their ordeal and the way he had disposed of Latschenko. No hesitation, no wasted moves, no excess force. Just ruthless efficiency. As if handling armed thugs was nothing new to him…

With the truck speeding down the road and her mind

rehashing everything that had transpired, she realized one undeniable fact.

She had trespassed in the wrong damn place.

As Jared drove the truck, every muscle in his body was tense with frustration. Usually, he found rescuing a victim from a dangerous criminal deeply satisfying and one of the reasons he stayed committed to his job despite the long hours, reams of paperwork and internal politics. Today, however, that satisfaction was overshadowed by anger and self-recrimination. His altercation with Latschenko had ruined his chance to search the house and possibly uncover proof Sidorov had been involved in his younger brother's disappearance. But what else could he have done? The blonde trespasser had been in imminent danger. Her survival had to take precedence over his original plan, which was a long shot born of desperation. That logic was inescapable to any reasonable person. So why did a niggling voice in his head question his motives? Why did it accuse him of placing the well-being of a stranger over that of his own flesh and blood?

No, that was ridiculous. Despite the fact that he and Steve had a complicated relationship, colored with anger and resentment and hurt, none of that had influenced his decision to run interference for the woman. He had made the right call, according to his training and conscience. The noise in his head was caused by worry and uncertainty.

Next to him, his passenger was hyperventilating, her rapid breathing audible in the confines of the truck. She was obviously terrified, and her reaction didn't surprise him. Latschenko was a tough, scary dude, and Jared didn't regret knocking him out.

When the woman had first crawled out of the garden, he'd known her presence was a complication he didn't need, but he'd been confident he could control the situation. Her claim that Sidorov had drawn a gun on his visitor had substantiated his suspicions the supposedly retired mafia boss hadn't completely walked away from his criminal past. Jared had warned her to make a speedy exit. Everything would have been fine if she'd moved a little faster or if Latschenko had been content to hang out a little longer at the tennis courts. The difference of a few seconds had proved disastrous, a point driven home when Jared had spotted the two facing each other, the guard's gun aimed at the blonde's slender stomach. He could have walked away from the situation, but he'd felt compelled to intervene. What if he hadn't? Would the woman have managed to escape on her own? Or would she have ended up like Steve—missing, with family members trying desperately to figure out what had become of her?

There was no point dwelling on what-if scenarios; he had to decide his next move based on what had actually gone down. He would take her to her car so she could contact the police, even though the last thing he wanted was lawmen swarming all over Sidorov's place. If the former Russian mobster felt he was under scrutiny by the authorities, he wouldn't go about his usual routine or take part in the candid, potentially incriminating conversations Jared had hoped to record on the bug in his office.

When his passenger's breathing had evened out and

she was no longer gripping the dashboard, he spoke to her. "Where's your car?"

She expelled a long breath. "A couple of blocks south of Sidorov's property. You'll need to circle back."

He glanced over at her. Strands of pale blond hair, shaken loose from her ponytail, hung straight and delicate as corn silk around her face. A deep blue, sleeveless top hugged the generous curves of her breasts, and faded jeans emphasized her narrow waist and extremely long legs. She possessed a spectacular body that had felt awfully good pressed against his side.

He returned his gaze to the road, checked traffic and made a U-turn. "What type of vehicle am I looking for?"

"A white RAV4." She shifted around in her seat, probably still feeling the lingering edginess of adrenaline. "Thanks for helping me. If you hadn't stepped in… Well, I'm not even going to attempt to finish that sentence. Do you always think really fast on your feet? That lunch-toting, garden-loving girlfriend story was darn creative, and you told it so convincingly it seemed like the guard was going to let me leave."

He slowed the pickup to allow a van to merge. "I figured it was worth a try, but unfortunately, Latschenko didn't quite buy it." He added, "What's your name?"

"Brooke Rogers."

"You said your brother-in-law was being held at gunpoint. What's he mixed up in?"

"Nothing."

"Are you sure?"

"Yes…of course." Her slight hesitation indicated a little less conviction than her first denial.

"Why were you looking in Sidorov's window?"

She muttered something under her breath that sounded like "neurotic sister."

He shot a sideways glance at her. "I didn't catch that."

"It has nothing to do with you." Pink infused her cheeks, a sure sign she was embarrassed, but he'd been trained to get all the facts, and he intended to keep after her until she came clean.

"I ran interference for you and nearly got shot. The least you can do is answer my question."

A dark green Ford Explorer switched into their lane without warning, forcing him to brake hard to keep from rear-ending it.

"My reason for being there is personal," Brooke said. "What were you doing there? Why were you pretending to be a gardener?"

He shot her an offended look. "What do you mean, *pretending*?" Bracing the bottom of the truck's steering wheel with his knee, he held up his hands to prove his point. "There's nothing phony about these calluses. I cut grass, trim hedges—"

"—and warn off trespassers, which I doubt is part of your job description," she finished for him. "You walked up to a guy with a gun like it was no big deal, you tried to use his fear of his boss to manipulate him, and when that didn't work, you got the drop on him." She paused. "You're an undercover cop."

He stiffened. "You've got some imagination."

"You insisted I leave because you didn't want me to come into contact with Latschenko, and also because I was distracting you from your assignment."

Damn right, she'd been distracting. Then again, any

man with a pulse would've had a tough time ignoring a woman whose face and body were more striking than any Hollywood starlet's.

"How long have you been watching Sidorov?" she asked.

He needed to shut down her curiosity, without letting her know she was on the right track. "Hey, I'm not watching anybody, Blondie. I get paid to do lawn maintenance, and that's what I do."

"Yeah, right. I don't want to seem ungrateful for your handling of Latschenko, but my brother-in-law is in danger, and I need to know what's going on."

He kept his eyes on the road and his manner benign. "I understand your concern, but I'm the wrong person to ask."

"I don't believe you. And until you admit the truth about why you were on Sidorov's property, I won't talk about my reasons for being there." She sat up straighter and pointed through the windshield. "That's my vehicle."

He checked his rearview mirror, then slowed the Green Thumb truck to a crawl while he scanned the immediate vicinity. There were no occupied parked cars and no one hanging around who could have her SUV under surveillance. Satisfied with his findings, he pulled to the side of the road opposite it.

The instant he parked, Brooke jumped out. As he joined her on the street, he noticed her top had slipped down, exposing pale pink bra straps and the upper swells of her breasts. His body hardened as if she were topless, which annoyed the heck out of him. Work boots clomping, he crossed the street ahead of her.

"What are you doing?" she called out.

"Making sure your SUV hasn't been tampered with. I assume you wouldn't want me to drive off and then discover you have a flat."

"No, that would be bad. Thanks." Her lips curved in a smile that shimmered through his body.

Whoa. That felt good. *Too damn good.*

He must have looked at her for a few seconds too long because her smile faltered as she stared back at him. What was she thinking? More important, what was she feeling? The same attraction he was?

Eventually, she cocked an eyebrow as if to say, "What are you waiting for?"

What, indeed? With her blond hair, long legs and dynamite figure, she must have guys gawking at her all the time. The thought that he was one of a crowd of admirers cooled his ardor like a few ice cubes tossed down his jeans, and he jerked his gaze away from her.

"Move your car after you call the police," he told her. "Latschenko might wake up and come looking for you."

While she unlocked the driver's door, he circled the vehicle, checking each tire in turn. At the last one, he leaned down and attached a GPS tracking device to the underside of the car. Now wasn't the time for a lengthy conversation, but he definitely wanted to talk to her again and check out the contents of her camera. Based on their earlier exchange, her cooperation was unlikely unless he produced his FBI credentials, which he wasn't in a position to do; he'd left them in his car at the lawn-maintenance company when he'd gone undercover. And there was another reason he needed to keep track of her. She was related to the guy in the suit who had been threatened by the Russian mobster he'd been watching. Maybe he could learn more about Sidorov by questioning her sister's husband.

Chapter 3

Brooke tugged her purse out from under the front passenger seat, where she'd hidden it, and dug around inside until her fingers made contact with her cell phone. As she touched the digits 911, a flash of silver in her peripheral vision caused her to look up from her phone. A familiar sedan had just reversed onto the street. *Trevor's car.* But was her brother-in-law behind the wheel, or was it someone else moving the Lexus away from Sidorov's property?

The front headrest obscured the identity of the driver, but then the brake lights came on, the car jerked to a stop, and the driver's door opened. A man wearing steel-rimmed glasses and a gray suit lurched sideways and vomited onto the asphalt road.

"Trevor," Brooke breathed, her forehead sagging against the steering wheel in relief. Had he escaped or been released? There was no way to know, but it didn't matter. All that mattered was that he was unharmed.

"This is 911 dispatch. What's your emergency?"

She jolted at the voice coming from her cell phone. She'd been so focused on the sedan and Trevor that she'd forgotten she'd placed the call. She started to answer, then hesitated as Joe's words played back in her mind. *What's your brother-in-law mixed up in?*

She'd been quick to defend Savannah's husband, but it had been a knee-jerk reaction. She didn't really know the man. He came across as a bland, unexciting guy, and, over the years, she'd come to appreciate his stability and even temperament because that was exactly what her volatile sister seemed to need. As for what he needed or wanted, apart from Savannah, she had no clue.

Why had Trevor met with Sidorov? If it had been a business meeting, why had they met at the Russian's home instead of at the bank? If it wasn't a business meeting…she didn't want to think about what it might have been. If she carried on with this call, she'd set in motion events over which she'd have no control, and those events would give rise to consequences she couldn't foresee. What impact would that have on her sister? She needed to talk to Trevor and understand the situation fully before she decided whether or not to involve the police.

"Do you have an emergency?" the calm voice prompted again.

Hoping she wouldn't regret her decision, she said, "Sorry, my mistake. There is no emergency." Then she hit End and tossed her cell phone into the cup holder between the seats. When she glanced up, Trevor's car door had closed, and the Lexus was pulling away from the curb. She watched the right signal light blink on and the vehicle execute the turn before she started her engine and followed.

Within the next few minutes, Trevor's erratic driving confirmed his attention wasn't on the road. He kept veering to the right, then swerving back to correct. If she hadn't known better, she'd have suspected he was drunk. Other drivers in his vicinity must have reached the same conclusion because a few hit their horns in angry response to his edging into their lanes. Finally, he seemed to gather his wits and drive in a competent fashion. The traffic was light at this time of day, forcing her to keep a considerable distance between them or risk being spotted. She wasn't ready to confront him yet. At this point, she preferred to stay back and keep tabs on where he was going.

It was quickly apparent his destination wasn't the local police station. If he'd intended to go there to report the incident with Sidorov, he would have followed the sign posted at the main intersection downtown, instead of driving past it. What was his plan? Would he return to the bank this afternoon? Given what had happened to him, it was hard to imagine he could be productive workwise. But where else would he go? Lots of men under stress would head to a bar and drink to forget their worries. Trevor never drank to excess at social gatherings, but today he might feel he had reason to make an exception. Or maybe he wasn't in the mood to drink in public. Maybe he'd stop in at a liquor store. His usual drink of choice was scotch, she remembered absently.

Up ahead, he blew through a stop sign, turned left

without signaling and then ran a red light. Horns blared, and two cars swerved to avoid hitting him. It was impossible for her to follow; the risk of getting T-boned in the intersection was too high. Sitting at the red light, waiting for it to turn green, she was only moderately annoyed she'd lost him. Trevor wasn't some stranger she was tailing who might disappear forever. She knew someone whose call he would always take, no matter how stressed or distracted he was.

Brooke pulled into a plaza, parked her SUV and opened the window of her vehicle to let in some fresh air. Then she pressed her sister's number on her cell phone. When Savannah came on the line, Brooke got straight to the point. "Trevor isn't having an affair."

"Are you sure?"

She wanted to yell, *Damn right, I'm sure*, but she curbed the urge to vent her frustration and answered quietly. "Yes, Savannah."

"Don't use that patronizing tone with me. You can't begin to understand how I feel. There's no one special in your life. No one who could break your heart."

Not anymore. Chad had dumped her a few weeks after she'd been shot. Brooke pushed away her own hurt to focus on her sister. "You'll wreck your marriage if you keep being jealous. Trevor doesn't deserve it."

"Yeah, well, it's hard for me not to worry. Women flirt with him all the time. It happened the other day in the grocery store. I came back from getting cereal, and some woman in a low-cut top and a skintight skirt is asking his opinion about melons."

Her sister's tendency to blow things out of proportion usually amused her, but not today. "I swear to you that his trip to Langeville today had nothing to do with a woman."

Silence on the other end of the line. Then a long sigh. "Trevor and I used to be so happy," Savannah said wistfully. "What's happened to us?"

Brooke felt a rush of sympathy. Her sister might be melodramatic, but she was really hurting and needed some encouragement to get through this rough patch. "Maybe you and Trevor should spend some time together and figure out how to connect again." Well, listen to her. Giving advice to the lovelorn when her only serious relationship had ended badly.

"I like that idea," her sister said. "Maybe we could go away somewhere."

Somewhere far away, Brooke thought suddenly. A place where they'd be safe from Sidorov, Latschenko and their guns. A plan began to form in her mind, and she spoke in the compelling voice she'd perfected during her stint as a police officer. "I need you to call your husband and tell him to meet you at—" she dipped her head to better see the red-and-white sign at the far end of the plaza "—Dean's Diner. Immediately. It's located in a plaza near Highland and Conestoga."

"Why? What's wrong?"

"I can't discuss it over the phone, but it's extremely important you get in touch with him and insist he do this."

"He won't answer his cell phone if he's driving, and even if he does pick up, he's not going to like being asked to come to some diner. He'll want to know why."

"Tell him it's an emergency and if he truly loves you, he has to come without knowing the reason. As for you, leave your house right away. I'll explain everything when I see you."

"Jeez, Brooke. You're starting to worry me, and that's not like you. You're the one always telling me to lighten up."

"Not this time," she said grimly and disconnected.

Satisfied she'd done all she could for the moment, Brooke gazed at the diner she'd decided on as their meeting place. She'd have preferred the comfort and privacy of her sister and Trevor's home, but she couldn't be sure it would be safe there. Who knew what Sidorov was capable of, especially after he discovered his security guard had been attacked?

She felt her eyelids droop and determinedly forced them back open. Her lack of sleep was making it hard to stay alert and focused. She needed a blast of cold water to her face and a jolt of caffeine to her brain, but the effort required to walk over to the diner seemed as monumental as running a marathon. A five-minute rest. That was all she needed. Then she'd push herself to keep going.

Jared approached Brooke's SUV from an angle with as much stealth as possible, considering he was still wearing work boots. The last thing he wanted was for her to notice him and take off out of the plaza parking lot. He'd already returned the Green Thumb truck, given its owner two hundred bucks and an apology for the complaint about him that would surely be forthcoming and picked up his own car, a blue Mustang.

When he drew level with the open driver window, he glimpsed Brooke slumped against the car door. His heart rate kicked up a notch, and his training took over; he reached inside the SUV and laid his fingers across the base of her throat to check for a pulse. Her skin was soft and warm from the sun, her heartbeat a steady rhythm.

She jolted upright and shoved his hand away. “Don’t touch me.” The alarm in her voice turned to confusion as recognition dawned in her eyes. “You! What are you doing here? How did you find me?”

He opened his mouth to answer her, but she didn’t give him a chance. “You couldn’t have followed me. I’d have noticed a Green Thumb truck on the road anywhere behind me.”

“I took the truck back to the lawn company and picked up my own car.” He pointed to his vehicle parked several spaces away.

Her eyes narrowed in suspicion. “How have you turned up here? That can’t be a coincidence.”

“I put a GPS tracker on your SUV.”

Her skin flushed with anger. “Okay, that’s creepy, but it also explains why you made a point of checking my tires. It was just an excuse to get close enough to my SUV to attach something. I knew that Boy Scout routine was too good to be true.”

“Sorry about the deception, but I knew I had to talk to you again.”

“As I recall, our last conversation ended because you weren’t being honest with me. If that hasn’t changed, then we’re done talking.”

Her blunt words didn’t surprise him. She seemed to be the type of woman who wouldn’t take crap from anyone. Normally, her straightforward manner would strike him as annoyingly brusque, but instead he couldn’t help admiring her guts. "Okay, let's start over. You were right. I'm not a gardener."

She looked pointedly at his Green Thumb shirt and grass-stained jeans. "Nice disguise. What's your name, and who do you work for?"

"Jared Nash. I'm a special agent with the FBI."

Her dark blue eyes shone with satisfaction. "I knew it. You were way too calm about Latschenko and his gun, and you lie really convincingly. Speaking of lying, I'd be naive not to ask to see some ID."

He retrieved his credentials from his jeans pocket and passed them over. She studied them carefully, then returned them to him.

"Now that we've established I'm not a creep stalking you for nefarious purposes, will you let me sit in your vehicle while we talk?"

She nodded, and as he moved to the passenger side of the SUV, he heard the door locks release with a click. Once he'd settled next to her, she asked, "Would you mind taking off those sunglasses? I'm tired of seeing myself in them."

He removed his mirrored glasses and tucked them in the neck of his T-shirt. "Is that better?" he asked, giving her a long, penetrating stare. Most people tended to shy away from his intent gaze, but not her. She didn't look away or even blink. Once again, he felt a grudging respect for her. Not that it mattered. He was here because she had information he wanted. "You said you were going to call the police. Did you?"

She shook her head. "I started to, but Trevor drove away, so I decided to hold off for a while. Now that I know the FBI is involved, I'm not sure if that's necessary. But before I decide what to do, I have a few questions. Why is Sidorov under surveillance?"

He was tempted to tell her it was none of her damn business, but if he wanted her cooperation, he had to give her something. "He's a person of interest in an investigation."

"What kind of investigation?"

The most important one of my life. Blocking out the sudden churning in his gut, he answered. "A man's missing, and Sidorov might be involved. That's all I'm prepared to say." Time to change the subject. "You mentioned you'd taken a picture of Sidorov threatening your brother-in-law. I'd like to see it."

"I haven't had a chance to check it out myself."

"Now seems like a good time to do that, don't you think?"

"I suppose so." She twisted around in her seat, her breasts coming within inches of his arm as she reached back for the camera. She didn't seem to notice, but he sure did. His heart rate picked up and the interior of the SUV began to feel like a sauna. He told himself she wasn't being intentionally provocative, but his body wasn't listening. It was enjoying the view too much.

When she settled back in her seat and rested the camera in the cradle of her thighs, he swore softly under his breath. Oblivious to his discomfort, she stared at the back of her camera with a frown, shifting closer to him to move out of the sunlight streaming through the windshield. She let out a frustrated sound. "It's too bright. I can't see the display properly."

He knew how to fix that problem. He reached over, cupping his big, wide hands over her smaller, narrower ones to make a better shield against the sun. Her closeness made him aware of her scent. It wasn't strong like perfume, more like a lingering soap or shampoo. Could it be watermelon? Yeah, that was it. He'd always liked the juicy fruit, and next time he ate some, he'd think of her.

Her startled blue eyes lifted to his. They maintained eye contact for a good long moment, neither one of them speaking. Eventually she fidgeted in her seat, and the camera shifted under their hands. "Look again," he murmured.

She dropped her gaze to the camera, then groaned softly. "The shot shows the gun, but Sidorov's face is so blurry it's unrecognizable. I can't believe I screwed it up."

"Don't be so hard on yourself. You were shocked by Sidorov's actions, which is completely understandable."

"Now I don't have proof of him threatening Trevor."

"I have some software on my laptop that might be able to sharpen the image." He breathed in her scent again before moving back to his side of the vehicle. "Why were you looking in his office window?"

"It has nothing to do with your investigation."

"That wasn't our deal. You said if I told the truth, you'd do the same."

She remained silent, her lips pressed together in annoyance.

Prepared to wait her out, he rolled down his window. Birds chirped in a sprawling oak tree close to the road. The smell of burgers grilling on a barbecue somewhere reminded him he hadn't eaten since early morning.

After a few minutes, his gaze strayed to his passenger. He took in her high, sculpted cheekbones, her thickly lashed eyes and her flawless skin. No doubt about it. Brooke Rogers was drop-dead gorgeous—and as stubborn as she was beautiful.

Eventually, she huffed out a breath. "Okay, I was there because of my sister. She has this crazy notion her husband is having an affair."

"With whom?"

She didn't offer up the culprit, so he threw out a few possibilities. "Sidorov's daughter? The housekeeper?" Another option occurred to him, and he figured he might as well voice it. "Sidorov himself?"

"Heavens, no," she sputtered.

"Tell me who she suspected."

"Savannah only gave me the address, not the name or description of Trevor's supposed lover."

"So you brought a camera along to get a shot of your brother-in-law and his lover together."

"My sister insisted," she admitted, "but I knew there wouldn't be any naked bodies cavorting about. Trevor's priorities are Savannah and his bank career, in that order."

A banker. Why had Sidorov pointed a gun at a banker? Had he lost money due to bad investment advice, or was he simply disappointed by the services he'd received? His reaction seemed extreme, but an ex-mafia boss might be accustomed to threatening those who didn't live up to his expectations.

"I want to talk to your brother-in-law. Find out why he met with Sidorov and what caused the guy to draw a gun on him."

"I've been wondering about that, too. In fact, I've arranged for Trevor and my sister to come to the diner in this plaza. It seemed safer than meeting in their home."

He couldn't fault her reasoning, given what Sidorov had done. "When do you expect them?"

"Hopefully within the next half hour or so. I figured I'd get a coffee while I waited for them."

"Good idea. Let's go."

They left her SUV and headed across the parking lot to the diner. Inside, the place had a late 1950s, early 1960s vibe going on. Oversize photos of movie stars and rock-and-roll idols of that era hung on the walls. The floor was black-and-white tile, and red vinyl covered the chair seats and booth benches. The place was nearly empty, the lunch crowd having already cleared out, and the jukebox in the corner quietly played an old Elvis song.

Brooke excused herself, pointing to the restroom sign. "I'll be back in a minute."

Jared headed for a booth near the back of the diner, wanting privacy for the upcoming conversation with Brooke's brother-in-law and his wife. A waitress came over, dressed in a white cotton blouse, short flared skirt and ankle socks. She gave him a friendly smile, even though he saw signs of fatigue: dark circles under her eyes, a yellowish stain on her shoulder and mussed hair that had barely been brushed today. As she placed the menus on the table, he noticed a light stripe on her ring finger.

"Two decaf coffees," he said.

Her smile faded, probably anticipating a poor tip, yet another disappointment for a new mother whose marriage or engagement had broken down. Her next words were a valiant effort to change his mind. "Our sandwiches are like nothing you've ever tasted. We use the highest-quality ingredients as well as bread baked daily by a local, award-winning bakery."

His stomach responded to the mention of food with a few hunger pangs, and the diner's offerings sounded infinitely better than the take-out meals he'd eaten over the past few days. "Okay, your sales pitch has won me over. I'll take three sandwiches. A BLT, a grilled cheese and a roast beef. Hold the mustard." Brooke was welcome to eat whatever appealed to her, or she could ask for something else.

The waitress's smile was back in full force as she jotted down his order. "I knew you looked hungry when you walked in. Your meal won't take long. In the meantime, I'll get your beverages."

The coffees had been delivered by the time Brooke returned from the restroom. He watched her add a generous helping of cream and three packets of sugar to hers.

"Don't judge," she muttered. "I need a pick-me-up."

"When did you last eat?"

"I had an apple when the sun came up."

"That's hours ago. I've ordered enough food for both of us."

"Thanks, but Latschenko's gun pointed at my stomach killed my appetite."

"You should eat whether you feel like it or not. Low blood sugar is probably the reason you passed out in your SUV."

She rolled her eyes. "I didn't pass out—I fell asleep. And that only happened because I pulled an all-nighter for work."

Now probably wouldn't be a good time to mention the coffee he'd ordered her was decaf. He and insomnia had been keeping each other company till the wee hours of the morning lately, so he'd started cutting out caffeine after noon. "What kind of work keeps you up all night?"

She took a moment to answer him. "I'm a PI."

He noticed her fiddling with her mug, not meeting his eyes. "You seem reluctant to mention it. Why is that?"

"My profession has a somewhat sleazy reputation."

He could tell that bothered her. It surprised him a no-nonsense woman like her cared about other people's opinions. Or maybe it was his opinion she cared about. After all, it was his eyes she was avoiding. It wouldn't take much to ease the awkwardness she was feeling.

"I don't consider your work as sleazy." He added, deadpan, "Even if you were sneaking around with a camera trying to get an X-rated shot."

She laughed, her whole face lighting up. Damn, she had a pretty smile. Up until now, it had been understandably absent, but he hoped she'd have reason to smile more in the not-too-distant future. "By the way, I was impressed by your fancy camera, even if Latschenko wasn't."

"A tool of the trade that cost me a small fortune. I'm grateful it wasn't confiscated, although I guess if it had been, that would have been the least of my worries." She tapped the table with her fingers, unconsciously keeping rhythm with the song on the jukebox. "Thankfully, my clients aren't all jealous spouses wanting proof their significant others are cheating on them. I do jobs for insurance companies, lawyers, whoever needs info and is willing to pay for it."

The waitress arrived with a platter of sandwiches cut

into wedges. He transferred a few roast-beef wedges to his plate, then nudged the platter closer to Brooke. She didn't take the hint. Instead, she took a sip of her coffee, grimaced at the decaf's mild taste and set down the cup. "Enough about me. How long have you worked for the FBI?"

"Twelve years." He took a bite of his sandwich.

"What office do you work out of?"

His mouth was full of roast beef and bread, so he didn't respond immediately. The food was delicious, and he was going to take his time savoring it. His companion should take a break from talking and do the same. An apple at dawn wasn't enough to keep a mouse going for hours, much less a tall, athletic woman. But because she was stubborn, the only way he was going to get her to eat was to insist. "The waitress wasn't kidding about these sandwiches. They're fantastic. You really should try one...especially if you want me to give up information."

"I guess that's a bargain I can accept." She looked as if she was trying not to smile, but her lips wouldn't cooperate and curved upward as she selected a grilled-cheese sandwich from the platter. One bite later, she was devouring it with relish. "These are exceptionally good," she admitted, reaching for another wedge. "I taste a couple of different types of cheese."

"Then I don't regret nagging—I mean negotiating—for you to eat." He added, "I work out of the Cincinnati office."

She wiped her fingers on a paper napkin. "What did Sidorov do to become a person of interest in your missing-person case?"

He shook his head. "Can't answer that one."

"Can't or won't?"

"Take your pick. The matter is off-limits."

"Okay, but you can't blame a girl for trying, especially when a member of her family was threatened by your 'person of interest.'"

"Trevor is the one you need to grill for answers, not me."

She nodded. "Oh, I plan to. In the meantime, I want to thank you again and also to apologize. I realize by coming to my rescue, you ruined your cover. I'm sorry about that."

She sounded sincere, but *sorry* didn't fix the damage her presence at Sidorov's place had done. *Sorry* was just a word people used when they screwed up. He'd heard that word uttered by his brother more times than he could count over the years, and each time it irritated him more than the last. But it wasn't Brooke's fault he had a bad history with the word. They finished eating in silence, and there wasn't enough remaining to need take-away containers.

The waitress came by to clear the table and deliver the bill, telling them to take their time settling up. A few minutes later, a woman entered the diner, dressed in a floral skirt, pink frilly blouse, high heels and silver bangles on her wrists. She waved away the hostess and strode purposefully toward their table. As she got closer, she called out in an annoyed voice, "What's the big emergency, Brooke?"

This had to be Savannah, the jealous sister who had unknowingly sent her sibling on a perilous errand. The designer clothes she wore were on the opposite side of the fashion spectrum compared to Brooke's tank top, jeans and sneakers, but the family resemblance was unmistakable. Savannah was a shorter, plumper version of her sister with a wider face and green eyes.

Brooke looked past her to the diner's entrance. "Where's Trevor?"

Savannah huffed out a breath. "I suggested he wait in the car while I talked to you. His color is off, and he's not acting like himself at all. I think he's picked up a flu bug and should be home in bed."

The banker might be feeling unwell, but a virus was hardly to blame. Jared addressed the banker's wife. "Trevor isn't sick. He's terrified."

"What? Who are you?" Her lip curled as she took note of his grass-stained shirt and jeans. Her gaze settled on the embroidered name on the shirt's pocket. "What are you talking about, *Joe*?"

Brooke spoke before he had a chance to. "Don't let the grimy clothes fool you. This man was working undercover when he very possibly saved Trevor's life."

That was stretching the truth a bit, Jared thought, but certainly dramatic enough to get her sister's attention. Interesting how Brooke had failed to mention she'd been in danger, too. He could only assume she didn't want her sister to be stressed out about more than one member of her family at a time.

Brooke continued in a low, determined voice. "Go get your husband, Savannah. We need to talk to him."

Chapter 4

When Savannah entered the restaurant the second time, her hand was curled possessively around the arm of the briefcase-carrying man Jared had last seen entering Sidorov's mansion. As the couple approached the booth, a pale-faced Trevor smiled faintly at Brooke, but directed his words to Jared. "I understand you want to talk to me. Who are you?"

Jared introduced himself and, for the second time in an hour, dug out his FBI credentials. As Trevor glanced at them, his skin went even paler, revealing freckles that hadn't been noticeable before. "You're with the FBI?"

When Jared nodded, he and Savannah exchanged uncertain glances before looking at Brooke curiously.

"Please, sit down," she urged. "Both of you." She moved to the opposite side of the booth and slid in beside Jared so the couple could sit together facing them.

They took their seats silently, then waited for Jared to speak.

He had conducted hundreds of interrogations during the course of his career, and his next words rolled off his tongue without conscious effort. "What's the nature of your relationship with Dmitry Sidorov?"

"Why are you asking?"

Trevor's curiosity was understandable, but Jared was in no mood for it. He pinned the man with a withering stare. "I'm asking because that's my job. You have two choices. Answer my questions in a direct manner or refuse to cooperate with an FBI agent. The latter will have consequences I promise you won't enjoy."

Trevor lifted his hands in a take-it-easy gesture. "No need to get testy. I'll cooperate fully."

"Talk to me about you and Sidorov."

"Sidorov is a prospective customer. I met him for the first time today." His tight expression indicated he wished he hadn't.

"How did the meeting come about? Did you make initial contact, or did he?"

"He called me, saying he was a wealthy retiree who was considering changing banks. He asked me to put together a proposal of the services my bank could provide and bring it to his home to discuss."

"Tell me about your meeting."

"It started off fine, and he seemed receptive to my proposal, but then he went off on a tangent and asked me for information that had nothing to do with his finances."

"Can you be more specific?"

"He wanted to see the loan applications of companies the bank had decided against extending credit to. I told him I couldn't do that. The loan applications contain sensitive material about the companies' operations and financial position. My bank's policy strictly forbids me from sharing that information with anyone other than bank personnel."

Jared had been watching carefully for any signs Trevor was lying by omission or exaggeration, but the man's facial expressions and body language were consistent with his telling the truth. "How did he take your refusal?"

"He offered me money to bend the bank's rules. He said the bank didn't pay a smart man like me enough, that I deserved more. He knew things about me, personal things he shouldn't have known."

"Can you give an example?"

Trevor didn't answer right away. Finally, he spoke in a low voice. "He knew my wife and I had visited a fertility clinic last week."

Jared turned his head in time to see Brooke's mouth drop open in surprise. Her sister reached across the table and squeezed her hand. "I wanted to tell you, but the next step hasn't been decided. I'm game to go ahead, but Trevor has reservations because it's really expensive, and there are no guarantees."

Her husband shifted uncomfortably. "I want a baby as much as you do, sweetheart, but in my line of work, I've seen many people who overextend themselves moneywise, then get into dire straits and lose everything. I don't want that to happen to us, but I also hate the idea of disappointing you."

Although the conversation had shifted away from Sidorov, Jared decided the couple needed a few moments to clear the air. He wasn't surprised the Russian knew so much about the banker he intended to bribe. The guy was a pro and would, therefore, be familiar with every possible way to turn the screws in his victims.

Savannah untangled the bangles on her arm, then looked up at Trevor. "Is that why you've been so distant lately?"

He nodded. "I know once we start treatment, it'll be nearly impossible to stop until we're holding our own baby. I just need time to come to terms with spending all that money on something that, if unsuccessful, could break our hearts."

"Those last few nights you worked late… I thought you were being unfaithful."

The horrified look on his face proclaimed his innocence more eloquently than words. "No, never. I worked late those nights preparing for my meeting with Sidorov, trying to figure out what it would take to bring him on board. I had no idea at the time Sidorov was doing his own research into me. In exchange for that confidential applicant information, he offered to cover a year's worth of clinic treatments."

It was Savannah's turn to be surprised. "That's tens of thousands of dollars. He must want the information really badly."

Apparently, Trevor hadn't confided in his wife yet about the extent of Sidorov's desire for that information, so Jared decided to enlighten her. "When your husband turned down his bribe, the Russian resorted to threats and pulled out a gun. Isn't that right, Trevor?"

Savannah let out a gasp. "What's he talking about, Trev? Tell me it's not true."

Trevor wrapped his arm around her as if to protect

her from his next words. “I wish I could, but I can’t. Sidorov put the barrel to my temple, saying he wouldn’t take ‘no’ for an answer. He gave me five days to get hold of the information, choose several of the financially weakest companies and set up meetings with the owners. At the meetings, he wants me to vouch for him as a legitimate venture capitalist.”

Brooke had been sitting quietly, but now she spoke up. “Why would he want to invest in bad companies?”

Jared voiced the theory he’d been mulling over in his mind from the moment he’d heard Sidorov wanted confidential applicant information. “Sounds like a new twist on an old business—loan-sharking. He’s counting on these owners being so desperate for cash they’ll accept it from an unknown third party based on a reputable banker’s recommendation. After a few months, they’ll be hit with expensive repayment terms they have to meet or else Sidorov’s muscle will pay them a visit. Or Sidorov might use his involvement in their companies to pressure them into laundering illegal proceeds. I’ve seen that happen, too.”

Magnified a little by his glasses, Trevor’s brown eyes revealed anguish and fear. “If I don’t do what he wants, he promised to hurt me and Savannah. He showed me a folder full of info about us—where we live, the names of our family members, friends and my coworkers, what we owe on our mortgage and credit cards. He told me if I went to the police, I’d die before I had a chance to report him.”

Savannah let out a gasp of dismay and reached for her husband’s hand. Trevor swallowed with difficulty, before continuing. “I left his place, totally freaked out, not knowing what I should do. I drove around for a while before I realized all I wanted was to go home and hug my wife. When Savannah called, I was turning onto our street, so I picked her up and we came straight here."

"Who is this Sidorov?" Savannah demanded.

"The FBI has him tagged as one of the bosses of the Bratva—the Russian mafia," Jared said. "Last year, he almost died during a power struggle within the organization, so he came to Langeville to recover and, supposedly, to enjoy early retirement. But based on your meeting with him, he seems to have been working at his own criminal operation."

"I wonder if Trevor is the first banker he's contacted," Brooke murmured.

"Can't the FBI arrest Sidorov?" Savannah asked. "Based on what he did to my husband?"

Jared frowned. "He released Trevor without a scratch, and he could deny he poses any threat to him. Even if a prosecutor was willing to charge him, a judge might release him on bail until the trial. If that happened, Sidorov would pose even more of a danger to Trevor and you."

"What about witness protection?" Trevor asked.

The banker had apparently watched too much TV. "The federal government has very strict guidelines. Lots of people witness crimes, but it's rare they receive assistance. From what you've said, you don't know enough about Sidorov's operations to qualify for the program."

"Maybe I could learn more," Trevor offered. "Go along with whatever he tells me to do until there's enough evidence for him to be held without bail and convicted."

"That would be extremely dangerous for you. And even if you were successful and approved for witness protection, it's a life-altering change. After the trial, you and Savannah would have to relocate to another state, you could never work in banking again, and neither of you could ever have contact with your family or friends again."

Savannah gazed at her sister with tears in her eyes. "That sounds more like punishment than assistance. What are we supposed to do?"

"I think you should go away," Brooke said.

"Where?"

"How about Hilton Head? You've told me a few times your friend Amy has offered to loan you her condo there."

"If we did that, how long would we need to remain there?" Trevor asked Jared.

"I can't say definitively. I'll be continuing with my investigation of Sidorov related to another matter, but it'll take time to build a case against him. For now, be grateful you have somewhere to stay that's off the grid."

"What do you mean, *off the grid*?" Savannah asked.

"Your friend's condo is a private residence, as opposed to a hotel that would record your ID and keep your credit-card information on file. You don't want to leave a paper trail Sidorov could follow, if he chose to. The safest course of action would be to pay for everything with cash from this point forward."

"Can we afford to do that?" Savannah asked Trevor. "You've mentioned before that, even if we sold some investments today, it would take at least a few days to raise the money."

He gave her a reassuring smile. "I'll take a cash advance on our line of credit. As for work, I'll tell my boss there's been a family emergency, and I need to take two weeks off. He's been pushing me to use up the vacation time I carried over from last year."

"Sounds like you have a plan," Jared said.

"Savannah, why don't you contact Amy and make sure her offer still stands?" Brooke suggested.

"Good idea. Excuse me while I step outside to make the call."

Savannah slid out of the booth and headed for the front of the diner. Trevor waited until his wife was out of earshot before he turned to Jared. "I didn't want to scare my wife, but several members of my local bankers' association have died in the past six months. I didn't pay much attention to it at the time, other than feeling bad for their families, but now I can't help wondering if they'd had any dealings with Sidorov."

"Do you remember their names?"

"I can ask somebody at the association. All I know is they were all middle-aged and regular attendees of the meetings. Is it just a coincidence they died after Sidorov moved to Ohio? Maybe I'm being paranoid, but it would put my mind at ease if I knew their deaths weren't suspicious."

Jared pulled out a notebook and passed it to Trevor. "Make the call and write down their names and anything else you think is pertinent. Where they lived. What banks they worked for. I'll try to find out what happened to them, but it might take a while."

"Whatever you can manage is fine," Trevor said.

Brooke exited the booth. "I'll go check on Savannah."

Within minutes, she was standing outside the restaurant in the bright sunshine, waiting for Savannah to finish her call. After a quick "goodbye and thank you again" exchange, her sister dropped her cell phone into her purse, her bangles jangling. "Okay, Trevor and I are all set. Amy gave me the condo's address and the spot where she keeps her spare key. She's happy we're finally going to enjoy the place and wishes she could join us, but she's too busy organizing a charity gala."

"That's great." Brooke hugged her sister. "I'm glad my suggestion worked out."

Savannah held her close for a few extra seconds. "You should come to Hilton Head with us. When Sidorov figures out Trevor and I have left town, he's going to try to find us, probably by contacting our family and friends."

"He won't find out about Amy's condo from me," Brooke said firmly.

Savannah rolled her eyes. "I'm not worried about that. I'm worried about you. This guy sounds utterly ruthless. You could be in danger, too."

Her sister had no idea Brooke had already been detained at gunpoint by Sidorov's security guard, and she sure wasn't going to tell her. "I appreciate your offer, but I'm not coming to Hilton Head with you. You and Trevor will finally have some time alone together. The last thing you need is me tagging along."

"Don't worry about that. This is hardly the way I envisioned a romantic getaway with my husband," Savannah muttered. "On the run from a death threat."

Brooke patted her arm sympathetically. "I know, but try to make the most of it. Remember what Mom always used to say. Make lemonade out of lemons, right?"

"I suppose so." She frowned. "If you won't come,

then, please, don't stay at your place. Find somewhere else for a while where you're sure you'll be safe."

"I'll think about it." Although her sister's suggestion held some merit, she wouldn't feel right about couch surfing at her friends' houses. Apart from the imposition of a last-minute houseguest, what if her presence brought danger to them? She'd never forgive herself if someone got threatened or hurt on account of her. The alternative—renting a hotel room for an undetermined length of time—wasn't viable either. Her line of credit was already maxed out to keep her business afloat. Establishing her reputation as a PI had taken more time—and the start-up costs had been higher—than she'd expected. Even so, she didn't regret her decision to be self-employed.

Savannah stabbed a finger in her direction, a gesture she felt entitled to as the older sister. "Ask that FBI agent for a suggestion. Or better yet, stick close to him. My impression of him is he's smart, competent and determined. A guy with his training would be really good at fending off bad guys and protecting you. He also has seriously impressive muscles, no wedding ring and a sexy mouth."

Savannah couldn't know her conjecture about Nash's skills had already been put to the test and proved true. And the rest of her description of the man was valid, too, including the comment about his sexy mouth. His occasional smiles had sent tingles up Brooke's spine, which was crazy given the circumstances.

"He is totally male and totally hot. Don't tell me you haven't noticed, sis."

She was tempted to deny it, but Savannah's expression told her that she'd be wasting her breath. What the heck. It was nice to see a twinkle in her sister's eye. For a brief moment, she'd forgotten about the threat from Sidorov, and Brooke wasn't going to spoil her fun. "Yeah, Savannah, I noticed. He is totally male and totally hot."

The sound of a throat being cleared made her jump. Oh crap. Jared Nash was standing a few feet away, having exited the diner without her noticing. What exactly had he heard?

Apparently, enough to be entertained. His lips curved in a slow, knowing smile. She felt her face flush and darted a look at Savannah, who had been facing the diner and must have watched him approach. Her sister gazed back innocently. *Too* innocently. Savannah had set her up.

The awkward moment was broken by the arrival of Trevor. He and Savannah headed across the parking lot with Brooke and the FBI agent trailing afterward. When they reached the Lexus, the two women embraced again while the men exchanged cell-phone numbers.

"He likes you, too," Savannah whispered to Brooke. "He was staring at you intently every time you spoke. So take the advice you gave to me and 'make the most of it.' Stay close to him and I mean really close. I'll want the juicy details from you later."

"Not going to happen." The sex or the gossip.

"Prude," her sister teased.

Brooke's only reply was to say, "Call me when you're settled at the condo."

When Nash opened the passenger door for Savannah, she thanked him, then blurted out, "When Sidorov finds out Trevor and I are gone, he might take out his anger on our families. Trevor's all live in England, so I'm not worried about them. But my sister's here. Please, keep her safe."

"I'll see what I can do," he replied.

"Hey," Brooke objected, blindsided by her sister's direct plea to the agent, "I can take care of myself."

"Against a Russian mobster?" Savannah's head shake conveyed her disbelief as she buckled her seat beat. "That's optimistic, even for you. I almost lost you once. I can't stand the thought of you getting hurt again."

Her sister's words were ones of concern, but Brooke didn't appreciate the reminder of her mortality or the curious look Nash gave her. Trying not to show her annoyance, she said, "I promise I'll be extra careful." Then she closed the passenger door and turned away from her sister.

Chapter 5

"I think we should go back to my place," Nash said, after Savannah and Trevor had disappeared down the street in their Lexus.

Brooke shot him a sideways glance. Now that her sister and brother-in-law were on their way to safety, she could fully appreciate the looks of the man who had rescued her. His hair, minus the baseball cap he'd worn when they'd first met, was a rich cocoa color. His tanned arms were rippled with muscles a bodybuilder would envy, and his flat stomach and thick thighs looked great in denim. Add to that, his height placed him among the small percentage of men she didn't tower over.

Every bit as superb as his physique, his face boasted a broad forehead, high cheekbones and a granite jaw. But his eyes were the real kicker. The color of polished metal, they reminded her of one-way glass that allowed him to see while offering only a reflection in return. What had he seen with those eyes? Probably lots, given his line of work. Her short time as a cop had introduced her to a whole other world most people weren't familiar with, a world teeming with criminals prone to violence and bloodshed. Her job as a protector of innocent people, working to keep them safe from that world, had given her a sense of pride as well as periodic doses of excitement. That had all ended the night she'd been shot, when she'd changed from protector to victim.

The dark mood came out of nowhere, dragging her down. As she fought against it, she realized Nash was watching her with an unreadable expression. Did he sense the turmoil in her? Or was he just waiting for a response to his question?

"Why should we go to your place?" she ventured. Was he flattered by her comment about him being totally male and totally hot? Or was he opportunistic? Did he believe if she were alone with him in a private place, she'd act upon the attraction that those words implied?

The guy obviously didn't know her. She didn't do casual sex. Actually, she didn't do any kind of sex anymore, at least not for the past two years. After Chad had dumped her, she'd preferred to remain alone. But maybe enough time had passed, and she should consider ending her hiatus. A hunky specimen of a man like Nash didn't come along every day, and it was only natural she'd be tempted.

He rubbed the back of his neck, the movement flexing a magnificently sculpted bicep Brooke pretended not to notice. "I want to try to sharpen up that shot of Sidorov."

She should have felt relieved by the impersonal nature of his comment, but instead she felt disappointed. She could lay blame for that at Savannah's door. Her sister's suggestive comments had steered her thoughts in a direction that was rash and inappropriate. She was grateful he wanted her camera, not her body. Of course she was. A onetime sexual encounter was not the way to heal what was damaged in her.

"Follow me," he said, before ambling over to the blue Mustang that was parked next to her RAV4.

Within minutes, they were retracing the route that led from Columbus to Langeville. He drove fast in his sporty car, and she swore under her breath as she realized she'd forgotten to get their destination for her GPS. Her leg began to tire from keeping so much pressure on the gas pedal, but she was determined to keep up. Finally, on the outskirts of town, he pulled into a motel parking lot.

Her surprise was fleeting, as she recalled he worked—and most likely lived—in Cincinnati. It made sense he'd stay locally, not commute and waste valuable time. She peered through her front windshield at the neon sign above the office. Twisted Pines Motel. No trees, twisted or otherwise, could be seen on the property. Apart from the misleading name, the motel looked fine, not shabby or run-down. There was fresh green paint on the doors to the units and well-tended shrubs on the walkway to the office. The parking lot was in the midst of being repaved, so there was only a narrow strip of undisturbed asphalt in front of the motel rooms. To avoid taking anyone's spot, Brooke parked close to the street on a patch of dirt.

As she left her SUV, she saw a guy in a red bandanna fixing the light fixture outside one of the units. When he glanced over at her, she was suddenly conscious she had no luggage, and Mr. Fix-It probably thought she was here for a romp in the sack. Great. Today she was both a trespasser *and* a tramp.

Nash had unlocked and opened the door to Number Seven and was waiting for her, so she quickly pressed her key fob to lock her vehicle and went to join him. With a wave of his hand, he motioned for her to go ahead of him, and she did, advancing into the motel unit.

Inside, the room was far from luxurious, but at least it looked functional and clean. The furnishings consisted of two double beds covered by blue-and-gray-striped comforters, a blue upholstered wing chair, a dresser topped by an oval mirror, a minifridge and TV. A laptop lay open on a pine desk with a straight-backed chair tucked underneath. On the walls, framed photos showcased horses of different colors and sizes running in the desert at sundown.

A decent-sized room, she thought, setting her camera next to the laptop. But when Nash closed the door and engaged the security chain, the space seemed to shrink by half. She pivoted on her heel, seeking to put more distance between them. Being alone with him was awkward enough without tripping over him in the close quarters.

He pulled his cell phone out of his pocket and ducked into the bathroom. After a minute or two, she heard muffled talking behind the closed door. Hardly an ideal arrangement when the only place for a person to have a private conversation was the john. She sat gingerly on the wing chair and waited. By the time he reappeared, she was wound tight as a yo-yo.

He propped his butt against the dresser and crossed his ankles. "Your sister's worried Sidorov will come after you."

She was tense enough without dwelling on her sister's concerns. "Savannah is a sweet person, but she's also a chronic worrier. She sees a disaster waiting to happen in almost every situation."

"That may be so, but it doesn't change the fact that she might be right this time."

Brooke's heart rate kicked up a notch. "I don't find that kind of speculation very useful."

"I agree. We need to know Sidorov's intentions toward you."

She smoothed her hands over her thighs, then gripped the arms of the motel chair. "How can we do that?"

"Early this morning, I bugged his office."

He looked pleased with himself, and she didn't doubt it had taken courage and ingenuity to outmaneuver Latschenko. There was just one little problem she felt obliged to mention. "How does that help? I assume, when Latschenko regains consciousness and tells Sidorov what happened, they'll be speaking Russian." She paused. "Will you be able to translate their conversation?"

"I won't need to. During my first day on site, I overheard the two of them talking in English. When I mentioned it later to Latschenko, he said after the age of ten, he was raised by his American mother and rarely saw his father. The first time he tried to speak Russian to Sidorov, the guy told him to stop because he was mangling the language."

"Well, that's a lucky break for us. Except how do we access what's been picked up by that bug?"

"It's being recorded on a flash drive in the shed behind Sidorov's garage."

"We have to go *back there*?" Despite her best efforts, she couldn't keep the dismay out of her voice.

"No, I need that bug to stay active. If we're seen returning to the property by Latschenko or Sidorov, it'll raise suspicions about why we're there. And, of course, then there's the issue of our safety."

"Yeah, there's that," she agreed readily. He had been so calm and confident throughout the whole interaction with Latschenko that she thought he might be dismissive of the magnitude of the danger they had faced. It was good to hear him acknowledge their well-being had been at serious risk. "How are we going to get the flash drive?"

"I've arranged for someone to pick it up and bring it here."

That must have been the call he'd made in the bathroom. "Who is this 'someone'?"

He shrugged, the movement rippling through his broad shoulders. "His name isn't important, but he's someone I've known for years and trust completely."

Nash might trust him, but did the guy know what he was getting into? "Aren't you worried about his safety?"

The sexy mouth Savannah had pointed out to her earlier lifted in a half smile. "Nope. I've warned him about Latschenko, but the guy's been in places a hundred times more dangerous than Sidorov's backyard. He'll be in and out with no one the wiser."

"When is he coming?"

"In about twenty minutes." As Jared spoke, he emptied his jeans' pockets, setting his keys, credentials and wallet on the dresser. After a quick glance at his cell phone, he returned it to his pocket. Then he gathered up an armload of clothes from one of the dresser drawers.

"What are you doing?" she demanded, even though she had a darn good idea.

"I'm going to get cleaned up. Grass got down my shirt and it's making my chest itch."

That same chest had touched the side of her breast when he'd had his arm around her to keep her from doing anything rash. It had felt solid as stone, warm as fire, muscle-y as… She couldn't think of an apt descriptor, but she had no trouble imagining how magnificent it would look naked. She shoved the image out of her mind. "What about the camera? Aren't you going to try sharpening the shot I took of Sidorov and Trevor?"

"I'll get to it. Soap and water first."

She clamped her teeth together. There was no point protesting further. He would do what he wanted anyway.

He gestured toward the kitchenette. "Help yourself to a drink. There's coffee in the cupboard and cola in the fridge."

"Not thirsty." She didn't need his hospitality. She needed his cooperation.

His long legs carried him in the direction of the bathroom.

A thought occurred to her. "What if your guy shows up early?"

"Come and get me," he tossed over his shoulder, still walking away from her.

"In the shower?" She felt her cheeks heat. Damn, that sounded suggestive, but maybe he hadn't noticed...

His footsteps stopped. He turned and shot her a wicked grin. "Sure. I'm not shy."

Adjusting the showerhead to the *pulse* setting, Jared grimaced as the jets of hot water pummeled him. After a full morning of yard maintenance, his arms and shoulders ached as if he'd bench-pressed a piano. The motel's miniature bar of soap kept slipping through his fingers, and it took more effort than it should have to reach down and retrieve it.

Although he'd removed his watch, he was acutely aware of the time. Three o'clock. A half hour past the time of Sidorov's meeting across town. Despite the water streaming down his body, his muscles remained tense. He wasn't supposed to be showering in his motel room. He was supposed to be charming the housekeeper, then searching Sidorov's house. He was supposed to be leafing through the folders left out on the man's desk and digging through his file cabinet. Except a certain statuesque blonde had wreaked havoc on his plans. In spite of the irritation he felt, he couldn't stop thinking about her sassy, kissable mouth, her high, firm breasts and her sweetly curved backside.

He rinsed off quickly and stepped out of the shower. After he'd tugged on a clean pair of jeans, he eyed the stubble on his chin in the mirror. It looked a bit scruffy, far from the clean-cut, professional image he usually presented. He'd purposely stopped shaving for a few days to better fit with his manual-laborer role. Now that his cover was blown, the stubble was no longer needed, but it matched his current aggravated state of mind, and he couldn't be bothered getting rid of it.

After he buttoned up a shirt and ran a comb through his hair, he left the bathroom, calling to Brooke, "I'll be outside." While he waited in the parking lot, a light breeze ruffled his damp hair. He checked his phone. Alex Sheridan was running a few minutes late.

A high school friend of his brother's, Alex had worked overseas on and off for years as an independent security consultant before returning to the States a few months ago. Sociable and unconditionally loyal, he was the type of guy Steve must have wished he had for a brother. Not the blood relation who hadn't talked to him in months, who had been in no screaming rush to fix their estrangement and even now was wondering what his younger brother had done to end up missing. Had he made the mistake of crossing Sidorov, or had he only been letting off steam to their sister about the Russian? There were lots of other aggressive sons of bitches out there Steve could have run afoul of. If so, Jared could be on the wrong track entirely. However, it made sense to focus on the man Steve had identified until Jared could rule him out.

A white Dodge Ram roared into the dug-up parking lot, kicking up dirt and gravel. Alex emerged from the driver's side, the earbuds of his ever-present iPod dangling from his neck.

"How did it go?" Jared asked.

"Easiest job ever." With his deep, resonant voice, the security consultant could have been a theater actor before the era of microphones. "I swapped out the flash drive with another one as per your instructions." He handed over the tiny device with a flourish.

"Thanks. I owe you."

"Forget that," Alex scoffed. "You know I'd do anything for your brother."

Jared had always thought Alex and Steve were like an equation that didn't add up. Alex was responsible, tech savvy and goal-driven. Steve was fun-loving, preferred working with his hands and never planned beyond his next beer. But despite the two being like day and night in terms of interests, career choices and temperament, their friendship had endured over time and distance. "Yeah, you guys have a lot of history."

"Back in high school, Steve saved my sanity," Alex said. "All those weeks in the hospital when I thought I'd end up in a wheelchair forever, he'd distract me with bizarre but true facts or stupid jokes, then listen without judgment while I ranted about how my injury was going to ruin my future. I can never pay him back for that."

"He doesn't expect you to. Being his friend is enough."

Alex shoved a hand through his dirty-blond hair. "I'm just glad I was stateside when your sister texted he'd gone missing. Steve and I played pool about three months ago, and he seemed fine with everything in his life, except for the ongoing misunderstanding with you."

Misunderstanding? That was quite the euphemism for the Grand Canyon–sized rift Steve had caused between them. But now wasn't the time to get cranked up over past resentments. Ignoring Alex's comment, he said, "I appreciate your coming to Langeville to help figure out what's happened to him."

"I know Kristin believes with every fiber of her being he's missing, but what if she has it wrong? Couldn't Steve have left town without telling her?"

The same thought had occurred to Jared when his sister had first begged him to check into their brother's "disappearance." He'd arrived in Langeville, convinced he'd track down Steve in a matter of hours. Those hours had dragged into several long, frustrating days as the younger Nash's whereabouts remained elusive.

"Steve has called Kristin every Sunday night for years," he reminded Alex. "No matter where he was or what he was doing. She insisted on that stay-in-touch routine when he turned eighteen, and he agreed to it because he cares about her and knows her tendency to get worked up and go nuclear." His siblings' closeness was a sore point because Kristin didn't know a fraction of the crap that baby brother had pulled, mostly because Jared couldn't bring himself to ruin her illusions.

Alex shaded his eyes from the sun. "Maybe he got fed up following her schedule. Maybe he decided to change his check-in day to Thursday."

"So he does that with no warning, no call, no text, leaving her to agonize something terrible has happened to him?" If that turned out to be the case, Jared would wring his neck.

"No, that doesn't sound like him at all," Alex admitted. "Steve loves Kristin and would never be so inconsiderate."

Impulsive, irreverent, immature, yes, Jared thought. Blatantly inconsiderate, no. That distinction belonged to him. He hadn't returned any of Steve's calls over the past eight months. He'd been too furious, too disgusted to listen to the excuses and apologies and promises Steve was so good at dishing up. One thing he knew for certain. If his brother hadn't contacted Kristin, it was because he *couldn't* contact her.

He and Alex had spent the first day ruling out the obvious—serious injury or death—by calling hospitals and morgues within a hundred-mile radius. Steve hadn't passed through any of them in the past week. Relief that he wasn't injured or dead had quickly given way to confusion. Where in blazes was he?

Kristin had been the one to mention the name Sidorov. During their last Sunday-night conversation, Steve had told her that the Russian despised him, but when his sister asked why, he'd clammed up. Steve's unwillingness to confide in his sibling was out of character, which made Sidorov worth investigating.

Jared's thoughts were interrupted by Alex asking, "What do you want me to do next?"

"I think it's worth another canvass of Steve's apartment building. You might have missed talking to some of his neighbors if they were away or worked the night shift and wouldn't answer the door when you tried the first time."

"Sure. I can do that."

He expected Alex to hop back into his vehicle, but the guy seemed in no hurry to leave. After an extended pause, the reason became apparent. He had more questions. "You were planning to search Sidorov's house today. Did you find anything useful?"

"I never got the chance. All I had time to do was plant the bug."

"Are you going back tomorrow?"

When Jared had asked Alex to retrieve the flash drive, he hadn't revealed the reason he couldn't do it himself, and the other man hadn't asked, probably because he'd heard the urgency in Jared's voice. But now that Alex was asking, Jared felt he owed him an explanation.

"I can't. My cover's blown."

"That sucks."

An accurate assessment of the situation, Jared thought. He wasn't in the mood to rehash what had gone wrong, so he said instead, "What I did discover is Sidorov has been involved in illegal activities since he moved to Langeville."

"You think Steve might have found out?"

A chill went up his spine at the implications of that possibility. Based on Jared's interaction with the banker, Sidorov was the same ruthless criminal who had struck fear into the hearts of many during his years as mafia boss. Jared had no doubts the Russian would dispose of someone who posed a threat to him or his financial interests.

"If my brother had discovered Sidorov's criminal activities, he would have involved the police." A year ago, Steve might have contacted him for advice, but their estrangement had wrecked any chance of that.

Alex frowned. "Maybe there was no time to do that. Or maybe he wanted to know more details before he called them. If Sidorov caught him at it—"

Jared cut him off midsentence. "We need facts, not speculation." His suggestion wasn't only for Alex's benefit; it was a reminder to himself, as well. He had to treat this investigation like any other. Keep digging until he hit pay dirt. He only hoped the dirt he eventually found wasn't a grave.

Shoving the morbid thought aside, he said, "Steve will turn up alive."

"I hope you're right." Alex added in an undertone, "I've buried two friends already this year."

Would Steve turn out to be number three? Jared wondered.

The motel door opened and Brooke appeared. "I thought I heard voices." She smiled at Alex, whose answering grin spread as wide as a crocodile's. "I'm Brooke Rogers."

"I'm Alex Sheridan. Nice to meet you."

"I wanted to thank you myself for bringing the flash drive from Sidorov's shed here."

"You know about that, do you?" Alex shot Jared a look of blatant curiosity before he returned his gaze to Brooke. "You're welcome. Glad I could be of assistance." He rocked back on his heels while his eyes made a leisurely tour of her pretty face, shapely breasts and long jean-clad legs.

Jared didn't like the attention Alex was paying Brooke one bit. "I'll be finished in a minute," he told her. "Wait inside, will you?" His voice was pleasant, but his tone made it an order, not a request.

Her smile vanished. She stepped back and shut the door with more force than was necessary.

Alex let out a low whistle. "Ve-e-ery nice."

"She ran into trouble at Sidorov's place. I had to take her with me."

The security consultant nodded approvingly. "By all means, help her out. I hope, for your sake, she expresses her appreciation in more than words."

Jared knew exactly what the other man was thinking, but decided to let it pass. A woman who looked as smoking hot as Brooke tended to bring out men's baser instincts. He, too, had been having sexual thoughts about her. It was shockingly easy to imagine her naked, her heated gaze beckoning him to touch her in all the right places. But that was just a one-sided fantasy. Brooke had done nothing provocative to encourage him. He didn't count the "totally male, totally hot" comment she'd made to her sister. He could tell by her flushed cheeks he wasn't supposed to have heard it. Of course, if she'd said those words brazenly to his face…that would have sent an entirely different message.

After Alex drove off, he returned to the room. Brooke was once again parked on the blue armchair, this time contemplating the unremarkable beige carpet. Released from its elastic, her blond hair fell past her shoulders in soft waves.

She glanced up. "So…you're helping search for Alex's missing friend and you've reason to believe Sidorov is involved, right?"

Damn. Alex's deep voice must have penetrated the motel door. Luckily, she missed the earlier part of their conversation. If she knew the missing man was his brother, her curiosity would really go into overdrive. He ignored her question and connected the flash drive to his laptop. Opening the file containing the recording, he moved the cursor until the clock showed 1:15, which was just after he had knocked Latschenko unconscious.

"Ready to hear this?"

She laced her fingers over her knee. "Sure."

"You might want to shift your chair closer. My laptop speakers don't have much volume."

She dragged the armchair to a spot six inches from his straight-backed chair. Once she'd retaken her seat, he clicked on the audio file.

"What the hell happened to you?" The speaker

spoke with a strong Russian accent. According to the FBI file Jared had reviewed, Sidorov had immigrated to the States in his late twenties. Although he had acquired an excellent command of the English language over the next thirty years, he'd never lost his accent.

"The new yard guy, Joe, attacked me with hedge trimmers," Latschenko said, his voice strained. "My hand hurts real bad."

Sidorov offered no sympathy, asking only, "Why did he hit you?"

"He was protecting his girlfriend. She showed up on the property with a camera. I caught her and insisted she hand it over, so I could check what she'd been taking pictures of. When she resisted, he went after me."

"Where was your gun while all this was going on?" Sidorov demanded.

"I had it pointed at her, but he surprised me."

"Don't give me excuses," Sidorov bellowed. "You are paid to watch over my family and my property. Instead, you allow a stranger to wander around outside with a camera. What if she had had a gun?"

"If she'd had a gun, I would have shot her when I first laid eyes on her," Latschenko answered immediately.

Jared hit the pause button on the laptop.

"Why are you stopping?" Brooke asked.

"It just occurred to me there's no reason you have to sit through the whole recording. I can listen to it on my own and just give you the highlights afterward."

"No, it affects me. I want to hear it." She stared at him without blinking. "All of it. Not the sanitized version you think I can handle."

He wasn't really surprised by her decision, but he didn't like the fact that he had no idea what Sidorov and Latschenko were going to say about her. She'd already been through a lot today. She didn't need anything else to add to her stress level.

"Play it," Brooke urged. "I assure you I can take it."

In spite of his reservations, Jared started the recording again.

Latschenko was still speaking. "I decided to see what was on the camera before I brought her to you. I won't make that mistake again."

"This girlfriend. What did she look like?"

"Tall, blonde. Got a bombshell body."

The sound of papers rustling could be heard through the speakers. "Is this her?"

"Yeah. Why do you have a photo of her?"

"She is related to the money guy I was meeting with." Sidorov added, "I always gather information on family members when I plan to do business with somebody. Her name is Brooke Rogers, and she is a PI."

"She's a *what*?"

"A private investigator with her own business in Columbus. That explains the camera."

"Son of a bitch," Latschenko grumbled. "She didn't look like any dick I ever saw. She looked—and acted—like a blonde bimbo."

"Then she played you for a fool." Sidorov's voice held utter contempt for the other man. "Chernov would never have been taken in by her. It's only because he is away that I gave you this chance to work for me."

"I know, and I really like this job," Latschenko said. "I'll do whatever it takes to win back your trust." He paused. "Why do you think she came here? Because your moneyman asked her to?"

Sidorov made a scoffing sound. "He had no reason to be suspicious. He thought we were meeting about transferring my investments to his bank."

"Then somebody must have hired her. Who? Why?"

Jared glanced over at Brooke, curious to see her reaction to the two men discussing her, but her face was like a mask, showing nothing of what she was feeling.

A rhythmic sound, possibly a vacuum cleaner, intruded on the men's voices. The conversation became muffled, disjointed, only a few phrases standing out. "…family of that bastard…" and "…Chernov…" and "…threat dealt with…"

Jared cursed silently, straining to hear. There was more talking by Sidorov and Latschenko, but none of the words were clear enough to understand. Eventually, the vacuuming sound faded away, and their conversation could be heard again.

"I'm gonna get my cousin to stake out the PI's place and call me if she shows up," Latschenko said. "That way I can stay mobile and keep looking for her."

"That's good. I like to see you using your brain," Sidorov said with grudging admiration.

"You don't have to worry. I won't stop until I find her."

"You cannot do it alone. I will call some people I know to help you search. When she is found, bring her to me and don't forget her camera. I have many questions to ask her."

"What if she goes to the police?" Latschenko asked.

"I know someone there. I will tell him about her."

"What good will that do?"

The Russian laughed slyly. "No good for her at all. He will find out everything he can from her, then make sure she is no problem for me."

Chapter 6

With Sidorov's threat echoing in her mind, Brooke felt an overwhelming urge to throw up. She swallowed hard, blaming the queasiness of her stomach on the richness of the grilled-cheese sandwich she'd eaten. She should have stuck with coffee. Concentrating hard, she managed to keep her nausea in check, but not her fear. Anxiety wrapped around her like a python, squeezing her chest so hard she expected to feel her ribs crack. Her heart hammered and her vision blurred. Hard to believe she'd once received an award for bravery. Of course, she'd been a different woman back then. That woman had been changed irrevocably the night two bullets had slammed into her body, nearly killing her and destroying the mental toughness she had taken for granted.

Her breathing grew shallower as the airflow was

restricted by her tight chest. She became increasingly light-headed, on the verge of blacking out. *Oh God… could a person suffocate from fear?*

"Brooke?"

The sound of her name made her start. She'd forgotten about the FBI guy who sat close by, watching her.

"Nothing bad is going to happen to you." His fingers curled around her wrist.

He must be able to feel the frantic beating of her pulse, she realized. She should pull her arm away. Make some smart-ass remark to show she was fine, that she had taken the recording in stride like she'd assured him. But that would take breath—and moxie—she didn't have.

His touch was light. Gentle. Soothing. As warmth from his hand seeped into her skin, the pressure in her chest eased up. She sucked in desperately needed air.

"I won't let anybody hurt you." His voice was calm, confident.

She used to be the one to reassure victims of violence. Now the tables had turned, and she was the one needing reassurance. She couldn't make the transition in her mind. It felt so wrong. If only she could go back in time, she'd change the event that had changed her. But that was impossible, and she was foolish to keep wishing for it. Somehow, she had to learn to accept that the trauma of that night would forever be a part of her. And when something triggered a memory of it, it was okay to freak out inside, so long as she gritted her teeth and held it together on the outside until the fear and panic subsided.

She concentrated on her breathing, instructing her lungs to fill and empty so she wouldn't keel over like a fool. All the while, Nash stroked her hand as if he had nothing else to do, no better place to be. Her heart rate gradually slowed until it matched the unhurried pace of his fingers. How strange that a man she barely knew could ease her panic.

After a moment, his hand slipped away to rest on his jean-clad thigh. "Feeling better?"

She stared at him. Up close, his jaw looked wider and his lips fuller. She wondered how his mouth would feel pressed against hers. Based on the unhurried touches and intense stares he'd given her, she was pretty sure his kisses would be slow, deep, thrilling—

"What are you thinking?" he asked.

Heat flooded her cheeks, but she wasn't about to embarrass herself further. Fidgeting in the motel armchair, her gaze flitting anywhere but into those too-perceptive gray eyes of his, she caught sight of the flash drive attached to his laptop. "I'm thinking about Sidorov. Can he be arrested based on the recording we just listened to? You heard him. He threatened to kill me."

"He said you wouldn't be a problem for him."

"That's because he's going to get rid of me."

"I agree that's probably his intention, but we don't have enough to prove it." Nash continued in an even, unemotional voice. "The FBI won't lay charges based on a poor-quality audio recording with vague inferences. They know Sidorov's lawyer could rip apart their case at trial, arguing there are several ways to interpret his client's words. For instance, you wouldn't be a problem if his client compensated you to end your investigation."

"Maybe if I went to the police, the recording would be enough to convince them to keep an eye on Sidorov," she suggested.

"Remember what he told your brother-in-law. That if Trevor involved the police, he'd die before he could report what had happened. Sidorov implied the same thing on the recording. The only way for Sidorov to make good on his threats is if he's paying someone on the police force to watch out for his interests."

She thought for a moment. "I could mention that to the police chief. Surely, he's not the one on Sidorov's payroll."

"We can't know that for a fact, but assuming he isn't, I think he'd be skeptical that one of his men is corrupt unless you can provide him with a name and evidence of bribery. Even if Sidorov were arrested for uttering a threat, he'd likely be released on bail because he has no criminal record. Rumor has it he's always paid others to do his dirty work, and they're willing to do prison time rather than cut a deal and rat him out."

"So you're saying our justice system hasn't managed to punish a ruthless mob boss for his crimes and everybody is okay with that?"

His response was immediate and unequivocal. "I'm not okay with it."

She was silent for a moment, then issued him a challenge. "You think you can connect him to your missing person, Nash? Find ironclad evidence that will stand up in court?"

"I won't rest until I do."

She saw his determination in the line of his jaw and the seriousness of his eyes. "What am I supposed to do in the meantime?"

"Stay out of sight, so his men can't find you. That means you should avoid working, in case he tracks you down through your clients."

"What about the meetings I've booked?" she asked, dismayed by the thought of disappointing those who had hired her.

"Postpone them. Your safety is more important than work right now."

True, but time off meant time unpaid. "That's really going to mess with my cash flow," she grumbled.

"You're welcome to stay here if you want. There's an extra bed, and the FBI's picking up the tab, so it won't cost you anything."

She studied him, wondering if there was any underlying reason for his offer. On the surface, it made sense. She would save money and be safer with him than on her own. Even so, the room was not very big for two people who were strangers. The cohabit arrangement could get really awkward, especially if the periodic flashes of attraction she felt for him grew any stronger.

"I appreciate your offer," she said, "but I'm going to have to decline."

"The choice is yours, of course, but think how pleased your sister will be when she calls and finds out she doesn't need to worry about you."

He had a point, dammit. Savannah would be over-the-moon relieved—and delighted—to hear her sister would remain under the watchful eye of a hunky FBI agent. Given the circumstances, was it worth the risk to go it alone? It also occurred to her that if she remained with Nash, she'd be able to keep tabs on his efforts to get Sidorov arrested.

"Once again, I'm impressed by your negotiation skills," she commented. "Thanks. I'll stay for a few days." She let out a frustrated groan. "You know, what's really maddening is that I'll be stuck here while Sidorov and Latschenko are free to come and go as they please."

Nash touched her arm, his rough palm sending a tingling sensation all the way to her fingertips. "I understand your anger. What's happened isn't fair. But life rarely is, is it?"

Her thoughts went immediately to the night she was shot and the aftermath of her injury that included losing her career and her fiancé. Nash was right. Life wasn't fair, but that wasn't the point. The point was to deal with whatever crap happened and not whine about it.

Nash's words broke into her reverie. "If you hadn't come to Sidorov's place with a camera, he wouldn't be so determined to find you now. Why didn't you refuse when your sister asked you to spy on her husband?"

"I tried to talk her out of it, but Savannah's had a lot to deal with this year, and she was really wound up. I couldn't just ignore her concerns."

"Sure, you could have. Her request was unreasonable, given the only way you could get the proof she wanted was to trespass on a stranger's property."

"Savannah's my only family. Do you have siblings?"

"A sister…and a brother." He looked away, a closed expression on his face.

"Have you ever acted against your better judgment because you couldn't bring yourself to disappoint them?"

"I suppose so," he admitted grudgingly.

"Then you've just proven my point."

"What point is that?"

"When it comes to family, the heart—not the head—calls the shots. I feel lucky to have a sister, even if she sometimes makes me crazy." She added, "I agreed to run that errand for her today because I thought getting yelled at by an annoyed home owner was the worst thing that could happen. Boy, was I wrong."

He shook his head ruefully. "That's an understatement."

"Look, despite what happened, I don't regret being there."

"What?" His voice rose, as if he couldn't believe he'd heard her right. "Why not?"

"If I hadn't gone to Langeville, I wouldn't have found out Trevor was in trouble. He would've had to deal with the threat from Sidorov alone."

"Not exactly. I was going to run his license-plate number and pay him a visit."

"I'm not sure how much he'd have told you, Nash. You wouldn't have known to ask about Sidorov and his gun. I think the only reason Trevor spoke so candidly to us was because he felt he had no choice. We already knew he'd been threatened, and he couldn't get away with keeping quiet about it."

"Maybe."

"The good part is Trevor and Savannah are safe and on their way to Hilton Head together."

"And you're safe, as well." After a moment, he added, "If you stay here, there is one condition."

She lifted an eyebrow, curious to hear what he wanted. "What's that?"

"You have to start calling me by my first name. You do remember it, don't you?"

The devil rose up in her. "Joe?" she offered mischievously.

"Very funny." His tone was dry, but the edges of his mouth curled upward.

She liked his name. Actually, she liked a whole lot

more about Jared than just his name. But she should forget about that, given they'd be staying in close quarters for the foreseeable future.

Fatigue from the prior night's stakeout washed over her. The job had entailed locating a skip accused of scamming his insurance company before leaving town. Instead of chasing all over the place looking for him, Brooke had researched his personal life. Then she'd made like an owl, watching from a parked car in front of the guy's girlfriend's place. When the guy had arrived at dawn to wish his beloved a happy birthday, Brooke had called the police and her client.

Awesome job, the CFO of the insurance company had told her. Praise like that stroked her needy ego and made the all-nighter worth it. If not for Savannah's call, she'd have quit working at noon and gone to sleep. Instead, she was caught up in a nightmare she couldn't awaken from.

Nightmare or not, she could feel herself fading. The adrenaline that had kept her alert and wired was gone. Her eyelids drooped. Her body swayed in the chair.

A deep voice penetrated the fog in her brain. "You look wiped."

No point denying the obvious. She peeled her eyes open in time to see Jared point to the bed nearest the window. "Go lie down before I carry you there."

The possibility of his hands on her body galvanized her into action. Sort of. Wobbling on legs like the newborn foal in the photo on the wall, she made it over to the bed.

"I just need a short nap," she muttered.

As she curled up on the comforter, she told herself

she'd be home in her own bed soon. Assuming her FBI protector was as competent as he was hot.

Latschenko chewed the last bite of his burger and washed it down with a long slurp of soda. He was dreading the phone call he had to make, but there was no way around it. He had been searching for the blonde PI all afternoon with nothing to show for his efforts. And the guys that Sidorov had helping out had texted him a few minutes ago that they had come up empty, too.

He pulled out his cell phone and called his wife. They had been separated for a month, and he hated everything about the arrangement, especially the part where he had to schedule times to see his son. A boy needed his father a lot more than twice a week, but Marcella had dug in her heels. He had been abiding by her timetable while he tried to worm his way back into her good graces, but this evening he had other priorities. "I can't make it tonight," he told her. "Something's come up."

"You're supposed to be here in half an hour," she shot back. "You can't just call and cancel last minute. I have plans."

Jealousy pricked him, and he reacted before he could stop himself. "What plans? Where are you going?"

"That's none of your business. We're not together anymore, remember?"

How could he forget? He was sleeping alone every night and hadn't had sex since she'd thrown him out. "Our situation is only temporary. I want to come home and be your husband again—and a full-time father to Franco."

"That's not happening unless I see some major changes."

"You can't be serious about—"

She cut him off midcomplaint. "Don't act like you don't know what I'm talking about. I told you what I want a hundred times, but you've spent the last three years tuning me out like I don't matter."

Women loved making mountains out of molehills, and his wife was no exception. Even so, he knew he'd better say something nice or she'd curse him and hang up. "You do matter. You and Franco are my family, and I need you."

She made a scoffing sound. "Those are pretty words, but I know if I take you back, I'll regret it. Nothing will change."

"That's not true. I've been working hard at those changes you want."

Just as he'd hoped, curiosity got the better of her. "What changes have you made?"

"I quit smoking." A decision he was sorely regretting today because of the pressure he was under from Sidorov.

"Yeah? For how long?"

"Four days." He added quickly, "I know that's not very long, but I also know how much you hate it. I promise this time I'm gonna kick the habit for good."

"That one change isn't enough."

"Okay, then listen to this. I got a job." Before she could fire off a dozen questions, he answered the one he knew would be uppermost in her mind. "It's not permanent. Actually, it's only for a few weeks, but it could work out to be longer." Of course, that was only a possibility if he got back in Sidorov's good graces by finding Brooke Rogers.

"What kind of job is it?" Marcella asked.

"Private security." He liked the way that sounded. So much better than "hired muscle." The work consisted of protecting Sidorov and his family and making sure people who owed his boss paid their debts on time. If they didn't, he roughed them up a bit, then waved around the gun Sidorov had provided. That always won him their respect and cooperation. "When I get paid at the end of the week, I can give you enough for next month's rent and food. The reason I can't come tonight is I'm working overtime."

She was silent for a moment, probably shocked by the good news he was earning again. He hadn't been employed much since he'd got out of prison. His ego and his marriage had been hit hard by that period of his life, but he was making money now and that was what counted.

"Don't you need that money to live on?" she asked.

"Nah, my deal includes room and board." The apartment above Sidorov's garage was nothing compared to the luxurious rooms inside the main house, but it was a step up from some of the cockroach-infested places he'd lived in when he was single. And it was a big improvement over crashing at his buddy Mike's place and getting dirty looks from Mike's girlfriend whenever he forgot to use a damn coaster under his beer bottle.

Marcella let out a sigh. "I know you're busy, but can you come over here for an hour? Franco has been jabbering all day about seeing his daddy. If you don't show, he'll cry his eyes out. You don't want that, do you?"

He didn't know if Marcella was exaggerating or not, but the thought of his son being unhappy stabbed him in the heart. His little boy had shed enough tears in the past month. Little kids didn't understand why their parents sometimes had problems. They only knew they missed the one that moved out. "All right, I'll be there in fifteen minutes. Make sure he has his soccer ball. I'll take him to the park."

Marcella and Franco were waiting outside their five-story apartment building when he turned into the parking lot. Franco wore his favorite Spider-Man T-shirt, and he was holding a soccer ball that looked huge in his small hands. As soon as Latschenko stepped out of his vehicle, the boy dropped the ball and ran flat out for him. "Daddy," he shrieked with unbridled enthusiasm.

There was no sweeter sound in the world than his son calling his name. He missed that high-pitched, innocent voice and the sunny smile that reminded him of his younger brother. One day in the future, he and Franco might butt heads as fathers and sons often did, but today he knew his son was overjoyed at the chance to spend time together. Excitement giving him wings, Franco vaulted into the air. Latschenko caught him, curling his left arm under his little rump, and hugged him close.

"You got a boo-boo, Daddy." His son pointed to his bandaged right hand. "Does it hurt?"

"Not too much," he lied.

"Head rub?" Franco asked tentatively.

"Sure." With his sore hand, he gave him a gentle head-knuckle rub. The boy giggled and mimicked him, twisting his tiny fist on his father's head. Carrying his son in the crook of his arm, Latschenko crossed the asphalt to speak to his wife.

She had her dark hair scraped back into the bun he loathed, but otherwise she looked great in tight jeans and a black striped top whose low neckline showed off her luscious cleavage. As he approached, her expression was stern, and he figured she was still mad about having to cancel her "plans" tonight. What plans were so important to her? Was she dating somebody?

His guts twisted at the prospect of another man's hands on her, and he wondered if she had decided to betray her wedding vows. No, she wouldn't do that, especially now that she knew how hard he was trying to fix their marriage. He wanted to grab her and kiss her until she begged him to move back home, but he restrained the urge. "You look pretty. If I didn't have to work, I'd be tempted to stay longer than an hour."

His compliment made her blush, and she gnawed at her lower lip, a nervous habit of hers as familiar to him as the contours of her face. Before their separation, he'd have nuzzled her neck and patted her butt, but he didn't want to risk her wrath.

"I'm glad you could get away," she said. "Franco really wants to show you some new moves with his ball, and I can keep my hair appointment with the woman who lives in 2B. She used to work at Giovanni's salon, and I'm desperate for a change."

"You're not gonna chop off all your hair, are you?" He hated short hair on women. It made them look like men, which was a crime against nature.

"So what if I am?" She arched an eyebrow. "It's my hair. You don't get a say anymore about what I do."

He changed tactics, realizing too late he'd made a mistake by offering an opinion, even if it was a right one. "Okay, okay. Just don't do anything you'll regret, okay?"

"Mommy, Daddy, don't fight." Franco's head swiveled between the two of them, his eyes wide and sad.

"We're not fighting, little man."

"That's right," Marcella chimed in. "Daddy and I are just talking."

His son's mutinous expression announced clearly that he didn't believe them.

"Give us the ball," Latschenko said to his wife. "We men have some running and kicking to do at the park. Isn't that right, Franco?"

"Yeah. I am so fast now I can beat you." He stretched out his thin arms to take the soccer ball from his mother.

"I can't wait for you to show me." After a nod to Marcella, Latschenko headed in the direction of the park, his arms full of the little boy who was his pride and joy. There was nothing he wouldn't do for his son. Nothing. He would work hard to get back together with Franco's mother, so his son would once again have a whole family, not a broken one. And he would work hard to support that family properly. The job with Sidorov was a good one, and the guy had hinted he was expanding his business and might need to hire an extra man to help Chernov. Finding the PI would prove Latschenko was that man. What happened to her afterward wasn't something he wanted to think about, especially while he was holding his sweet little boy.

"What time is it?" Brooke mumbled, her voice groggy from sleep.

Jared didn't glance up from his laptop, even though his heart skipped a beat at the sound of her voice. "Seven o'clock."

"In the morning?"

Her guess suggested she'd noticed the sunlight streaming through a crack in the curtains.

"Your short nap turned into a very long rest."

Last night, he had made the mistake of looking at her stretched out on the bed. Asleep, with her blond hair fanning out like a halo, Brooke appeared angelic. But the instant his gaze strayed from her face, the ethereal comparison vanished. Her shapely breasts and showgirl legs, still clad in tank top and jeans, were sinful, not saintly. He'd jerked his gaze away, but for the rest of the evening, her soft breathing and frequent shifting of position had messed with his concentration, which made no sense at all. She was unconscious, for Pete's sake. How could she be such a distraction? As ridiculous as it was, his awareness of her hadn't diminished until he'd fallen asleep himself at midnight in the second double bed.

The bed creaked as she sat up. "Is there anything to eat?"

"There are blueberry muffins in the bag on top of the minibar. If you want coffee, I made some fresh twenty minutes ago."

"Thanks." Her voice was still a little husky from sleep, which he liked more than he should have. She surged off the bed, and he heard her helping herself to a muffin and a cup of coffee.

"Your phone buzzed while you were asleep," he said.

"Did you pick up?"

"Yeah. It was your sister. She and Trevor drove all day and have arrived at the condo in Hilton Head."

"Okay, that's good to know."

After a few minutes, her footsteps crossed the room again and then stopped nearby. His skin prickled, but he didn't glance up, hoping she'd get the hint that he was busy and she shouldn't talk to him.

She cleared her throat. "Do you think the guy Sidorov referred to during the muffled section of the recording could be Alex's missing friend?"

Her thoughts were in sync with his, dammit. All night, the possibility that Steve had been the *threat dealt with* by Latschenko's predecessor, Chernov, had weighed heavily on Jared's mind, but he'd told himself the words' meaning was inconclusive without hard evidence.

"The guy's family must be so worried," Brooke continued, her voice placing her as having moved close to his chair. "How long has he been gone?"

Jared answered without intending to. "Three days for sure. Maybe up to ten."

"What's his connection to Sidorov?"

Again, words tumbled out of his mouth before he could stop them. "The guy's sister said there was trouble between them."

Jared glanced over in time to see Brooke slip her hands into her pockets. The movement caused her jeans to ride down. Another inch or two and her belly would show beneath her top. He wondered if the skin would be pale or tanned—

"That's it? She didn't give you anything else?"

He dragged his attention back to their conversation. "She didn't know any details, but it was enough to get my attention. That's why I came to Langeville."

"Do you believe the guy is still alive? Given Sidorov's money and his armed thugs, he has the means to make anybody disappear. Permanently."

Jared couldn't fault her logic, but it fueled his darkest fears and made it difficult to think objectively. He couldn't afford to wallow in emotion, so he took a deep breath, reminding himself there was no proof Steve was dead.

"If Sidorov ordered a hit," she speculated, "I wonder where the body is."

Her blunt words were like physical blows, chipping away at his defenses, inflicting damage that hurt like hell. He had to shut her down. "I shouldn't be discussing this with you."

"It doesn't hurt to brainstorm possibilities, does it? I've got nothing better to do."

Pressure built up inside Jared, threatening to explode. If she kept at him, he was going to blurt out the truth—that he was terrified she was right, that his brother had been killed and was lost to him forever.

"Your boredom isn't my problem. I have a case to solve, and your comments aren't helping."

She was silent for a long moment, considering him. "It's going badly, isn't it?"

"Yes," he admitted. He'd tried and failed to locate Chernov, and he wasn't sure what he should do next. Meanwhile, there was a clock ticking away in his head. For every hour that passed, the chances Steve would be found alive and well diminished.

Brooke tucked a strand of blond hair behind her ear. "I know finding out what happened to this missing person is your top priority, but if there was another way to get Sidorov arrested, would you be willing to spend some time on that?"

"You're talking about the bankers Trevor mentioned."

She nodded. "If their deaths could be linked to Sidorov, those murders could bring him down."

"Yes, they could," he agreed. "Unfortunately, the

local police don't like to help out the feds without a ton of paperwork. That's why I told your brother-in-law it would take a while."

"I still have contacts at the Columbus Police Department. I could ask for the incident reports as well as the medical examiner's findings."

Interesting, Jared thought. Her words implied she'd been a cop prior to becoming a PI. "That might speed things up," he admitted. He retrieved the list of names Trevor had written down.

With a smile, she picked up her phone and headed into the bathroom to make the call. A few minutes later, she was back. "Okay, we're all set. The reports will be sent to my email account in the next couple of hours. I'll need to borrow your laptop to access them."

"Sure. We can go through them together."

She smiled again as if the idea of their collaborating on a task pleased her. He wondered if there was anything else she'd like to do together. Giving in to impulse, he got up from his chair and approached her, not stopping until he was standing directly in front of her. "I've been meaning to ask you something. When you were outside the diner with your sister, who were you talking about?"

Her face flushed a deep rose color as she laid her cell phone down on the dresser. "Ah, I don't remember."

Her proximity was having a predictable effect on his anatomy, but he didn't mind. Not at all. "Really? Your choice of words made it pretty clear you're attracted to this guy. Do you know what my first thought was?"

She shook her head, her eyes wary. He realized he wasn't the only one aroused by their nearness. Her breasts rose and fell quickly, their peaked nipples showing plainly through the silky material of her top.

"My first thought was 'I hope she's talking about me because I'm really attracted to her, too.'"

Her eyes darkened, and he sensed her waiting to see what he'd do next. He stared at her mouth. Would she be okay with a direct approach or should he give her some time to make up her mind? He opted for the latter and brushed his lips over her jaw. She jolted as if zapped by an electrical charge. He felt it, too. The zing of mutual attraction. Nuzzling her neck, he breathed in her fragrant scent. "You smell really good." He edged back to look at her. "I wonder how you taste."

She wet her lips, an invitation he didn't hesitate to act on. He kissed her softly until her lips opened with a low, needy moan. Slipping his tongue inside, he took his time caressing every moist contour and delicious curve. She had an addictive taste, he decided, one that made him want to go slowly and keep on kissing her. Meanwhile, his hands were stroking her back, pressing her against him, letting her feel the strength of his arousal. Eventually, she grabbed hold of his shoulders, and her body strained against his, showing him that he wasn't the only one with needs.

He devoured her until he had to break off in order to breathe. Her gasps told him she'd run out of air, too. Hungry for more of her, he slipped his hands under her top and touched her bare stomach. His fingertips encountered puckered skin—

"No," she cried out. She shoved him away and fled to the far side of the room.

He was too taken aback to say anything.

From a safe distance, she smoothed down her top

and addressed him in a cool tone of voice. "That was too far, too fast, mister. I'm not having sex with you."

She made it sound as if he had been overly aggressive, which wasn't fair. Yes, he'd held her tightly and got hard. Yes, he'd kissed her deeply, erotically. But if she'd wanted to stop, she could have just said so. There was no need for her to sprint across the room and deliver that disapproving lecture. She had been with him, kiss for kiss, the whole way. She had been passionate and willing right up to the very last second. She just didn't want to admit her feelings to him or herself.

He opened his mouth to clarify the situation for the Queen of Denial but stopped when the motel phone rang. Brooke was closest, so she answered it while he realized the only person who knew that number was—

Brooke turned to him, her eyes wide with alarm. "It's the motel manager. He says a big guy in a leather jacket is asking about me."

In less than twenty-four hours, Latschenko had discovered their hideout.

Chapter 7

Brooke swallowed hard as Jared took the phone from her trembling fingers.

"Thanks for the heads-up," he told the manager. "Add fifty bucks to my bill and say you never saw her."

Jared's deep voice barely registered past the roaring in her head. *Latschenko is here. Run.*

She jumped as Jared's hands gripped her shoulders. "I know you're worried, but you need to listen to me."

"Let's not waste time talking, okay? We need to get the heck out of here."

"That's definitely part of the plan," he said, stroking his hands down her arms.

The gesture was one of reassurance, but even in the urgency of the moment, she felt a frisson of something else. Sexual awareness. Wildly inappropriate under the circumstances, yet undeniably present.

"What's the rest of the plan?" she croaked.

"You take my car through the motel's back alley and park behind the Dumpster."

"What about you?"

He smiled grimly. "I'm going to fix the sonovabitch's car so he can't follow us."

The idea of a stranded Latschenko appealed to her, but not the possibility that he might catch Jared sabotaging his vehicle.

She shook her head. "I don't like the plan. It's too dangerous."

"So is a high-speed chase if he comes after us."

"True, but—"

"Wait ten minutes," he continued, as if she hadn't spoken. "If I don't show, leave."

Abandoning him felt flat-out wrong. "No."

"If I'm late, there's been trouble. Trouble I can deal with better if I know you're far away from it."

The fact that he viewed her as a liability hurt because it was justified. She had panicked yesterday when faced with danger. Why would he think he could trust her to help him, if needed?

"Ten minutes," he insisted. "Then you head to safety, no matter what. Please, do this for me."

Despite her misgivings, it was senseless to argue with him. "Okay."

He released her. "Grab my bag from the closet, will you?"

As she rushed to do that, he went to work clearing off the desk. A moment later, he had his laptop case hanging over his shoulder by the strap and a gun in his hand.

Her heart lurched.

"Don't forget your camera."

She retrieved it from the dresser, thinking of the trouble it had brought her.

"Ready?" Jared asked, his voice calm, his gaze focused.

Mouth too dry to make a sound, she nodded. If she had to be running for her life with anyone, she was glad it was Jared Nash.

He cracked open the door, then beckoned to her. "Go."

Sergei Latschenko knew he had a short fuse, but the motel manager at Twisted Pines was making him nuts. Before he'd made it halfway through his description of the female PI, the moron in the red bandanna had insisted on getting his reading glasses from the back room. Finding them had taken him a good five minutes, and the guy was now staring at him, not searching his ancient-looking computer.

"I'm gonna ask again." Latschenko leaned his bandaged hand on the counter, resisting the urge to shout. "You got a really tall, hot-looking blonde staying here? Her name is Brooke Rogers." He and Sidorov's men had split up the yellow-pages listing of local motels, and they were checking them out one by one. When he had pulled into Twisted Pines, he'd immediately recognized her vehicle from the description Sidorov had provided. If she wasn't here now, she'd be coming back at some point to pick up her SUV. And when she did, she'd find it undrivable, all four tires punctured. Slamming his knife deeply into them had relieved some of the frustration he'd been feeling, but the idiot in front of him was cranking him up again.

"What's her name again?"

"Brooke Rogers. Her SUV is out front."

The guy finally got pecking at his keyboard. "Nobody by that name is registered."

Maybe the chick had paid cash and made up a name. "You wanna make some money?"

"How much?"

He dropped a hundred-dollar bill on the counter.

The guy perked right up. "What do I have to do?"

"You give me the master key and tell me which units are occupied."

The guy behind the counter blinked like an owl. "Most of the people staying here are couples. And they don't want to be disturbed, if you know what I mean."

He knew, all right, having banged plenty of chicks in worse dumps than this. He'd stopped doing that when he met Marcella. But after eight years of marriage, she'd thrown him out. Now he had to arrange times to see his kid. His own damn son.

He dug five more twenties out of his wallet. "If anybody complains, give them this." Sidorov had told him to be generous with bribes to get the information he needed.

The office was hot as hell in spite of a fan humming on the counter and a partly open window. The fact that he wore a leather jacket to conceal his piece made the heat worse.

"Make a list of the rented rooms and bring it to me," he said, eager to catch a breeze outside.

In the shade of the overhanging roof, he was itching to light up a cigarette, but he didn't have any with him. This was the wrong damn week to try to quit. Too much was going down. To keep his job, he had to show Sidorov that he could find the PI fast.

He glanced over his shoulder. What the hell was keeping the manager? The moron must be yakking on the phone. Then he noticed something. A blue Mustang was missing. When he'd arrived, it had been parked in front of the second set of five units.

Nothing could have left the lot earlier without him hearing it because of the motel office's open window. The Mustang must have gone in the opposite direction. Why would it do that when there was no exit?

He set out for the units, then veered around the side of the building where a dirt alley stretched along the edge of the property. An eyesore of a green Dumpster cast a bulky shadow on the ground—the perfect place to hide a vehicle. He broke into a run.

Brooke drummed her fingers on the Mustang's steering wheel, then checked the digital clock again. Six minutes had passed, the red numbers changing faster than she had believed possible. Her nerves wound tighter and tighter as Jared's ten-minute deadline approached.

She stared out the Mustang's windshield at the deep gully separating the motel's property from the adjacent vacant lot. Strewn with broken glass, rusty equipment and wooden boards with protruding nails, the terrain was an obstacle course she didn't look forward to navigating. If she misjudged the slightest bit, the debris could damage the vehicle's tires and undercarriage.

She checked the clock again. Three minutes left. Obviously, Jared hadn't given himself enough time to sabotage Latschenko's car and rendezvous with her behind the Dumpster. His plan had been too hastily conceived. Ten minutes wasn't enough time; he should have allowed fifteen. Even so, she knew he'd be furious if she didn't follow instructions. But how could she just leave him when he was risking his life to protect her?

Come on, Jared.

The clock seemed to be speeding up, so she closed her eyes—

The passenger door opened. She exhaled a pent-up breath. "I was getting ready to leave," she said, opening her eyes.

It *wasn't* Jared getting into the car, and her relief turned to terror.

"Thanks for waiting," Latschenko said, his eyes as cold as she remembered.

Move!

Heart pounding, Brooke shoved open her door. Her sneaker touched down on dirt and her shoulder cleared the frame of the car, but then her momentum suddenly reversed direction. The thug had tangled his hand in her hair. He jerked her head back so brutally, she cried out.

"You're not getting away this time," Latschenko growled. "The more you fight, the more it's going to hurt."

She threw her weight sideways, trying to wrench herself out of his grasp. His grip didn't falter. She was like an animal caught in a trap, and she was experiencing the same panic at being unable to break free. A vicious tug dragged her backward into the car. She screamed as excruciating pain exploded in her neck.

Using her elbows like weapons, she punched backward. Her efforts were rewarded by a grunt of pain, then the blare of the horn as her arm connected with the steering wheel. She pressed down harder.

"Stop that." Knocking her arm away, Latschenko held her back against his chest. The smell of his sweat made her gag.

"Give me one good reason why I shouldn't knock you out." His bandaged hand brushed the underside of her breast.

Revulsion rose in her—but she knew if she were rendered unconscious, there was no chance of escape. An idea came to her, and even though it made her cringe, she had to try it. She forced herself to relax against him. "If I'm out cold, we can't go back to my motel room and make use of the bed."

He let out a harsh laugh. Shoving her back into the driver seat, he braced his arm across her collarbone to keep her there. "Is that why the lawn guy protected you? Because you promised him sex?"

She licked her lips, watching Latschenko's eyes track the movement. "He enjoyed his time with me, and so will you." She knew she was playing a dangerous game, but based on the conversation Jared had caught on tape, Sidorov was more dangerous than this man.

She faked a seductive smile. "There's no need to do it in a cramped car when there's a comfy room close by."

She expected him to cop a feel, but instead his hand curved around the column of her neck. "If my wife wasn't so hot, I might be tempted. Besides, I think you're trying to play me, and I'm not dumb enough to let that happen again. Mr. Sidorov has got some questions for you."

"I don't know anything. This has all been a mistake." She risked a sideways look at the open car door. Freedom seemed close by, but his hand on her throat kept her captive as well as the knowledge that he carried a gun. He hadn't used it up to now, but that didn't mean he wouldn't if he lost control over her.

"You brought a camera onto his property." A blunt finger lifted her chin. "Who hired you to spy on my boss? Was it the Nash family?"

Her whole body jolted in shock. The missing guy's name was Nash?

"Your silence tells me I'm right."

"I'm not working for the Nash family or anybody else," she insisted. "I was just too surprised to answer."

He let out a curse. "I don't believe you."

"But—"

He cut off her denial by seizing her throat, his fingers digging into the sensitive skin. "You talk too much."

She tried desperately to break his choke hold, but he was strong, and no amount of clawing at his hand or pounding on his arm had any effect. He was going to make her black out, so she'd be easier to deliver to Sidorov. She couldn't let that happen. Calling on every bit of self-control, she forced herself to close her eyes, stop fighting and go limp.

He didn't ease off. Not at all.

Stay still, she told herself. Her head pounded. Her throat burned. Her lungs begged for air. Oh God, what if he held on too long and killed her by accident?

Suddenly, there was a thudding sound and the pressure left her neck. She knew she had to act immediately or lose the element of surprise, so she flung herself toward the open door. This time, she was stopped by a strong hand on her wrist and a familiar voice saying, "Don't go. You're safe."

She turned back to see Jared looming over Latschenko's slumped body, his SIG Sauer in his free hand. Her heart leaped at the sight of him.

"I'm sorry I didn't get here sooner." Releasing her wrist, he touched her flushed cheek. "I didn't realize you were in trouble until I heard the horn."

"You came…in time," she croaked. The pain from Latschenko's choke hold was terrible, and talking magnified its intensity tenfold. She would thank Jared with words later. For now, her eyes would have to express her gratitude.

His gaze locked with hers. Something stirred in her, and she forgot all about being grateful. She wanted to be close to him, to feel his heart beating against hers, to inhale his scent. Like a flower seeking the sun, she reached out for him.

He gently eased her back into her seat. "The dizziness will pass in a moment. Just breathe deeply."

He thought oxygen deprivation had made her move toward him? Obviously, she needed to make her feelings clearer…except she didn't actually know what those feelings were. And she had no clue what he was feeling either. Those gray eyes of his were no window to his soul. Instead, they were enigmatic, mysterious, secretive.

"Who hired you to spy? Was it the Nash family?" Remembering Latschenko's words gave her a much-needed reality check.

"I'll drive." Jared backed out the open passenger

door. "Why don't you switch seats while I dispose of Latschenko?"

Good idea. She wasn't up to concentrating on traffic. She watched, her mind racing with questions, as Jared dragged the unconscious man out of the car.

If a familial connection existed between him and the missing person, how could Jared be the agent in charge of the investigation? That would be a conflict of interest, and the FBI would likely have a policy prohibiting his involvement. He had to be acting without official sanction.

A feeling of dread lodged like cement in her stomach. She knew, from her brief stint as a cop, gathering enough evidence for the arrest of a man like Sidorov was a painstaking, time-consuming process. It usually took a team of dedicated professionals to pull it off. And despite Jared's amply demonstrated competence, he was only one person.

When he returned to the car, he looked surprised to find her still behind the wheel. She climbed over the gearshift to the passenger seat, and he slid his long, muscular body into the seat she'd vacated.

Suddenly she was grateful he'd misinterpreted her reaching for him as a reaction to her ordeal. And maybe it was. She shouldn't be cozying up to a stranger, especially one with a hidden agenda. From now on, she'd keep her distance—and her hormones in check.

He started the engine and turned to her. She shifted over against the door.

His expression was grim as he eyed her throat. "We'd better get ice on that right away."

Ice would help with the swelling but not the bruises that would soon develop. Or the anger she felt at his deception. At least her injury gave her a good excuse to stay silent and mull over what her next move should be. Her companion's deceit reinforced a truth she had learned when she was shot two years ago.

The only person she could rely on was herself.

Chapter 8

"Where...?"

"Where are we going?" Jared finished Brooke's sentence, as he'd been doing ever since they'd left the motel. He didn't want her talking more than necessary. He could tell it hurt her by the way she winced when she spoke.

Damn, he hated that Latschenko had laid his hands on her, and he blamed himself for not preventing it. He shouldn't have allowed her out of his sight. Not even for a few minutes. But his self-recriminations couldn't change what had happened. All he could do now was take care of her while she recovered.

They stopped at a gas station where he bought cold water bottles and ice and called Alex. The two discussed various options for accommodations. When he returned to the car, he passed Brooke a drink and set to work fashioning an ice pack out of one of the T-shirts he pulled from his suitcase.

"Where next?" she prompted again.

"In fifteen minutes, we'll head north and meet Alex." He passed her the ice pack, and she pressed it against her throat.

"Another motel?"

"No," he said, his voice grim. He wasn't making that mistake again.

"FBI safe house?"

Not an option. But a place could be safe without being owned by the Bureau.

"It's private and secure," he assured her.

Alex had invited them to stay at his cousin's, where he was crashing while he helped look for Steve. The cousin was a teacher and had gone to France for the summer, so they'd have the run of the place with no questions asked. Alex couldn't meet them for half an hour and the key was with him, not under a doormat or inside a ceramic frog in the garden.

Brooke shifted in her seat. The sunshine through the windshield lit up her hair, rendering the blond strands as fine as spun gold. It made him think of song lyrics he'd once heard. Something about a *treasure beyond compare.* He wasn't prone to whimsical musings. Funny the song should come to mind when he was looking at a woman he'd known for such a short time. Then Jared noticed the ice pack had dripped onto her blue shirt, rendering it translucent and causing her left nipple to pebble from the cold. His heart beat faster as he wished her whole breast had been revealed.

He yanked his gaze away. What was wrong with him? The woman needed safeguarding, not ogling. But every minute he spent with Brooke Rogers fired up his testosterone as if she were an aphrodisiac.

Maybe it was his body objecting to a long stretch of abstinence. After discovering his longtime girlfriend had cheated on him, he'd been so angry and disappointed he'd immersed himself in work. Months had passed with no sex and no interest in changing his celibacy. But close proximity to a knockout like Brooke flooded his head with erotic fantasies.

The new place had another advantage. Alex Sheridan. He would be the proverbial third wheel, an unwitting chaperone to his two houseguests—

Brooke's hoarse voice broke through his thoughts. "Why didn't you tell me…the missing guy's name is Nash?"

His head whipped around. "What?" he said, not because he hadn't heard her, but because she shouldn't know that info.

"You should have been…honest with me. Instead, I had to hear it…from Latschenko."

Jared's hands tightened into fists, and he wished he'd tossed the bastard into the Dumpster, instead of leaving him next to it. Sidorov's orders had been to bring Brooke back for questioning, not strike up a conversation with her. However, events had unfolded differently for everybody concerned. Because Latschenko had shot off his mouth to Brooke, Jared now had a damage-control issue.

"The guy nearly strangled you," he said. "I wouldn't consider him a reliable source."

"Who is? You?" Her voice was raw, but there was a sarcastic bite to her words.

"I haven't lied to you."

Her blue eyes narrowed. "No lies…but no straight answers."

"I told you before. You don't need to know."

"Too late. I *know* you're related to—"

He cut her off, saying, "That's not relevant. I will find evidence against Sidorov. All I need from you is to lie low while I do it."

She reached for her water bottle. Took several slow sips.

Jared could hear her swallowing from the other side of the car. Talking had to irritate her throat. And although it made him a heartless bastard, he hoped the discomfort would put an end to their conversation. Discussing Steve with Alex ripped him up bad enough. He wasn't going to let Brooke get in on the act, too.

She returned the bottle to the cup holder. "Sidorov isn't…on the FBI's radar. Nobody there…is after him."

Her statement took him aback, but he kept his expression impassive. "Not true. I am."

"Not in an official capacity. You need more resources than yourself to take him down."

"No, I don't."

She pointed to herself. "I have law-enforcement experience and I'm available."

"I'm not looking for a partner."

Her mouth tightened into a flat line. "You could do worse."

"You're a civilian and Sidorov wants to kill you."

"That makes me motivated to see him behind bars."

"I'm not arguing with you anymore."

"Good." When her lips curved, he realized she'd misinterpreted his remark. "Tell me what leads you've got."

"Forget it."

"You talk, or I walk."

He didn't like the fierce resolve in her eyes. "What do you mean?"

"I won't sit idle while you search for evidence to nail Sidorov. If I can't be involved, then I'm gone."

"Gone where?"

"You don't need to know."

Stubborn woman. If she thought issuing an ultimatum would change his mind, she would be sorely disappointed.

And yet…she was about to make a dangerous mistake. "You shouldn't be alone. It isn't safe."

"I'll pass your concern on to the police when I see them."

"You can't rely on them to protect you," he said, alarm deepening his voice. "You heard Sidorov. He has someone on the inside watching for you."

"I'll have to take my chances." She reached for the door handle, lifted the lever. Was she really going to leave?

A second later, her hand dropped away and the breath he'd been holding rushed out. Smart lady. She'd come to her senses and decided to remain with him.

She turned her face to him, mustered up a small smile. "Thanks for saving my life. I won't forget it."

It. Not *him*. The impersonal pronoun was distinctly unsatisfying. He wanted her to remember him, not what he'd done for her.

She shoved open the car door, her golden hair swinging. She wasn't bluffing about leaving.

"Wait," he called out.

She glanced over her shoulder at him, still poised to exit the car. Damn, was he really going to cave to her demand? Yeah, he was. Because if he didn't, he knew he'd feel the same regret for turning his back on her as he felt for Steve.

"You can..." His voice trailed off.

"I can...what?" she asked in a low voice.

"You can know details of my investigation." That wasn't exactly accepting her offer to help, but at least he wasn't totally shutting her out.

She considered him. "Tell me who in your family is missing."

There was no way around it. He had to tell her or watch her walk away. He cleared his throat. "My brother."

Her eyes widened in surprise. "That's why you looked so upset back at the motel."

He was tempted to deny it, but he doubted she'd believe him.

She eased back into her seat and closed the door. "I'm really sorry for what I said. I shouldn't have speculated so negatively about what might have happened to him."

He didn't reply, just steeled himself against the compassion in her voice.

They sat in silence for a few moments.

She drank more from her water bottle. Fiddled with the lid. "I'm right about you not having FBI support, aren't I?"

He nodded. "Sidorov has been retired from the Russian mob for a year, so the FBI has no interest in him."

"But your brother has gone missing," she said indignantly.

"There's no real evidence of that." He rolled his shoulders, trying to ease the tension in them. "I went to the room Steve was renting. Even though his stuff is gone, I *know* he didn't leave voluntarily."

"You think somebody moved his belongings to make it look that way?"

"Yeah, I do. The lock on the door is junk. Anybody could have jimmied it."

"Who saw him last?"

"His landlady talked to him a week ago before she went to visit her sister. She wasn't aware anything was wrong until I showed up Monday saying his family was worried about him. That's when she let me in and discovered the room had been cleared out."

Brooke's blue eyes searched his, and he noticed the color of her irises darkened to cobalt when she was concerned. He could lose himself in those eyes…

"What was your brother doing in Langeville?"

"Working for a local contractor. According to my sister, he was hired to do minor repairs and paint houses."

"Did you talk to the guy?"

"Of course. He thinks Steve got bored and took off—with two hundred dollars he'd been given to buy supplies."

"Is that a possibility?" she asked.

"Steve might have pocketed some unearned money, but that doesn't explain his being out of touch. He calls our sister every Sunday like clockwork. He didn't do that, and he's not answering his cell phone." He dragged a hand through his hair. Every hour that went by increased the odds he wouldn't find his brother alive.

"We should go," he added. "Alex is going to wonder what's keeping us."

"That's your brother's friend? The one I met at the motel?"

"We're staying with him."

"He doesn't mind last-minute guests?"

"He's happy to help out, although he did ask if you could cook."

"I think my time is better spent looking for Steve."

"About that—"

"Don't even think about reneging on our deal." She fastened her seat belt with long, elegant fingers. "You may not be expecting much from me, but I intend to surprise you."

He didn't doubt that. Brooke Rogers had surprised him plenty of times since they'd met. The biggest surprise was his relief she wasn't leaving. And although he told himself he was merely worried about her safety, the rationalization didn't quite ring true.

Right after Alex Sheridan gave them a tour of his cousin's contemporary split-level, Brooke noticed the man edging toward the door.

"I have to leave," he said. "My uncle has suffered a heart attack."

"How awful," she replied. "How's he doing?"

Alex shook his head. "It doesn't sound good. After my dad left, he stepped in and did so much for us. I want to try and see him, and if he doesn't recover, I need to stay with my mom for a while."

She nodded sympathetically. "Of course you do."

He turned to Jared. "I feel bad about bailing on you."

"Don't," the other man said immediately. "You go be with your family. It's the right place for you."

"I'll text you when I know more. Hopefully, I'll

only be gone a few days. I want to come back and finish this with you."

"Thanks. You've already been a big help."

"While I'm gone, you two can get settled into the place. There's beer and juice in the fridge, as well as some breakfast food. Help yourself to whatever you want. As for dinner, I saw restaurant menus in one of the drawers." He regarded Jared with a wide, unblinking stare.

Brooke sensed some silent communication passing between the men but was unable to interpret it. "We appreciate you letting us stay here."

Alex shrugged. "No problem."

After Alex left, Jared sank into a black leather chair and closed his eyes. He looked tired, and Brooke wondered if he had spent the past few nights awake, worrying about his brother. She felt the sudden urge to hold him, reassure him, but that was what girlfriends were for. Given his good looks, muscular physique and undeniable masculinity, she couldn't imagine him lacking female companionship. Or if he did, it was by choice.

She thought about their passionate interlude at the motel. She had enjoyed touching him and kissing him, but then his fingers had touched the scar on her stomach, and her attraction had fizzled like flat cola. She could tell her cool treatment of him afterward had confused and annoyed him, but she'd done that for his benefit. He could do so much better than cozying up to a woman who was a train wreck, both inside and out.

No, he wouldn't want her to comfort him. The best way to thank him for saving her life was to come up with a new angle on his sibling's disappearance.

She sat on the couch and mulled over what she'd

learned. What if Steve had been abducted from a place other than his room?

"Do you still have that contractor's number?" she asked.

Jared's eyes fluttered open slowly as if he'd dozed off for a second.

Man, he has thick, sexy lashes. And that not-yet-fully-awake expression was a turn-on. She was pretty sure that would be the way he'd look in the morning after a long night of lovemaking.

"What did you say?" he asked.

She repeated her question, her mouth going dry as he leaned forward to answer, his biceps flexing.

"Sure. Why do you ask?"

"I think we should search the last house Steve worked on."

Jared frowned. "The focus has to remain on Sidorov. My brother's cell-phone records showed he called Sidorov's house the week before he disappeared."

He was brushing her off, going back on their agreement in the car. Evidently, he didn't realize the deal wasn't negotiable.

"What's the contractor's name and number?" she persisted.

Annoyance tightened his face. "Ed Keesing is *not* going to cooperate. He's mad as hell about the money that vanished when Steve did. I already asked to see the house, and he told me to forget it unless I had a warrant."

"I've dealt with obstinate people before." Like the man in front of her.

"You'd be wasting your time."

"It's my time to waste, isn't it?"

A broad shoulder lifted in a shrug. "Knock yourself out."

He passed over his cell phone, telling her the block-number feature was activated and the fifth number on the list was the contractor. Then he heaved himself out of his seat and headed for the kitchen.

She held the phone, weighing what words to use to Steve's boss. What would get her inside that house? She could say she was a friend of Steve's who had visited him there and accidentally left something behind. The only problem was she didn't know the address. Then she thought about Sidorov's assumption she'd been hired to find Steve.

As she made the call, Jared appeared in the doorway holding a can of Coors, his hooded eyes watching her. Why the sudden interest? Did he want to witness her fail? *Not going to happen.*

When a gruff voice answered, she spoke confidently. "Hello, Mr. Keesing. My name is Brooke Rogers. I'm a private investigator hired by the family of Steve Nash. I understand he was last seen working on one of your jobs."

"He painted a house over on Middleview Road for me," the man told her grudgingly. "But I already told his brother I don't know where he is."

"I'd like to see the place."

"What for?"

"There might be something there that could help me locate him."

"I've been through it since he left. There's nothing."

"I'd like to look for myself. And I'm prepared to give you two hundred dollars for your time." If this ploy worked, she'd have to ask Jared for the cash.

Keesing made an impatient sound. "I'm too busy to give you a tour."

"I don't need a tour, just a key. I'll return it when I'm finished."

"I'm not handing over a key to a complete stranger."

"His family is really worried about him."

"They don't need to be. He'll turn up."

She tried again. "He isn't answering his cell phone—"

"Dodging creditors, no doubt."

The guy was royally teed off, but she couldn't let his anger stand in her way. "Listen, they're terrified something's happened to him."

"If that's true, why haven't the police contacted me?"

The question caught her off guard for a second. "They will in short order, Mr. Keesing."

He snorted.

She sensed he was a split second away from hanging up on her. "You should be aware the family is making a lot of noise at the police department. They won't stop until a search warrant for that house is issued."

"Good luck to them."

"Actually, it won't be good luck for you if they succeed. When the police conduct a search, they look everywhere. And I do mean *everywhere*. They tear up floorboards. They punch holes in walls. In short, they make a complete mess."

Keesing cursed in loud, colorful language.

"You have the power to prevent that," she noted.

"What do you mean?"

"You let me look through the house. If I find nothing, I report back to the family, and they stop pushing for a search warrant."

Silence on the other end of the phone. Then, "I'm

just the contractor. I have to check with the company who owns the property."

"You do that. And be sure to warn whoever is in charge he's risking serious property damage if he's uncooperative."

"Why don't you talk to Martin Wilson? I hired Steve on his recommendation. Maybe Steve mentioned his plans to Wilson."

"Thanks for the suggestion, but I still want to see the house."

Another silence, this one shorter. "All right, but you'll have to wait till eight o'clock tonight. I'll meet you there."

"What's the address?"

"22 Middleview."

Ending the call, she felt like punching a fist in the air for victory. She settled for glancing at the doorway, where Jared still stood. His expression was no longer tight as he saluted her with his beer. "Okay, I'm impressed. Your arguments were very persuasive. Nicely done."

His praise was like sunshine, warming her skin, her bones, her insides. But it was stupid to read so much into his words. He was no different from the other men who had passed through her life. They made nice as long as they got what they wanted from her. When she disappointed them, they moved on.

"Are you hungry?" he asked.

"I'm not cooking," she said automatically.

The corner of his mouth kicked up. "I'm not asking you to. I found the stash of menus Alex mentioned."

"Nice investigative work," she murmured. "Let's check them out and pick a place."

She expected him to head back into the kitchen, but he stayed put. Only his eyes moved. From her hair to her lips. Then they journeyed over her body, tracing the contours of her breasts, her hips and her legs, as if he were a sculptor intrigued by her form. Heat licked every place his eyes roamed. She wanted to throw off her clothes just to cool off.

Oh, who was she kidding? Her wonky internal thermostat wasn't the reason. She wanted him to see her naked. Which made no sense. She hated her body. Avoided looking at it whenever she showered or dressed. She dipped her head and crossed her arms over her scarred midsection.

Footsteps sounded in the kitchen, which meant he'd stopped watching her. Good. The extent of her relief shamed her. She was so messed up. No wonder Chad had bailed on her and was now married to a skydiving instructor who bore no scars inside or out.

Jared returned with the menus. "Pizza? Burgers? Chinese?" His neutral tone belied the fact that he'd seemed hungry for *her* a few minutes ago.

She cleared her throat. "I don't care what I eat, as long as I can get some clean clothes for tomorrow." Belatedly, she remembered she had no cash in her wallet, and using her credit cards could be risky. "Ah, can I borrow some money? I'll pay you back when this is all over."

He nodded. "If you'd rather stay here, I'll pick up whatever you need."

She needed a complete change of clothes including pj's and underwear, but the thought of him choosing intimate apparel for her made her uncomfortable. "Thanks for the offer, but that isn't necessary."

"It's no big deal. I've shopped for women's clothing before."

She'd just bet he had. She stretched out her legs, trying not to think about him wandering through a Victoria's Secret store, choosing lacy bras and satin thongs for girlfriends, past and present.

His gaze moved to her legs and stayed there. Hmm, maybe he didn't have a current girlfriend. For no good reason, the thought gave her a much-needed lift in mood.

"How long is your inseam?" he asked.

Her mood crashed to the ground. He hadn't been eyeballing her legs because he was attracted to her. He'd simply been measuring them for a pair of pants.

"You don't need to know my inseam," she said. "I'm buying my own clothes."

"My sister says I have good taste."

Sister. Not girlfriend. Oh, stop with that.

"Your sister could like sequined tops and stretch pants, for all I know," she muttered.

Crinkle lines appeared at the corners of his eyes, and he chuckled. The sound had a rusty undertone, as though he hadn't laughed in a long time. "You're something else, Blondie."

He'd called her that when he'd given her a ride to her car. The nickname made sense for someone with such fair hair, she supposed. So why did it sound like an endearment on his lips?

Because she foolishly wanted it to be.

Chapter 9

The line for tables in Chuck's Chicken Hut was so daunting they decided to get takeout and bring it back to the house. Half an hour later, Jared set his plastic plate on the end table and wiped his hands on a napkin. "That hit the spot."

"You must be psychic," Brooke said, easing back onto the couch. "I was thinking exactly the same thing."

She looked pretty relaxed. Funny how buying a few new discount-store clothes could dramatically improve a woman's outlook. Or maybe it was the food. He knew he always felt edgy when he hadn't eaten for a while.

The meal had satisfied his appetite for food, but his proximity to Brooke stoked a different kind of hunger. She took a sip of her cherry drink. The liquid stained her lips a deep red, and they looked moist and luscious. He wanted to taste them. Oh yeah. He wanted to taste so much more of her than just her mouth.

"The meeting with the contractor is at eight," she said. "What should we do until then?"

Make out on that wide, comfy couch.

He cursed under his breath. Brooke would be surprised by the response his libido very much wanted to give her.

She shifted, drawing his attention to parts of her anatomy he had no business looking at. Fortunately, she seemed clueless about her effect on him. He wanted it to stay that way. If she knew how hot he was for her, she might try to manipulate him. Like Ashley had done.

He hadn't thought about his ex-girlfriend in months, and he sure didn't want to start now. Even so, her memory reminded him to be wary. Hormones could persuade a man to imagine qualities in a woman that just weren't there.

"May I borrow your laptop?" Brooke asked. "Hopefully those reports from Columbus PD will be waiting in my in-box."

Jared set up his laptop so she could access her email. "The first one is Lance Tucker," she said, her gaze scanning the laptop screen. "His death was caused by massive internal bleeding, due to a hit-and-run."

Jared sat up straighter. "That sounds promising. Sidorov could have arranged it."

"The driver turned out to be an eighty-year-old woman who left the scene because she thought the bump she heard was a dog. She couldn't bear to stop and look, so she drove home. Her son spoke to the police after hearing about the hit-and-run on the radio and noticing extensive damage to her car."

"What's the story on the other two?"

Brooke's fingers flew over the keyboard. "Terry Glavin died of a heart attack. Lots of family history of heart disease, so it's unlikely Sidorov had a hand in his death. Eric Henderson was building a barn on his country property when an improperly braced beam fell and crushed him."

"Were there any witnesses?"

"Yes, the two neighbors who were helping him. Henderson lasted two days in the hospital and blamed himself for the accident." She closed the laptop, looking disappointed.

"It was worth a try," Jared said quietly.

"I suppose so."

"I want you to know, even if my brother turns up unharmed, I'll make sure Sidorov is arrested for threatening and trying to bribe your brother-in-law."

Her expression conveyed admiration and gratitude. "I like the thought that his actions won't go unpunished."

It wasn't easy keeping eye contact. He didn't deserve her looking at him like some kind of hero. Not when he felt such antipathy for his own flesh and blood. Feeling the need to change the subject, he asked, "You mentioned you were a cop in Columbus."

She nodded. "For six months."

"Why did you quit?"

Her eyes slid away from his. "Who says I quit? You've seen how useless I can be in a crisis. Maybe I got fired."

His gut told him differently. "That's not true, is it?"

"No," she whispered.

"Then what?"

He remembered the puckered skin on her stomach.

Had she been injured while on duty? Had that made her reconsider a career to "serve and protect"? If so, there was no shame in that. Law enforcement wasn't for everyone.

She got up from the couch. "Since you paid for dinner, I'll clean up."

"Tell me what happened. Were you hurt on the job?"

Her head dipped down, her hair slipping over her face like a mask. "I never talk about it."

He knew he shouldn't keep pressing, but he did anyway. "You could tell me. I'd understand."

The silence stretched between them. Finally, she lifted her chin and regarded him with blue eyes as hard as sapphires. "I'll say it again. I *never* talk about it."

Picking up their dirty plates, she disappeared into the kitchen. Her refusal to talk, combined with the lack of a denial, convinced him that he was right. And he was pretty sure he knew why she wouldn't discuss the specifics of what had happened to take her off of the job. Whatever the nature of the injury, her physical wounds might have healed, but it was obvious she was still struggling to cope with the aftereffects.

"How much longer do we wait?" Jared asked Brooke.

The Mustang's clock showed 8:20. Keesing was either running late or had stood her up.

"I'll call him," she said.

He watched her pull out her cell phone and punch in the contractor's number. They were parked on the street near the two-story rental Steve had been painting before he disappeared. The house had no garage, and only ten-foot strips of grass on either side separated it from its neighbors. He glanced at the sky. Gray clouds churned overhead, promising a storm would arrive soon.

"I'm at the house," Brooke said into the phone.

She was silent for a moment, listening. A second later, she closed the phone. "He can't make it."

She didn't seem particularly upset, which was surprising since she'd been so intent on searching the house. He started the engine, resisting the urge to say, "I told you so."

She shoved the car door open.

"Ah, Brooke—" What was she intending to do? Break in?

She glanced over her shoulder. "He told me where the spare key is hidden and said it was okay to look around."

He watched her walk away, his blood heating at the sway of her hips and the snug fit of her jeans over her backside. But it was more than her sexy body that attracted him. Her quick mind was equally appealing. And she'd survived an experience that still had a hold on her. Just like him.

By the time he joined her on the porch, she'd retrieved the key from a clay pot. She unlocked the door, and they entered the house, their footsteps echoing in the unfurnished space. He switched on the lights to relieve the gloom. White blotches dotted the living room walls where holes had been filled in but not yet sanded. In the kitchen, a new countertop leaned against the cabinets, awaiting installation. The faint smell of paint lingered in the air.

They moved upstairs. In the first bedroom, no curtains or blinds covered the window, and wires protruded from the ceiling where a light fixture should have been.

Pale blue sheets and a foam slab formed a makeshift bed in the corner.

"Maybe Steve set this up so he could crash after working late," he commented.

Brooke approached the expanse of blue, stopping in front of a small, white object. She knelt, her face dipping close to it. "He wasn't here alone."

"What makes you say that?"

"The pillowcase is edged with lace, and this candle smells like vanilla. Someone went to the trouble of bringing this stuff here, which suggests to me it was more than a one-night stand. Does your brother have a girlfriend?"

"He never mentioned anyone to me." Not that he would have, but if Kristin had known, she'd surely have told him. "If someone stayed here with him, we need to talk to her."

"No clue to her identity here except for a few long, dark hairs."

As Brooke bent over the pillow, he got an eyeful of her curvy butt. Rational thought deserted him, and his imagination took over, stripping those curves of their barrier of clothes. His fantasy didn't stop there. He'd tumble her onto those sheets. And nuzzle her nape and kiss along her spine all the way down to the juncture between her legs. Then he'd coax her to open for him and stroke her secret flesh until she was wrung out and gasping.

The image was so intense, so vivid, he nearly groaned aloud. Oh man, he had to put some distance between them. That was the only way he would be able to stop visualizing hot, sweaty sex with Brooke.

"I'll search the next room," he muttered, forcing his feet to remove him from temptation.

He stalled out in the hall, his pulse racing, his body aching for release. His reaction to Brooke was flat-out wrong. Not only because his focus should be on solving his brother's disappearance, but because she had made it clear she didn't like him touching her.

He could change her mind about that. He *knew* he could. But now wasn't the right time.

Entering the bedroom closest to the stairs, he could only make out shadows. Darkness had fallen early because of the approaching storm. Fortunately, this room had a light fixture. He hit the switch, then looked around at the sand-colored walls. The edges where the walls met the ceiling and baseboards were perfect. A professional paint job. No wonder Steve could find work anywhere he chose to roam.

Would his brother ever paint again? Or had Sidorov killed him and left his corpse rotting somewhere? The thought hollowed him out, made him feel as empty as the room.

He headed into the third and final bedroom. This one was a work in progress containing painting supplies and plastic sheets lining the perimeter of the room. One wall showed new paint in sweeping swaths over the underlying dark color. The presence of those roller tracks didn't make sense. No pro painter would leave a wall unfinished unless he had a damn good reason.

Jared's shoes made rustling noises as he walked across the plastic to the paint can and nudged it with his toe. The weight suggested it was almost full. So, lack of paint hadn't been the problem. Something else had caused Steve to stop working.

He hunkered down, using the Maglite he always carried to examine the drop sheets. No blood on them, at least none visible to the naked eye. Of course, its absence didn't rule out other possibilities. A gun or knife could have convinced his brother to put down his roller and go with his attacker.

When he came to a stretch of exposed carpet under the window, his skin pebbled with goose bumps. Had Steve left this spot bare because he'd run out of plastic sheets? Or had someone removed the sheet to dispose of evidence?

He studied the carpet fibers, coming up empty. A noise like the slamming of a car door had him straightening to look outside. His heart leaped at the sight of Latschenko and two tough-looking men passing under the streetlights, all of them walking in a way that suggested they were armed. He left the bedroom, calling softly but urgently to Brooke.

"What's wrong?" she said, appearing in the doorway.

"Latschenko's here—and he's brought some friends with him."

Her body tensed. "How did they find us?"

"We can worry about that later."

As they raced downstairs, he drew his SIG Sauer from his holster. The stairs ended near the living room. Through the large picture window, he could make out dark shapes coming up the driveway. The layout of the main floor was open concept, leaving them as vulnerable as fish in a barrel. If their attackers were equipped with semiautomatics, they could shoot out the window and riddle the interior with bullets. He and Brooke wouldn't survive the barrage. He pivoted on his heel and hustled her ahead of him toward the patio door at the back of the house.

"There's a wooded ravine beyond the yard," she said. "I saw it through the bedroom window."

"Okay, we run for it. If we get lucky, they'll search the house first." Even a few minutes' head start could make the difference between escaping…and not.

At the patio door, he turned and looked at her. Her eyes were wide with fear, but she wasn't paralyzed by it as she had been at Sidorov's place. She was ready to act, a fact she demonstrated by unlocking and tugging open the patio door.

He touched her cheek, a surge of fierce protectiveness moving through him. "I'll be right behind you." That way, if their pursuers caught up with them and opened fire, he would be the one to take the hit.

He and Brooke took off across the backyard, racing single file for the dense foliage of the ravine. A shout alerted them that they'd been spotted. Glancing over his shoulder, Jared saw two of the men emerge between the houses. Latschenko had probably assigned them to guard the back exit. No need for that now or for anybody to search the house. Their quarry was in direct line of sight.

The sky darkened further, then opened up, releasing a deluge of rain. Blinded by the downpour, he nearly plowed into Brooke, who had stopped running. He soon discovered why. Beyond the yard was a twenty-foot steep slope down to the ravine.

"Keep going," he urged her. Their only hope of escape lay in reaching the cover of the woods fast.

Taking a deep breath, Brooke stepped over the edge. Within seconds, she was fighting to keep her feet underneath her, her sneakers slipping on a combination of soaked ground cover and mud. Jared holstered his gun, then followed, throwing his weight backward and grabbing on to low bushes to slow his descent. A rank odor wafted up from the disturbed ground. Brooke pitched forward suddenly, and he let go of the anchoring greenery to grab hold of her. Together they plunged downward, a bruising, painful experience as branches scratched their faces and jabbed their bodies. All the while, the rain beat at them mercilessly.

Upon reaching the bottom, Brooke let out a low moan. He squinted through the rain. His mouth went dry at the sight of her right foot twisted underneath her. He helped her up, tensing as he heard voices drifting down from above. They needed to keep moving, no matter what her condition. If her ankle wouldn't support her weight, he'd have to carry her.

That didn't turn out to be necessary, although she did lean on him, her arm going around his waist. It was hardly the way he'd envisioned her touching him—because she was forced by an injury to do so. He regretted the reason, but not the reality. She felt good, tucked against his side, her hip aligned with his.

A trail of sorts wound through the trees. Did it lead to the edge of the ravine or circle back? There was no way to tell, but because it made for easier going, he steered Brooke onto it. She limped along at an impressive pace, barely slowing him down. The effort was valiant and, without a doubt, painful and exhausting for her.

The sound of breaking twigs mixed with profanity warned of their pursuers' descent into the ravine.

"Split up," Latschenko called out. "Don't let them get away."

Narrow beams of light flickered through the leaves. Flashlights to combat the growing darkness.

The trail was too open, too exposed. The thought must have struck them simultaneously because as one, they turned and plunged into the woods, dodging trees and shoving aside branches. The rain masked some of the noise they made, but not all of it. If Sidorov's men wanted to pinpoint their location, they had only to stand still and listen.

The vegetation became thicker, richer, denser. Pushing through it felt like wading through sludge. Sludge with sharp edges. Even so, he welcomed it. Foliage so tightly packed made for excellent camouflage.

After a few yards, Brooke jerked to a stop. "My leg's caught."

Whatever blocked her way blended perfectly into the leafy backdrop. Unfortunately, that wasn't true for her red shirt, which was still visible in the fading light. A rubbing sound reached his ears above the drone of the rain.

"What is it?" he asked in a low voice.

"Feels like canvas… I think it's a tent."

A tent? What was it doing so deep in the woods? Then he remembered the houses lining the top of the ravine. A neighborhood kid had probably set it up as a fort.

"Help me find the opening," Brooke whispered.

His first instinct was to insist they keep going, but then he thought about her sore ankle and bright shirt. She'd be safer in the tent than on the run.

His hands joined hers, searching the heavy, soaked

material. When he found the zipper, he undid it and held back the flap so Brooke could enter. A tug on his pant leg signaled she expected him to follow. He hesitated. Should he go with her? Or remain on guard outside?

He hated dark, close spaces. Had nearly died in one—

Twigs cracked nearby. No animal would be wandering around in this rain. The sounds were man-made—and close enough to make his heart race.

Hide.

The impulse was nothing short of a survival imperative, and he couldn't ignore it. But once inside the tent, he felt as if he were suffocating. His breaths came hard and fast. His sweat glands worked overtime. His muscles quivered.

Gritting his teeth, he fought his fear. He was experiencing a flashback, that was all. He wasn't tied up; he had crawled inside voluntarily. His knees weren't being bruised by a metal floor; they were cushioned by a sleeping bag. He wasn't breathing gasoline vapors, only musty air. Added to that, he wasn't alone. Brooke was with him. That thought settled him down. He had to stay in control. She was relying on his protection.

As he shuffled in backward, her hands guided him to the right, but the space was so cramped, he wound up lying mostly on top of her. His chest pressed into her back, his legs entwined with hers. A lovers' embrace—except they weren't spooning after a night of passion. They were being hunted by men with guns. He couldn't be distracted by her long, lean body under his. His focus had to be on what was happening on the other side of the canvas.

Were the sounds he'd heard fading or becoming louder? Were they made by one man or more? It took several long, tense minutes before he had his answer.

Louder. Two men.

He eased his gun out of his holster and held it in a two-fisted grip, ready to fire.

Chapter 10

"Shine your flashlight up there," a smoker-raspy voice called out. "The batteries in mine have crapped out."

Jared didn't have to wait long for the second man to speak.

"Where? I can't see a damn thing in this rain."

"Straight ahead. About twenty feet."

A single beam of light played over the tent, mere inches above their heads. Brooke went rigid underneath him, her muscles so tight she'd likely ache later. That assumed she'd survive the night. Seconds ticked by with only the patter of rain falling on earth and vegetation—and canvas. Would the men notice the different sounds? Would they come investigate?

Finally, a disgruntled voice answered. "There's nothing there."

"I'm sure I saw something."

The light zigzagged back and forth across the tent. Jared curled his finger around the trigger of his gun, hardly breathing.

A snort of disgust cut through the rain. "Well, if you did, whatever it was vamoosed. Which is what I'm about to do."

"Latschenko said we can't leave till we find them."

"Latschenko can kiss my butt. I didn't sign on for damn near breaking my neck tripping down that cliff and hiking miles through the bush."

"We won't get paid if we quit now."

"We won't get paid, period. They got away."

A loud, drawn-out curse followed that pronouncement. "I need the cash, man."

"Come on, I'll buy you a beer. Then you can cry in it."

The lone beam of light grew dimmer as the men tramped back through the woods.

Jared eased his finger off the trigger and relaxed his outstretched arms. That had been close. Too close. Without the tent, they would have been discovered.

"Think it's safe to leave?" Brooke whispered in the dark.

"Let's wait a bit." The conversation they'd overheard had sounded genuine, but it could be a ploy to get them to reveal themselves. They weren't moving until he was sure Sidorov's men were gone.

Brooke stirred, and his body hardened in response. With his mind no longer consumed by danger—past or present—he was exquisitely conscious of her nearness. What he'd felt at the house was nothing compared to the lust he was experiencing now. His body urged him to make real his raunchy fantasies, but she had been put through enough tonight. She shouldn't have to fend him off, too. He shifted as far away from her as he could.

The rain slowed to a light sprinkling, the soft patter creating a cozy atmosphere.

"Come back here," she murmured.

Had he heard her right? Or was he imagining what he wanted to hear?

Bemused, he shuffled sideways, stopping when his thigh bumped against hers. She stirred again, and he realized she wasn't just fidgeting—she was shivering. The temperature had dropped, and her clothes, like his, were soaked from the rain.

"That's better," she said. "I got cold when you moved away."

Damn. She wasn't after his body, only his body heat. On the other hand, at least she needed something from him.

"Give me your hands," he said.

When she did, he was shocked by her chilled fingers. "I'm putting my arms around you," he said. "The heat will transfer faster that way."

She didn't object. In fact, she snuggled up close, facing him this time. He looped his arms around her and massaged her sides, his fingers digging in to help with circulation. She groaned softly.

He eased off. "Too hard?"

"No, that feels good."

Good was an understatement. Her breath puffed against his neck. Her scent shot up his nostrils. Her tight nipples poked his chest. He was torn between the desire to hold her and the desire to shove her away. He wasn't an electric blanket, dammit. He wanted to do more than wrap himself around her. He wanted to kiss her hard and deep. He wanted to peel off her wet, tissue-thin shirt. He wanted to slip his hands under her jeans. And that was just for starters.

Giving free rein to his baser instincts would be a surefire way to warm her up. He was getting hot just *thinking* about the things he wanted to do to her. The reality would be incendiary.

What about Brooke? What did she want? Was she simply being practical by tolerating his proximity to ward off the chill? Or was she as turned on as he was?

It was too dark to see her face, much less read her expression. "Still cold?" he murmured.

"Not so much." She wasn't shivering anymore. In fact, the area between their bodies was downright toasty.

"Glad to be of service." Except the service he wanted to provide was much more than heat transfer. His lower body hardened further, a swollen, aching bulge inside his soaked jeans. She had to feel his arousal; he was cradled between her thighs. If she didn't want him there, she only had to move away. Unless she couldn't because she was trapped by his weight.

"Am I too heavy on you?"

This was her chance. A single word, and he'd back off.

"I don't mind."

What did *that* mean? Was it ambivalence or subtle encouragement? Maybe she was having trouble admitting she wanted him. Only one way to find out. He lowered his head. Bumped noses with her.

She laughed softly. As her stomach muscles contracted against his belly, he suppressed a groan. She was killing him. And didn't even know it.

"I hate the dark," he muttered, but this time he had a whole new reason for it.

"Pardon?"

"Nothing." The last time he'd fumbled a kiss was when he was a teenager, making out in the backseat of his dad's Impala after evening football practice. He hadn't thrown a pigskin in years, but he hadn't forgotten the thrill of victory on or off the field.

His next effort to home in on her mouth resulted in a touchdown. Her lips were full and sweet. He nibbled at them, coaxing her to make a pass of her own. She was soon doing exactly that. He savored her taste as she tangled her tongue with his. Then she changed angles and dived back in with a champion's determination. She didn't let up, and he vowed never to criticize that stubborn streak of hers again.

After a while, he craved more than kisses. A change in the playbook was called for. Levering himself onto his forearms, he licked a path down her throat toward her breast. She was wildly responsive, arching her back and panting as if she were running flat out for the goalpost. The darkness magnified touch and sound. Her legs spread wider, and he sank in with a groan. The urge to penetrate her pulsed in his body, in his blood. It wouldn't take but a minute to rid them of their jeans. Then he could go deep and send them both over the finish line.

His sneaker caught in the canvas, jarring him into awareness of their surroundings. Did he really want their first time to be in a soggy tent in the middle of nowhere? He thought of the fancy linens and scented candle up at the house. He didn't know if the trappings of romance mattered to Brooke, but she certainly deserved better than this tent. When they finally got naked, he'd make sure a big, soft bed was nearby. They'd be able to stretch out and roll around as much as they wanted without the risk of knocking down tent poles. And there would be no bumping noses because it was too damn dark for him to see. There would be light. He didn't care if it was sunlight, artificial light or candlelight, just as long as he could feast his eyes on every lovely inch of her. When he stroked her secret places, he wanted to watch her eyes darken with desire and her skin flush with passion. And after she came apart, he wanted to revel in the dazed expression on her face and know he was responsible for it. For that scenario to play out, he had to ignore the clamoring of his raging hormones.

Untangling his legs from hers, he eased back. "I think it's safe to go."

A soft fingertip traced his collarbone. "Let's wait another couple of minutes."

If she continued with those tantalizing touches, his good intentions were done for. "The rain's stopped. It makes sense to leave before it starts up again."

Her hand fell away from him, just as he'd intended. So why did he suddenly want it back again?

"Why so antsy?" she asked.

"I think things are headed out of control."

"What things?"

"You and me."

"Ah." He detected a smile in her voice. "Those 'things.'"

Her levity irked him. Didn't she realize she was

playing with fire? "We're stopping now because if we don't, we're not going to."

"Hey, we were only kissing."

"That kind of kissing could lead to me buried inside you."

She responded tartly to his bluntness. "You've got some ego, buster."

"It's not ego. It's honesty."

"No, it's fantasy, because I wouldn't have let you go that far."

"You want me. Otherwise you'd have pushed me away, whether you were cold or not."

When she didn't deny it, he gave her arm a gentle squeeze. "We'll start over once we're somewhere nice and dry and have protection."

She shrugged off his hand. "No, we won't."

"If this is cold feet, I know how to warm them—and you."

"Thanks, but dry socks are all I need."

Her haughty tone didn't change the fact that she had been the one reluctant to leave the tent a few minutes ago. "Remember the first time we kissed?" he said. "You backed off then, too, and acted cool as a cucumber when moments before you had been a red hot chili pepper."

"I'll admit you're attractive and I was tempted."

It was his turn to smile. She'd just handed him the perfect ammunition. "Aren't you *tempted* to know what it would feel like to go all the way together?"

She hesitated a heartbeat too long. "I'm okay with not knowing."

"Wouldn't you rather be satisfied by knowing?"

A long exhalation. "It's crazy for us to get involved sexually."

"We already are."

"I've only known you for two days."

"Two long, eventful days," he pointed out.

"I can't disagree with that assessment."

"I saved your life. If you can think of a better character reference, I want to hear it."

Silence. He'd finally stumped her.

He shifted closer and bent his head until he touched soft skin. Her cheek. "You have some pretty sexy moves. I especially liked the way you arched your back and wrapped your legs around me."

"The dark loosened my inhibitions," she admitted.

He detected surprise—and relief—in her voice. As if she hadn't believed her actions possible and was grateful to discover otherwise. A crazy thought occurred to him. "You haven't been with a man since you got injured, have you?"

"Okay, that's it. Time to go."

She struggled to get up, but he kept her pinned. Her impatience to leave confirmed his suspicion. She needed the dark to relax enough to become aroused. Why? Because the dark concealed what she couldn't accept about herself.

His sister, Kristin, had been self-conscious about her scars, too. When she was twelve, her bike hit a patch of oil on a driveway and skidded, causing her to fall through the side window of a house. The neighborhood boys had nicknamed her Scarface because of the disfiguring marks to her cheek and neck. She'd worn turtleneck sweaters even in summer and styled her hair to hang like a curtain over the right side of her face, but nothing she did could hide the damaged skin completely. She'd been miserable, saying she felt like a freak, that no man would ever date her, much less fall in love her. His reassurances that one day she would marry a great guy were dismissed as kind white lies. Fortunately, she'd been proved wrong. A firefighter named Heath Darren had come to the high school where she worked as a teacher. He'd been immediately drawn to her athletic body and dry sense of humor. Having seen his share of burn victims, he saw past the superficial scars to the essence of what she was. Just like it should be—but often wasn't.

Had Brooke experienced rejection at the hands of a lover?

The thought enraged him. She had trained to be a cop. She had put her life in danger for others. She shouldn't feel inadequate because of a few scars. He wanted to tell her so but sensed she'd misinterpret his words as pity. The ultimate insult. It'd be preferable for her to think he was just plain horny.

"Move it," she said, smacking his shoulder.

"Why so antsy?" he asked, throwing back her earlier words.

"I'm tired of you talking nonsense."

"It isn't nonsense. I'm finally starting to understand you."

"You don't understand anything about me."

"You're wrong about that. I understand you've been avoiding sex because your body's no longer perfect."

"It was never perfect," she shot back.

"You're splitting hairs. Most women would be thrilled to look like you."

"You haven't seen me minus my clothes," she muttered.

"We can fix that. I promise I won't faint from shock. In fact, I can practically guarantee I'll enjoy the sight very much."

"Thanks for the vote of confidence, but I won't be stripping for you."

"Or any other man, right?"

Her sharp intake of breath told him he'd hit a bull's-eye, but his intent wasn't to score points. It was to make her reevaluate her self-doubts.

"Are you going to insist on sex with the lights out for the rest of your life?" he asked quietly.

"Of course not."

"If you don't get rid of this hang-up soon, it'll have such a stranglehold you won't be able to break free."

"Not your problem. According to my fiancé, doing it in the dark adds a sense of mystery."

The mention of a fiancé caught him off guard. Had he jumped to wrong conclusions about her? Did she have a lover? His temper soared like a kite in strong wind, twisting to break free. Why the hell had she let him kiss her, touch her? Had she got him all worked up just to see if she could?

No, the passion had been intense and mutual. She was blowing smoke to protect her pride. Someone like her wouldn't want to admit to any weaknesses.

"I seriously doubt your fiancé enjoys doing the wild thing in the dark. Men are visual creatures. They get stimulated by what they see, especially their lover's body."

"That's quite the generalization."

"It's a scientific fact."

"Says who? *Playboy* magazine?"

He decided to change tactics. "I notice you're not wearing a ring."

A long pause. "We split up." The fact that she'd admitted the fiancé was past history was a triumph of sorts, and he took a moment to savor it.

"I know what you're thinking," she said, her tone defensive, "but it was for *lots* of different reasons. Not just because the sex wasn't great."

That last bit was music to his ears. "I can help you get over your body issues."

She scoffed. "I don't need your help."

"Oh yes, you do. You just need some time to come to the same conclusion."

"I won't be 'coming' to any kind of 'conclusion' with you."

He grinned at her innuendo. Brooke seemed to have forgotten one small detail. She wasn't the only stubborn person in this tent. "Oh, it'll happen, all right."

"Don't hold your breath. On second thought, go ahead. I'll enjoy the silence until you give up."

His elbows were starting to go numb from bearing his weight. "We both know a more pleasurable way to make me breathless."

She turned her head away. "In your dreams, FBI guy."

"I'd wish you sweet dreams," he said, as he finally shifted off her, "but I'd rather you had sweaty ones involving me."

As she scrambled out of the tent, he could swear he heard the gnashing of her teeth.

Chapter 11

The blast took Brooke by surprise. One moment she was crossing the street; the next, pain exploded in her side. She fell backward, her head slamming against the ground before the rest of her body caught up. Blackness beckoned, a tempting refuge. But she knew instinctively she couldn't allow herself to float away. If she did, she'd never return.

Saliva flooded her mouth, a telltale sign she was about to throw up. Her nostrils detected a metallic smell that made her nausea worse. She swallowed convulsively, her forehead clammy with sweat.

Get up. Get up.

She tried to move, but the signal from her brain got lost somewhere along the way. She concentrated fiercely. This time one arm managed to separate from her side. Her fingers landed in something wet. Weird. She hadn't even realized it was raining.

She lifted her wet hand and saw red. Not rain. Blood. Her *blood.*

Although the blow to her head had slowed her thought processes, she knew she had to stanch the puncture wounds in her side. Applying pressure to them, she gasped at the sheer agony of the experience.

Yeah, it hurts, but you're tough. You can take it.

What she couldn't take was the feeling of being helpless, vulnerable, weak. Since she'd joined the Columbus police force, her kick-ass attitude and fast reflexes had protected her. Not this time. This time she had miscalculated, racing from her cruiser without first donning her Kevlar vest. Hadn't thought she'd need it against a suspect who was supposedly armed with only a knife.

The sound of footsteps moved along the street toward her.

Help. *Her mind shouted the word, but her vocal cords managed only a hoarse croak.* Officer down. *She needed that passerby to take notice of her situation and call an ambulance.*

More slow, quiet steps.

Goose bumps raced along her skin as she realized a potential rescuer would be calling out to her, not approaching with the stealth of a predator. Craning her neck around, she glimpsed a shotgun cradled in filthy hands. She tried to throw herself out of harm's way, but only succeeded in flopping about. She felt like a fish out of water, caught in a net. Tears of frustration and fear mixed with the sweat on her face.

"Hey, open your eyes."

Did he expect her to watch him pull the trigger? Sadistic bastard.

The footsteps came closer. At this range, the shot would be fatal. She reached out, and her hand smashed into something hard. A fist-sized rock. Big enough to do some damage. As long as her aim was true—

"Take it easy. You're wrapped tighter than a mummy."

Her eyes shot open. A dark figure, unrecognizable in the sliver of light from the hall, loomed over her, but she knew that voice. *Jared.* Despite their earlier argument, she longed to curl up in his arms and bury her face in his neck. Instead she reached down and jerked her legs free from the tangle of sheets.

"You were really tossing and turning." He paused. "Bad dream, starring Sidorov and company?"

Of course he'd assume that. Yesterday had been two dangerous encounters with the man's thugs. But it was nothing compared to what had happened to her the last night she'd patrolled the streets of Columbus as a rookie cop. She'd been reliving that horror for over two years. The recurring nightmares left her tense, shaken…and shamed she'd lost the guts necessary to protect and serve.

"Sorry I woke you," she said, ignoring his question.

"That's okay. I'm a light sleeper. How about we get rid of this dark?" he said, reaching for the bedside lamp.

Her mouth felt like a dust bowl. "No, don't," she croaked. She was humiliated enough without him seeing her tear-streaked face.

"You sound a bit off. Want me to stay for a while?" His voice was a deep, comforting rumble.

She should turn him down flat, but the prospect of

being alone terrified her. If she drifted off to sleep, the nightmare would resume. The memory of the pain would be so intense, so *real* she'd jolt awake screaming. God, she hated that sound.

She must have hesitated too long because Jared turned to leave. The words shot out before she could stop them. "Don't go!"

He turned back. "You must really be spooked."

Her face felt hot from embarrassment, but she tried for a casual tone. "Yeah, well, it's been a rough couple of days."

"I won't argue with that." He approached the bed. "Scoot your legs up."

She propped herself higher on the pillow and bent her legs to the side. Her ankle protested, but it wasn't the stabbing pain she'd felt in the ravine. A moment later, the bed dipped with his weight as he sat sideways along the bottom and leaned against the wall. The hall light painted a narrow stripe over his bare torso and low-slung jeans. He must have tugged them on in a hurry because the top button was undone. The muscles in his chest were clearly defined. Her fingers itched to trace them. Bad idea.

Neither of them spoke, but the silence wasn't awkward. The churning in Brooke's stomach began to settle down. Using the edge of the sheet, she wiped the tears and sweat from her face. That damn nightmare. She hated the queasy, scared feeling it left her with. Why couldn't she stop reliving the past?

Jared shifted on the bed. Although he was being a good sport, he had to be anxious to head back to his own room and get some shut-eye.

"You must think I'm a major wimp," she blurted out.

"Because you had a nightmare?" He turned his head in her direction. "Nobody can control what their subconscious dishes up."

"I'll bet you've never woken up completely freaked out."

"You'd be wrong."

She didn't believe him. He seemed to thrive on dangerous situations. Maybe that was why he'd joined the FBI. Because the risks inherent in the job gave him a bigger rush than any extreme sport could deliver.

She punched her pillow. "You're just saying that to be nice."

"I *am* nice. But I've also had really bad nightmares."

"I'm not talking about when you were a little kid."

"Neither am I."

His tone was so serious she felt the first twinges of doubt. Maybe he was telling the truth. "How about offering up some specifics?"

"Why can't you just take my word for it?"

"Because I'm curious what would give you nightmares."

He blew out an exasperated breath. "I'm beginning to see why you and your fiancé split up. You're as stubborn as a pit bull."

"I take back that 'nice' comment I made earlier."

Her prickly words camouflaged the arousal growing within her. Although most of his body was in shadow, her imagination had no trouble filling in the gaps. She remembered every contour from those long minutes in the tent when he'd lain on top of her. The flat stomach. The lean hips. The hard bulge that had grown in size as he'd kissed her.

"Okay, I'll tell you," he said abruptly.

His change of heart surprised her, and his tone of voice implied what he was about to say was deeply personal. She suddenly felt dishonest. She had pressed him to open up with no intention of doing the same.

"No, forget I asked," she said.

"We're both wide-awake. We might as well talk."

He folded his arms over his chest, exhaled a breath. "Ten months ago, my partner and I went undercover inside a biker gang. For weeks, we collected hard evidence. Then things went south and our covers were blown. They killed my partner outright, but decided my death should be slow and painful. So they beat me senseless, drove me away from their hideout and locked me in a shed."

She should have respected his reluctance to talk. Now she owed him the courtesy of listening to an experience that seemed as horrible as her own.

"I came to with my feet and hands bound behind my back. It was pitch-black and hot as hell. I had to squirm around like a worm. Eventually I found a rough edge in the metal trim, but the ropes were thick, twisted nylon. The stifling heat made my stomach heave and my head spin. I took turns throwing up and passing out."

She'd been wrong to assume their experiences were comparable. Unlike her brief, intense stint in terror, he'd had to endure hours of torture. "What happened?"

"It took me most of the day to cut through the ropes. I tried to force the door open by throwing myself at it, but the lock was industrial-strength steel and wouldn't break." His next words were barely a whisper. "No matter what I did, I couldn't escape."

That sense of helplessness had probably been harder for him to bear than the agony of extreme heatstroke.

She swallowed past the lump in her throat. "But you survived. How?"

"When my partner and I failed to check in at our field office, a dozen agents were assigned to search our last known location. It was sheer luck one of the agents knew the area and remembered the shed. By that time, I was unconscious and so dehydrated I had to be hospitalized for three days."

"Do you still dream about it?" she asked.

"No."

"So the nightmares just stopped?" Why wouldn't hers? She clenched the sheets in her fists.

"I wish I could say they went away because I willed them gone, but it wasn't that easy." He shoved his fingers through his hair. "Nearly dying in that shed really did a number on me. A month after I returned to work, a suspect disappeared into a tight, dark tunnel and I couldn't follow him. That's when I knew I had to get professional help or quit the Bureau."

"You chose the help."

"An FBI lady shrink, no less. Her father was an agent, and she married a colleague of mine last year, so she really knows her stuff."

Unlike the psychologist Brooke had talked to in the hospital. "What did she suggest?"

"Exposure therapy."

"She shut you in her office closet with the lights off?"

He chuckled. "Something like that. Repeated, controlled exposure. Eventually, the situations that used to trigger memories of the shed stopped bothering me. The nightmares petered out soon afterward."

It sounded so simple—conquering fears through desensitization. Would it work for her?

She didn't realize she'd voiced the thought until Jared spoke. "I think that's already happening for you."

"What do you mean?"

"When Latschenko pulled a gun on you at Sidorov's, you were paralyzed with fear, then had a panic attack in the Green Thumb truck. But tonight when he and his men showed up, you kept your head, even came up with the idea of escaping into the ravine and hiding in the tent. That's a huge step in the right direction."

He had a point, she realized. Her reaction to danger had shifted a hundred and eighty degrees. Even the details of her nightmares had changed. She'd dreamed she had a weapon and could fight back.

"For the record, I don't think of you as a wimp," he said. "I think of you as a woman who can do anything she sets her mind to."

That was a far cry from how Chad had viewed her at the end of their relationship. He had loved having a fearless cop girlfriend with a bikini body. When that same girlfriend lost her nerve, gained a bunch of scars and quit her job, he couldn't handle the person she'd become. She'd spent a lot of time regretting she'd disappointed him before she'd realized what his "love" had actually been about: bragging rights and lust.

The other man in her life—her father—had never understood her dreams or encouraged her abilities. He believed being a cop was a man's job. Women shouldn't be packing guns and chasing down criminals. They should be making comfortable homes for their husbands and raising their children to mind their manners. When she'd been injured, his concern had quickly given way to smugness. He'd been proved right. Only those with the Y chromosome belonged in law enforcement.

Objectively, she knew his was an old-fashioned opinion, but her self-respect had still fallen off a cliff—especially when panic attacks had hit her after returning to work. She'd quit rather than risk endangering her colleagues or the public. Now she wished she had tried harder to find the right help like Jared had.

She looked at him, a dark form sitting motionless on her bed. He could have easily bailed on her, but instead he'd stayed. And despite her badgering, he could have avoided admitting he had wrestled with fears, too. Why had he done it? Why had he opened up to her?

He must have known his experience would strike a corresponding chord with her. Only survivors of near-death experiences could fully appreciate the toll it took, the fear that couldn't be completely excised. His understanding was welcome, but even more important was the sweet sound of his respect.

"I have a question."

His voice jolted her out of her reverie. She tensed instinctively. *Here it comes. How did you get those scars...?*

"Who called it quits? You or your fiancé?"

Her tension dissolved like jelly powder in boiling water. This was a topic she could talk about. "He dumped me. Neither my new body nor my change in careers met with his approval." Then because she didn't want Jared feeling sorry for her, she added, "We weren't a good match, but I was only able to see that afterward."

"Sounds like you're better off without the jerk."

Oh man, Jared was saying all the right things tonight. Maybe she shouldn't have rejected his offer in the tent. Based on his kisses, she had no doubt sex with him would be hot and exciting. Just thinking about it made her breasts tingle and her abdomen quiver.

If only he weren't so set on seeing her naked with the lights on. The very idea made her squirm. What if her scars turned him off? What if she saw the same look of revulsion on his face she'd seen on Chad's? She didn't need the humiliation, especially not when she was finally starting to feel a little better about herself.

"Are you okay now?" he asked. "Do you think you could get some sleep?"

"Yeah, I'm good. Thanks for the company."

"Alex sent me a text a little while ago. His uncle is doing better, so he'll be back in the morning."

Jared vacated the bed in one smooth movement. She stretched out her legs, regretting the empty space left behind by his body, wishing she had the courage to call him back.

At the doorway, he paused. "In case you're wondering, I don't usually spill my guts like that."

She suppressed a smile. "Don't worry. It hasn't ruined your tough-guy image."

"Glad to hear it."

Jared's words and actions had shown her two distinctly different sides of him. One as a gun-wielding savior. The other as a mentor offering insight. And though she wasn't entirely sure how she felt about it, there was a third part of his persona hovering on the periphery of her mind. That of a lover who could satisfy both her body and her heart.

The aroma of eggs and pancakes drifted up the stairs. Jared paused on his way down and sniffed appreciatively. Breakfast. How great that he didn't have to get in his car and drive to it. He continued down the stairs and headed into the kitchen.

Brooke stood in front of the stove, pouring batter into a frying pan.

"You said you wouldn't cook." He smiled at the smudge of flour on her cheek.

"I'm making an exception." Her eyes met his for a fleeting moment, then slid away. "Don't get used to it."

Despite her gruff tone, he knew this was her way of thanking him for the prior night. It wasn't necessary, but mentioning that would only make her feel more awkward. She had her pride, and he had no intention of undercutting it.

She'd already stacked plates on the counter, so he hunted through the cupboards for glasses and cutlery. After the table was set, he poured two mugs of coffee. His cell phone rang. "I'll keep this short," he promised Brooke, flipping open his phone.

"I've got the info on Sidorov you wanted." The voice on the line belonged to Brent Young, the colleague whose psychologist wife had helped him get over most of his fear of tight spaces.

"I'm putting you on speaker so I can take notes." Also, Brooke would be able to listen in. After what she'd been through yesterday, it seemed wrong to exclude her. He set his phone on the table, then retrieved a pen and notebook from his shirt pocket. "Go ahead."

"My search of our database shows Sidorov has become co-owner of about twenty small companies over the last six months. Interestingly, the companies' financials improved significantly after he invested his capital."

"Could he be using them to launder illegal funds?" Jared asked.

"No red flags are coming up, but it can't be ruled out." There was a short pause on the line. "Just so you know, no requests for time off will be granted until the serial killer working out of Toledo is caught. I heard Hilroy's been calling some people back from their vacations, too."

"I'm not finished here."

"If the boss man calls, you can't say no."

Jared closed his notebook with more force than necessary. "That's exactly what I *will* say."

His colleague was characteristically blunt. "Then you'll be ordered to talk to the boys on the Review Board. And that's usually a career-ending conversation."

"Thanks for the warning. Guess I'll have to lose my phone."

"That excuse won't wash with Hilroy, and you know it."

"Hilroy is the least of my worries."

"Not if he fires you," Brent shot back. "What if you can't find your brother because he doesn't want to be found? Are you sure you want to risk your career?"

Jared heard a clatter behind him and turned toward the noise. The utensil Brooke had been using to flip pancakes lay on the floor. He watched her pick it up and move to the sink to wash it.

"You didn't say 'yes,'" Brent went on, misreading his lack of response, "which means you need to rethink your decision. The Bureau can't afford to lose good agents."

"I hear you. Thanks for the info."

He pocketed his phone, then glanced at Brooke. "Is breakfast ready?"

"Everything's staying warm in the oven," she answered quietly. "Are you sure you're still hungry?"

"Why wouldn't I be?"

"You just found out you have to choose between your career and your family."

She sounded shocked, but he wasn't. He'd known his time off could be canceled at a moment's notice. That was why he'd involved Alex and Brent—to expedite the search. And no matter what ultimatums Hilroy threw at him, there was no doubt in his mind what he had to do.

"I've already made my choice. I don't stop until I find out what happened to Steve and help your brother-in-law."

Brooke's eyes still held concern, but her lips curved in a smile of respect and appreciation. "Somehow, I knew you'd say that."

She thought she understood him, but she wouldn't be smiling at him like that if she knew he was partly motivated by guilt. He should come clean with her. He should tell her the truth about his troubled relationship with his brother. But he didn't want to wreck her good opinion of him, so he stayed silent.

"Thanks," he said, as Brooke served up steaming scrambled eggs and golden pancakes.

Alex arrived a few minutes later. As he strolled into the kitchen, the corner of his mouth kicked up. "Looks like you two have big appetites this morning."

Jared knew exactly what he was hinting at, but Brooke didn't catch the innuendo. "I took you at your word and raided your supplies," she said.

"I'm just glad you made extra coffee." Alex helped himself to a cup, added some cream, then joined them at the table.

Jared watched the other man's gaze move over Brooke's face, no doubt searching for traces of whisker burn. *No, we didn't spend the night screwing like rabbits*, he was tempted to say. Maybe they had shared a bed for a while, but the intimacy wasn't sexual. It was... He frowned, at a loss to define what had passed between them. Not that he intended to explain anything to Alex. It just would have been good to know himself.

"How's your uncle?" Brooke asked Alex.

"Better than expected. When my mom mentioned a friend of mine had gone missing, he insisted I get my butt back here." He sipped his coffee. "Any new developments while I was gone?"

Jared reached for more syrup. "As a matter of fact, Brooke talked the contractor into letting us search the house Steve has been painting."

Alex gave her a thumbs-up sign. "Nice going."

Brooke's flush showed she was pleased by the compliment.

Jared finished chewing a mouthful of fluffy pancake. "Within twenty minutes, three of Sidorov's goons showed up and chased us into the ravine behind the house."

"How did they know you were there?" Alex demanded.

"The contractor said he was calling the company that owns the house," Brooke supplied. "I think we can safely assume Sidorov is connected to that company."

Alex gestured with his coffee mug. "Okay, Steve

was working indirectly for the Russian. So how did he piss him off? Screw up a paint job?"

Brooke crossed her knife and fork over her empty plate. "That would be the contractor's problem. And he'd have just fired Steve and hired somebody else."

"Did you find any clues as to what happened at the house?" Alex asked.

Jared spoke up. "It's not what we found. It's what we didn't find. Several drop sheets were missing from one of the bedrooms."

"And that's important because…?"

"It looked like Steve had stopped painting abruptly, which makes me wonder if someone showed up and interrupted his work. If that someone fought with him, Steve's blood could have wound up on the drop sheets. Those sheets might have been removed intentionally at the same time as Steve was abducted from the house."

"You never mentioned that possibility last night," Brooke said.

"I got distracted by those men showing up with guns." And later by her body pressed against his in the tent.

"Excuse me," Brooke said, pushing away from the table.

Frowning, he watched her exit from the kitchen. It wasn't like her to leave in the middle of a conversation. Was she annoyed he had waited to tell Alex and her now, instead of telling her when they'd got back last night?

When Brooke was out of earshot, Alex said, "I like her." That damn crocodile smile was plastered across his face again.

"So do I." Jared added sugar to his second coffee of the day. "And she likes me back, if you get my meaning."

"I won't do anything to mess with that," the other man promised.

Footsteps sounded on the stairs, and a moment later, Brooke hurried into the kitchen.

"You're not the only one who got distracted last night," she said, holding out her hand. Dangling from her fingers by a heavy gold chain was an oval pendant surrounded by small diamonds.

Jared headed back to the table. "Where did you get it?"

"Remember the room with the fancy sheets and candle? It was wedged between the pillow and the wall."

"Looks expensive," Alex remarked.

"Let me see." Jared examined it carefully, noting the initials *MS* on the back of the delicate pendant. "I'll be damned."

Brooke frowned. "What?"

"I recognize it."

"From where?"

"From a photo in Sidorov's office." He looked at her. "This necklace belongs to his daughter, Marisa."

"*She's* your brother's lover?"

"It would seem so."

Alex folded his arms over his chest. "Well, now. This is starting to get interesting."

"How old is she?" Brooke asked.

Jared knew from the background check he'd done on the Russian and his household. "Twenty-two."

"Then she's old enough to decide who she wants to sleep with."

He shrugged. "Sidorov may not see it that way."

"Most men have a hard time accepting their little girls have grown up," Alex agreed. "And although I think Steve is great, he's hardly ideal boyfriend material. He's got no real money, and he moves around often."

"I have no doubts this father made his objection known," Jared said.

"How would your brother have reacted to that?" Brooke asked him.

Jared turned to Alex. "How do you think?"

The other man rolled his eyes. "I think Steve would've told the guy to shove it somewhere dark and uncomfortable."

"That brings us back to the missing drop sheets," Jared said quietly. "Best-case scenario is Sidorov had him beaten up. Worst case is he had him killed."

"A beating wouldn't have stopped Steve from calling Kristin," Alex pointed out.

"No, it wouldn't," Jared agreed.

Brooke's fingers curled around her mug as if she were seeking warmth from its contents. No one spoke for a long while.

Jared forced himself to break the silence and voice the unthinkable. "Steve's body could have been wrapped in plastic, then disposed of."

Alex cursed under his breath. "Where?"

Brooke's response matched the one in his head. "The ravine."

Densely wooded with infrequent foot traffic, the ravine made a perfect dump site. Alex let loose with another curse, but Jared barely took it in. The delicious breakfast Brooke had cooked churned in his stomach as he remembered the disgusting odor he'd noticed when he'd first entered the ravine. Could it have been his brother's decomposing body?

He realized his horror must have shown when Brooke reached out to touch his arm. "The missing drop sheets could be meaningless," she murmured.

His gut and mind were both screaming the opposite. Steve was dead, and so was the hope he'd been carrying around that he could reconcile with his brother—

"Let's not get ahead of ourselves," Alex said, breaking through his dread. "Wild guesses aren't facts."

"Only one way to know for sure," he said with a calmness he was far from feeling.

Brooke was on her feet before he'd finished speaking. "We have to search the ravine."

Chapter 12

Brooke's heart beat faster as Alex parked his truck. His GPS had shown them a road wound down the hill to the base of the ravine. Considering her ankle still ached, she was glad they didn't have to attempt that treacherous twenty-foot descent again. She would have done it if necessary, because nothing was going to keep her from helping Jared look for his brother.

They exited the truck. Last night, the dark had made it impossible to judge the ravine's size, but today she could see it encompassed many acres. Acres that could conceal a dead body for a long time, if not forever.

"We'll cover more ground if we split up," Alex said, his voice grim.

Jared pointed to a water tower rising above the tops of the trees. "If we head in that direction, we'll end up near our entry point last night."

Trust Jared to have made note of a landmark even under the circumstances. She'd been too busy running for her life.

"If you come across anything suspicious," Jared added, "don't get too close. We don't want to contaminate any evidence."

Good advice, but she wondered how he could keep his emotions in check. If they'd been looking for Savannah's body, she wouldn't be showing such restraint. Her anxiety would have been written all over her face.

She set off, with the men fifty yards away on either side. The day was overcast, the threat of rain lurking in the clouds overhead. The raw dampness quickly sliced through her clothes and settled deep in her bones. Within a few minutes, she lost sight of her companions in the woods. Thankfully, their footsteps could still be heard as they forged ahead. Given what she was searching for, it was a comfort knowing she wasn't alone.

She scanned the ground, her gaze sweeping in a wide arc as she walked. Her ankle throbbed, but she ignored it. Several times she changed direction to look underneath clumps of bushes and peer into dark hollows. Corpses weren't necessarily dumped in one piece, she reminded herself, and wildlife often tampered with the remains. Those morbid thoughts added to the chill she already felt.

After climbing over a fallen tree, she paused. A rancid odor permeated the air. Feeling queasy, she sniffed until she located its source. A crevice at the intersection of two large branches. She found a stick and gingerly brushed aside fallen leaves. The remains of a squirrel came into view, its belly exposed, its internal organs crawling with maggots. She dropped the stick and turned away in disgust.

If Steve's body were in the ravine, its condition could be the same or worse, depending on the manner in which he'd been killed. It would be horrible for Jared to find him, horrible to have the memories of a lifetime tainted by a last, grotesque image. She would spare him that, if she could, even if the experience gave her more nightmares.

With renewed determination, she pushed on. If she hurried, she could finish searching her designated area and move into Jared's.

Eventually, the ground began sloping upward, indicating she'd reached the base of the hill behind the houses on Middleview. Anything tossed from the backyards above would end up in this section of the ravine. As she picked her way around a rusted oil drum, three broken chairs, a bed frame and various other castoffs, she inhaled a gross smell and braced herself for a gruesome discovery.

A flicker of movement drew her gaze. She stopped. Her heart gave a hard *thunk*, then began racing. Like a waving hand, a length of clear plastic fluttered in the breeze about twenty feet away.

It's probably the discarded packaging from a new mattress or sofa, she told herself. But her pulse kept up its maniacal pace, her body unwilling to accept that explanation.

She eyed the spot where the plastic appeared to be sprouting from the dirt like some weird vegetable. Part of the hill must have given way in last night's rain, she realized, with the displaced earth trapping the plastic. She edged closer. Something caked in mud protruded from the muck. It was rounded on one end with a web of thick strings. The object looked oddly familiar…

Her mouth went dry, and her throat constricted as she recognized what it was. A shoe. A man's shoe. And judging by the putrid stench wafting toward her, a foot was inside it.

She stared in horror at the mud. How deep did it go? Deep enough to conceal a whole body? She eased down into a crouch, her legs suddenly weak.

Until now, she'd believed it possible Jared's brother had simply left town, maybe spending a couple of days too drunk and hungover to remember he was supposed to call their sister. His inconsideration would have been wrong, but not unforgivable. In time, the story of his "disappearance" and Jared's search for him might have become a family favorite to be reminisced about when the siblings got together. Now her discovery could mean a family reunion would never happen.

She braced her hands on her knees and shoved herself upright. "Guys," she called out. Her voice was too hoarse to carry far. She cleared her throat, tried again. "Over here. I found something."

Alex arrived first. His eyes followed hers to the mud, then stretched wide. After a minute, he closed them as if the sight were too much to bear.

Jared appeared a few seconds later, approaching from the opposite direction. He took one look at Alex's bowed head and halted. Then he turned to Brooke. She couldn't speak, so she merely pointed at the shoe.

Shock registered in his eyes as he scanned the area and took in its implications. "No," he muttered. "Not like this." He moved toward the shoe as if pulled by an invisible force.

She had a sudden vision of him dropping to his knees and clawing at the mud. "Stop," she cried. "You have to stay back, remember?"

"What?" He glanced at her as if she were babbling in a foreign language.

"The scene must not be compromised."

"Last night's rain already did that." He started forward again.

She spoke fast, knowing she had only seconds to deter him. "Something important could still be there."

"She's right," Alex said, moving to block him. "We're done here. The only thing left is to call it in."

"Get out of my way." Jared's voice was a low, dangerous growl.

Alex maintained position, his body braced for attack. "Don't do it, man."

Neither wanted to fight, Brooke realized, but adrenaline increased aggressive urges. She had to end this standoff before it turned physical. *But how?*

She called out to Jared. "If you touch anything, the police could charge you with tampering with a crime scene and throw you in county jail."

His expression lost some of its fierceness. "I know that. I just want to look."

Alex turned away, massaging one shoulder. "I've seen enough," he muttered.

So had Brooke. She was thankful the mud had obscured everything except the shoe. Graphic visuals would have made the discovery much worse.

"The plastic seems to be the same stuff used at the house," Jared said quietly.

His tone was neutral, but Brooke knew he had to be hurting. The sooner he left the ravine, the better. "You don't need to stay," she said. "I found the…shoe. I'll wait for the police."

"Bad idea. Sidorov's inside man could get to you."

"Then I'll make an anonymous call."

"I'll make the call," Alex said. "It's my truck parked near the ravine. Somebody might remember it. You two should walk a few streets over, then call for a cab."

Jared looked at him. "Are you sure? Once the cops come, all hell will break loose."

"I know. I'll just tell them the truth. That I was searching the ravine because it's close to the last place my AWOL buddy worked."

Jared made a last-ditch protest. "You don't have to do this."

Alex's eyes were clear, his expression resolute. "I want to. For Steve."

"You were supposed to check in with me last night."

The hurt and accusation in his sister's voice were more than Jared could deal with right now. When he'd seen Kristin's number displayed, he'd been tempted not to answer. But he'd promised her regular updates, and that was a promise he had to keep. She was the reason he'd come looking for Steve.

"I got in late and didn't want to disturb you." When he and Brooke had returned to the house last night, it had been close to midnight.

"I wouldn't have cared what time it was. You know that."

Of course he knew. He just hadn't wanted to call her again without answers or, at least, significant leads. The last time they'd spoken, his lack of progress had escalated her already unbearable anxiety.

"What kept you out so late?" Her voice sounded tired, as if she were operating on very little sleep.

Muted noises came from the direction of the kitchen. Brooke must have been tidying up the breakfast dishes they'd left behind in their rush to get to the ravine—a place that would now be crawling with cops and crime-scene techs. He moved to the living room window and watched as a strong wind buffeted an oak tree. The weather was changing again and could interfere with the investigation. As if last night's rain hadn't already compromised any potential evidence.

"Jared?"

He refocused on his sister's question. "You know the last house Steve was working on? The contractor gave us permission to search it."

"*Us?* Was Alex with you?" Before he could confirm or deny, she added, "No, he couldn't have been. He called me from his uncle's hospital room to say he was staying with him overnight. So who went with you?"

Failing to answer would be like a flashing neon sign that he was withholding information. He decided to tell her the truth, without mentioning the extenuating circumstances. "I've enlisted the help of a PI."

His sister harrumphed. "First Alex. Now a PI. You must *finally* be worried about our brother."

He deserved her reproach—and worse. He should have trusted her instincts from the very beginning. He should have driven to Langeville to look for Steve Sunday evening right after she'd called. If he had, what might he have discovered? A killer clearing out his brother's rented room? Instead, full of resentment, he'd grudgingly made the trip the following afternoon.

Regrets were futile; he knew that. Just as he knew

the muddy grave in the ravine could mean he'd never have the chance to tell his brother, despite all the crap that had kept them apart, he loved him. There was no proof yet the corpse was Steve, but deep in his gut, he couldn't help but fear the worst.

Kristin's voice broke through his thoughts. "Did you find anything at the house?"

He swallowed. "A necklace belonging to Sidorov's daughter, Marisa."

"How did it get there?"

"It appears Steve and Marisa were sleeping together."

"*Were* sleeping together," she repeated. "Did they break up?"

He had no reason to believe that, hadn't even considered the possibility. The past tense had slipped out because of his fear that Steve was dead. But Kristin's question raised an interesting point. "Why didn't Marisa report him missing?"

"Maybe she thinks he dumped her. You said his belongings are gone, and he's not answering his cell. Taken together, those are pretty clear signs of a guy who no longer cares."

Was that how Marisa viewed Steve's desertion? Or did she suspect her father's involvement in ending their relationship? If that were the case, was she too loyal—or too afraid—to go to the police with her suspicions?

"I think you should talk to her," Kristin said, echoing the conclusion he'd just reached himself.

"I will."

"Maybe I should come to Langeville. She might respond more favorably to a woman."

"Stay home. The kids need you."

She sighed. "I feel so useless."

She wasn't the only one. He had nothing except suspicions. And his best lead was a woman who had reason to keep silent.

"Remember Harrison Ford's character in *Witness*?" Kristin said. "Maybe Steve's situation is like that. He's laid up somewhere, too out of it to call, but he's in good hands."

Jared flashed back to the scene in the ravine again and felt sick, but he couldn't shatter his sister's world without being certain. Instead, he closed his eyes and leaned his forehead against the glass pane, wishing its coolness could numb the pain inside him. "This isn't Amish country, Kristin," he said gently. "A Good Samaritan would've taken him to a hospital."

Neither of them spoke for a while.

"Do you think we'll ever know what's happened to Steve?" she murmured.

He spoke around the lump in his throat. "Of course I do."

"You sound weird."

"Too much coffee, too little sleep."

"That's all it is? You're not holding out on me?"

He couldn't talk about the ravine. If he did, Kristin would ask a million questions, none of which he could answer.

A loud squeal came through the line.

"Shh, Paige. Mommy's talking to Uncle Jared."

He felt his tension ease a little. His niece was nine months old, a blue-eyed miniature version of his sister who liked to be attached to her mom 24/7. Otherwise, she'd wail brokenheartedly. Kristin's demanding baby needed routine and familiar surroundings, so he was glad his sister had decided not to come to Langeville.

"What trouble did your daughter get into today?" he asked, partly because he wanted to divert Kristin from probing more deeply and partly because he'd enjoy hearing of his niece's latest antics.

"I found her eating out of the cat's bowl this morning. I swear she still smells like seafood medley."

"Stinky."

"Hey, her breath's nothing compared to the diaper waiting for her daddy when he gets out of the shower."

He couldn't help but smile. That last remark was more like the sister he knew. Their parents had been killed in a car crash when he was twenty-two. He'd left college to finish raising Kristin, a precocious fourteen-year-old, and Steve, a rebellious eleven-year-old. Unlike his strained relationship with his brother, the bond between Kristin and himself had always been uncomplicated and loving. He'd do anything for her. Let her hope a little longer. Let her believe Steve would show up with an apology and a doozy of an explanation. Let her enjoy the afternoon with her husband and her baby.

Another squeal, this time louder, conveying its meaning in no uncertain terms. *Get off the phone, Mommy. I want your full attention.*

"I should go," she said reluctantly.

"I'll call you again soon," he said, leaving the timing deliberately vague.

"If anybody can figure this thing out, you can, Jared."

Her faith in him made him feel guilty for his subterfuge, but he'd already made up his mind. "Try not to worry. Paige will pick up on it and stress you out even more."

"You've got that right," Kristin mumbled. "I love you, big brother."

"I love you, too."

He pocketed his phone, then turned from the window. Brooke stood in the kitchen doorway, drying her hands on a towel.

"Who's Paige?"

"My baby niece."

"That was your sister on the phone?"

He nodded. "She wanted an update. I mentioned Sidorov's daughter, and somehow we got talking about whether she and Steve were together or apart before he went missing. If they had broken up, it doesn't make sense that Sidorov would go after him."

"What if Marisa thought Steve used her, then dumped her, so she asked Daddy to teach him a lesson?"

Trust Brooke to come up with a new scenario. The "woman scorned" was as plausible as the others he'd been considering. He liked it enough to flesh it out a little more. "And Daddy got carried away and murdered him."

"Marisa might not know that," Brooke pointed out. "Or we could have this all wrong, and she really loved your brother. By packing up Steve's belongings, Sidorov tricked her into believing her feelings weren't reciprocated."

"I wonder how she'd react if she found out her father got rid of her lover."

"I doubt she'll believe us without proof."

The most convincing proof would be Steve's corpse with physical evidence tied to Sidorov or his men. The thought made him sick, but it also meant speaking with

Marisa should wait until after the autopsy was completed.

"How's your sister holding up?" Brooke asked.

"Not great," he admitted. "And in case you're wondering, I didn't tell her what we found in the ravine."

"No reason to. The owner of that shoe hasn't been identified. We could have this all wrong. It may not be your brother at all."

"The location and plastic suggest otherwise."

She frowned. "It's too soon to be sure. We need to give the police time to do their job. In the meantime, you're allowed to hope."

He just shook his head, refusing to give in to the desire to do just that, because he knew if he did, the uncertainty would eat at him like battery acid. Better to take the hit now, instead of wishing for a miracle that wouldn't materialize. Because the odds were overwhelming that the corpse the police had dug up was his brother.

Sergei Latschenko found his boss in the kitchen, sitting alone at the table, eating borscht and bread. The stench of cooked beets nearly made him gag, and he longed for a smoke, but his news was too important to wait.

"I talked to your cop," he said. "A dead body was dug out of the ravine behind Middleview a few hours ago."

Sidorov stopped chewing. "Do they know who it is?"

"Not yet."

The other man cursed in Russian. "I can't believe Chernov would be so stupid."

"What do you mean?"

"I told him I did not care how it was done, only make sure the body can never be found. Instead it turns up behind one of my company's properties."

"Sloppy job." Latschenko made sure to sound suitably disgusted, but inside he felt a tinge of alarm. He enjoyed intimidating people, liked the rush of power it gave him, but pointing a gun at someone was a lot different than using it to end someone's life. If this job with Sidorov became permanent, he'd be expected to do more than issue threats.

"He texted me after it was over," the other man continued. "Told me the job went perfect, no problems."

"He lied." Chernov didn't know it yet, but he should extend his hunting trip. Indefinitely. He had done more than disappoint his boss; he had deceived him.

Sidorov broke off a hunk of bread and dipped it in his soup. "When the body is identified, my daughter will be shocked. She thinks her bastard boyfriend left town. When she learns he did not, she will start asking questions. Did I know about them? Was I angry? How angry?"

That didn't sound good. "What will you say?"

"What I always say. She is more precious to me than all the diamonds in Russia. As her father, I have the right to protect her from men who would use her." His lip curled in distaste. "I still cannot believe she lay down with that painter."

Loyalty was important to a man like Sidorov, so Latschenko said what he figured his new boss wanted to hear. "Daughters should respect their fathers. They know what's best."

Sidorov grunted and shoved aside his soup bowl.

"Tell me about the girl PI. How could you and your idiots let her escape after I told you where to find her?"

He'd hoped news of the dead body would distract Sidorov from what had happened last night. No such luck. The reckoning had been postponed only because his boss had been holed up in his office all morning. "She ran into the ravine. It was dark, rainy. We searched everywhere, but there were many places for her to hide."

"Is she the one who found the body in the ravine?"

He shook his head. "It was a guy named Alex Sheridan. He says he got worried when he couldn't reach his friend and decided to look around the neighborhood where he'd been working."

The Russian wrinkled his beak of a nose as if detecting garbage. "He is lying."

"Your guy says the police checked with the painter's sister, and his story holds up."

Sidorov's expression became calculating. "I want to know more about him. Who is he? Where is he staying? Will he cause us trouble?"

"I'll find out."

"And keep looking for that PI. I want to know where she is."

"Don't worry," Latschenko said, determined not to strike out like his predecessor. "I'll make that bitch sorry she came snooping anywhere near you."

Caffeine was the last thing her nerves needed, Brooke thought, but that didn't stop her from scooping coffee into the coffeemaker. Making a fresh pot had given her an excuse to escape from the living room. She couldn't handle the tension, the uncertainty, the *waiting* any more. She could only imagine how much worse it must be for Jared, but at least he had his conversations with Alex at the police station and Brent Young at the Bureau to keep him busy; she had only her thoughts. Thoughts that had grown as dark and unpredictable as the storm clouds she'd glimpsed outside.

Jared had told Brent about the grisly discovery in the ravine. They'd discussed options in the give-and-take way of longtime colleagues and had finally settled on a strategy. Young would contact the Langeville PD to inquire about the autopsy findings. Local authorities, when faced with outside interest especially at the federal level, tended to act promptly and decisively. As soon as Young had details, he'd pass them along to Jared.

Brooke finished pouring water into the machine and pressed the switch. The coffee would take a few minutes to brew, so she sank into a chair at the kitchen table. Her gaze roamed around the room. Was it only this morning she had made Jared pancakes to thank him for staying with her last night?

Her mind flashed to the ravine. The police must have removed the body hours ago. Would it turn out to be Jared's brother? Was Steve Nash lying in the morgue at this very moment, waiting for dissection by the medical examiner's knife?

A shiver passed through her. Although she'd been the one encouraging Jared to hope, she couldn't shut out the fear that his suspicions were right, and he had lost someone dear to him. It wasn't fair. He deserved better. He'd come to Langeville willing to sacrifice his career to find his brother. He'd ended his surveillance of a suspect and exposed himself to danger to help her, a complete stranger. She would never forget his daring rescue, the first of several. His actions had been courageous, his motives unselfish. It seemed inconceivable to her that, despite all of Jared's efforts, his brother might be dead. Such an outcome would leave such a hole in his life and that of his family.

The last of the coffee sputtered into the carafe, rousing her from her depressing thoughts. It was the endless waiting that had her feeling anxious. She'd never been patient, had never been content to let life unfold at its own pace. When her father had undergone triple-bypass surgery, she and Savannah had kept a vigil at the hospital. If she'd been on her own, she would have gone out of her mind worrying, and she knew her sister alone would have fared no better. Fortunately, they'd had each other for companionship and comfort.

She thought of Jared. He was smart and disciplined, a man others could count on, no matter how terrible the circumstances. Yet despite all his toughness, he possessed surprising insight and sensitivity. Now he was alone and hurting. She wanted to go to him. Wrap her arms around him and give him the support she suspected he desperately needed but wouldn't ask for. What would be his reaction? Would he pull away? Or would he hold on tight?

Under the circumstances, she could understand how he might crave contact with another human being, how he might need someone else's warmth to help him ward off the cold dread inside him. Would he welcome her touch? Her heart skipped at the thought of his muscled body pressed hard against hers, and she chided herself for the instinctive response. She was talking about comfort, not sex. But sometimes one could lead to the other.

Last night, she'd been tempted to offer herself to him, but old fears had held her back. Today, she'd been reminded, in no uncertain terms, life was fragile and uncertain. She didn't want to die with regrets. She didn't want to miss out on wonderful experiences or pass up the good in life. And she knew without a doubt Jared Nash qualified as the good. Maybe even the best.

She moved to pour the coffee into mugs, having come to a decision she knew she wouldn't regret. She would reach out to Jared. And if he wanted more, she wouldn't refuse him. Not when she'd finally realized she wanted a lot more, too.

His cell phone rang in the other room. Her heart pounded faster in anticipation, in trepidation. *Calm down*; she tried to soothe her jittery nerves. It might only be Alex checking in. Or it might be someone else calling with information about Steve's disappearance.

Jared was facing away from her, but she could see his body, from head to toe, was a solid block of tension. And she knew that whoever was on the other end of the line, the call definitely related to the remains in the ravine.

Chapter 13

"Arc you sure?" Jared rasped.

"I spoke directly to the cop attending the autopsy," Brent said. "No positive ID yet, but the ME reported thc deceased is a white male with brown hair, six foot three, weight two-hundred-thirty, between thirty-five and fifty years old."

Not his brother. Not even close.

He grabbed for the wall, light-headed with relief. He hadn't been able to breathe normally since the ravine. With each breath, he'd imagined he could still smell the putrid odor of decaying flesh. The possibility that its source was his own flesh and blood had constricted his throat and tied his stomach in knots. Now his body felt so relaxed, so loose, it was a wonder he could stand.

"There were bruises on the vic's torso and arms,"

Brent continued, "and preliminary findings suggest the cause of death was suffocation."

Jared had seen his share of murder victims. The weapons of choice were mostly guns and knives. He thought of the size of the guy who had been killed. It wouldn't have been easy to hold him down and cut off his air supply.

A sharp intake of breath had him turning around in time to see Brooke reach out for him. Slipping an arm around her, he quickly ended his conversation with Brent. Then he pocketed his cell phone and drew her fully against him.

"What's the matter?" he asked, stroking her back. Through the thin cotton of her tank top he could feel her heart racing, her body trembling like the windblown trees outside.

"I saw you slump against the wall," she said, her words muffled against his throat.

She thought he'd been given the worst news possible, and her reaction made it clear that she cared more than a little about him. His spirits, already buoyed by Brent's call, lifted even higher. He set her back gently from him because, as much as he liked the feel of her embrace, she'd hugged him for the wrong reason.

"It wasn't Steve in the ravine."

She stared at him as if she couldn't believe she'd heard him right.

"The police don't know who it is," he added, "but it's definitely not my brother."

A smile spread across her face, making her skin glow and her eyes shine. She had never looked more beautiful to him. "I can't imagine how relieved you must be feeling."

He resisted the urge to kiss her—barely—by thinking about the other person who had spent the day waiting and wondering. "I have to call Alex."

Unfortunately, the man didn't answer his phone, so Jared sent him a text with the pertinent details before turning his attention back to Brooke.

"If you want to say 'I told you so,' go right ahead. I shouldn't have assumed the worst. I was just so afraid to hope."

"Believe me, I know all about that."

Her admission was at odds with her usual prickly manner. He wondered if she could be coaxed into lowering her guard further. "It turned out to be a mistake for me. How's it working for you?"

She considered him for a long moment, her expression enigmatic. "I'm thinking about trying another approach."

"And what might that be?"

Her lips curved in a smile that made his pulse beat faster. "Assume the best—and go for it."

Before he realized her intention, she stepped forward and looped her arms around his neck. His body surged in hungry response, a fact she couldn't help but be aware of as her embrace left absolutely no space between them. He groaned her name, his mouth seeking out hers in a kiss that quickly became fierce and wild. She urged him on, kissing him harder, pressing her breasts against his chest. The scent of her made his senses reel and so did the throaty sounds she made. From the moment they'd met, he'd been attracted to her, but it had taken the events of last night and today for him to see past the beautiful face and figure to appreciate the full extent of her determination and compassion. And even though he wanted to lose himself in the sensations coursing through his body, he couldn't quiet the questions in his head.

Reluctantly, he dragged his mouth away from hers. "What's happening here?"

"I thought that was obvious," she said, her voice low, her breathing unsteady.

"Explain it to me."

When she hesitated, a cold chill passed through him as he remembered how the dark had made her lose her inhibitions. Maybe relief had the same effect on her. "Today was stressful. Is this your way of blowing off steam?"

Her eyes widened. "What? No." Her cheeks flushed pink. "I want to be with you."

"I want to be with you, too." He rested his forehead against hers. "But not in the dark. If you have a problem with that, tell me now."

She swallowed. "There's no problem. I…I want you to see me."

What she really meant was she wanted him to accept her, imperfect body and all. He started to speak, then realized words wouldn't be enough to convince her. He needed to show her.

Brooke's heart raced as Jared took her hand and led her upstairs to the room where they'd talked late last night. When he turned on the bedside lamp, she had to lock her legs to resist the urge to bolt. Was this finally happening? Were they going to get naked and make love? She tried not to think about the naked part. Despite her bold words, she couldn't help but be nervous.

What if he was turned off by her scars? Or worse, what if she disappointed him sexually?

It had been a long time for her. And sex with her ex-fiancé had never been spectacular. She grew chilled, remembering. He'd called her a prude because she wasn't keen to try bondage and other kinkier acts, and his constant desire to push the boundaries left her cold. Maybe Chad was right. Maybe her body issues had always existed, and her scars had simply magnified them.

Then Jared stretched her out on the bed and kissed her again. It was hard to hold on to a single thought, much less inhibitions or worries, when his mouth was teasing hers so deliciously. She curled her arms around him, his body heat seeping into her like the steam of a sauna. Oh, this was heavenly. Her legs grew heavy and her toes curled. She stroked his shoulders where there was still some residual tension. The past few hours had been hard on him. Maybe he'd enjoy a massage. And the foreplay would give her more time to psych up to losing her clothes.

"Take off your shirt," she murmured.

As he sat up and discarded it, her mouth went dry. With his bare chest, tousled hair and stubbled jaw, he reminded her of a sultry Guess ad.

"Now what?" he asked, his eyes darkening.

"Lie down on your stomach." As soon as he complied, she straddled his hips and set her palms on his back, digging into his tight muscles with her thumbs. Rubbing. Kneading. His tanned skin was smooth and supple, his body hard and lean.

His low groan signaled his approval. "Don't stop. Your hands are pure magic."

Pleased by the compliment, she continued to work on him, alternating between firm pressure and feather-light strokes. Finally, she gave in to temptation and pressed her lips against his back.

Without warning, he flipped her beneath him. "Your turn."

The bed's duvet was soft and thick under her back. Obviously, her position ruled out a back massage, so he must have something else in mind. Something that involved her front. Her pulse beat in her throat.

He spread his fingers wide and stroked slowly over her breasts. Her body responded as if she weren't still wearing a tank top and bra. Her skin grew hot. Her nipples puckered into hard buds. He circled her pliant flesh, rubbing and caressing as she had touched him. As his gaze tracked the motion of his hands, she imagined what would happen when he finally tired of feeling cotton and wanted contact with her skin.

She closed her eyes, remembering the shock she'd felt upon viewing her scarred stomach for the first time. It had been awful. She'd felt as if she were looking at a stranger. Was that how Jared would feel? He was so damn good at masking his feelings. Would she be able to discern his true reaction? His face might not give him away, but there was one thing a man couldn't hide: his desire for sex.

Jared's voice startled her. "We're not so different, you and me."

She opened her eyes. Forced herself to respond in a light tone. "I'm surprised to hear you say that, considering what part of my anatomy you're touching."

"What I'm talking about is on the inside." He searched her eyes, his expression serious. "We both chose careers that put us in the line of fire. We got hurt and struggled to be whole again."

He laid a gentle hand on her cheek. "Your scars are proof of your courage and your will to survive. So no matter how bad they are, they make no difference to me. You're strong and sexy. And I'm the luckiest guy alive right now because you want to be with me."

Her throat tightened with unshed tears. "I'm the lucky one," she whispered.

After kissing his fingertips, she reached down and stripped off her top. His gaze lowered to the red, puckered ugliness that was her stomach. She held her breath, battling the instinctive urge to cover herself.

"You're beautiful, Brooke."

She wasn't sure she'd ever believe that, but the absolute sincerity in Jared's voice assured her that he meant what he said. Her heart soared into the stratosphere.

"I've been holding out on you," he said.

She stared at him, suddenly uncertain.

"I have a nasty scar on my right leg. If you think it'll gross you out, don't look."

His teasing smile made her own lips curve. "What else are you hiding from me?"

"Nothing a strip search wouldn't uncover."

She laughed. "You are *so* getting naked."

"Only if you join me."

In short order, his jeans and underwear went sailing across the room. Her remaining clothes soon followed. At last, she was able to revel in the delicious feel of naked skin pressed against naked skin.

As he laved her nipples with his tongue, exquisite sensations flowed from the peaks of her breasts to the rest of her body, gradually pooling in a throbbing ache at her core. His every touch excited her more than the last, and she writhed in wanton abandon.

"I want to taste you everywhere," Jared murmured, kneeling between her legs. Then he proceeded to do just that, his tongue delving intimately. It didn't take her long to tumble over the edge in a sensuous free fall.

While she recovered, he rained soft kisses on her eyelids and cheeks. Finally her body was ready to inflict pleasurable torture on him. She gripped the smooth planes of his back with hungry hands, then stroked lower till she reached his buttocks. She discovered what he liked by paying close attention to his breathing. A hitch in his breath indicated a pleasure point. Her fingers roamed and dallied over his entire body, discovering many pleasure points. The knowledge thrilled her, emboldened her.

He writhed and groaned in response. She rubbed her pelvis against his engorged flesh. Her skin may not have been smooth, but Jared didn't care and neither did she anymore. She wanted to join her body with his. She wanted him to bury his hardness deep within her.

Sweat darkened his hair, and an expression of fierce concentration hardened the planes of his face. He stared deeply into her eyes as if he had a direct link to her soul. What was happening between them felt right. So right she was starting to want more than just this one afternoon with him. But she couldn't think about the future when her body was clamoring again for release right now.

He pulled away to root through his wallet for a condom. Then he knelt between her knees and used himself to rub her. He whispered erotic words against her flushed skin. He praised her passion and urged her to confess her secret desires. Every word, every stroke drove her higher. Wet and ravenous, she spread her legs wider and arched her hips, trying to entice him to enter her.

He resisted, his restraint evident in his heavy-lidded eyes and clenched teeth. She hooked her heels around his calves and lunged upward, trying to obliterate his control. With an impassioned groan, he finally thrust into her, achieving full penetration with a single smooth stroke. She began to move, instinct guiding her to find the most satisfying rhythm—a rhythm echoed in their pounding heartbeats. The musky scent of their aroused bodies filled her nostrils, and she rejoiced in their earthy closeness. So much heat. So much pleasure. Responding to his urging, she rotated her hips faster. The friction drove her mad. She teetered on the brink, straining for release again.

Kissing her hair, Jared whispered her name and caressed her aching center. She couldn't hold back. A wave of heat slammed into her, turning the apex of her thighs into liquid fire. Her inner muscles clamped down on him like a vise, and she cried out in exultation as powerful spasms racked her body.

Within seconds, Jared's back went rigid under her hands. Then his own climax overtook him, and he shuddered again and again until he lay spent in her arms.

Through a sensuous haze, she realized this explosive lovemaking was the way it was supposed to be. And Jared was everything a woman could ask for.

Of course, lovemaking's afterglow could be influencing her. It was hard to think logically when her body still hummed from that mind-blowing climax. But sexual fulfillment couldn't fully account for the happiness she was feeling.

She inhaled sharply. She *wasn't* falling in love with Jared. She hadn't known him long enough for that. Only long enough for her to trust him—and have fabulous sex with him. The realization made her uneasy. She wanted to deny the significance of her actions, but the only convincing explanation was her heart was involved. Now what was she going to do?

As Jared's lips captured hers, her anxiety receded. She didn't have to *do* anything right now. She could just enjoy the moment.

Brooke awoke to a tickling sensation on her arm. Long masculine fingers were stroking her skin.

"We should get up," a deep voice rumbled.

She rolled over to find Jared lounging naked on the other side of the bed. The sheet rode low on his hips, blocking an X-rated view. "Alex will probably be back soon," he added.

She checked on the sheet's position in relation to her body. Her shoulders were exposed, as well as one breast Jared was eyeing appreciatively. Her pulse beat madly as every intimate thing they'd done came rushing back to her.

"Or we can stay put and risk giving him an eyeful." The mattress dipped as Jared shifted closer. "I'm leaving the decision entirely up to you."

"Because you're not shy," she said, her lips curving as she remembered his comment at the motel.

His expression turned mischievous. "Which I believe I proved to you in the last hour or so."

He sure had. And within minutes, she had shed her

self-consciousness like a butterfly emerging from its cocoon. What a flight she had taken. Soaring. Transcending. She'd never forget the experience—or the man who had shared himself with her.

She studied him. His chest gleamed like bronze against the white sheets, beckoning her to touch him. But if she did, he would reciprocate, and then touches would lead to kisses, and they wouldn't leave the bed for quite some time. And although making love again with Jared was incredibly tempting, their sexual relationship was too new, too precious, for her to be comfortable with Alex, or anyone else, knowing about it yet.

"We should get dressed," she said, sitting up reluctantly.

"How about a shower?" He traced her spine with his fingertip.

"You mean take one together?" She turned to face him. "Have you seen the size of that shower stall?"

"So it'll be a little crowded. I don't mind a tight fit. As you already know."

His words robbed her of speech—and the ability to think of a legitimate objection.

"It'll save on hot water," he coaxed.

His expression was charmingly innocent, but she was pretty sure his intentions weren't. Or was he just goading her with no expectation that she'd agree? Yeah, that was it. He thought he knew how she'd react. But she'd surprised him several times today and not just in bed. Why stop now?

She smiled sweetly. "By all means, let's share the shower and be eco-friendly."

His eyes widened. *Gotcha*, she thought. But the upper hand didn't stay with her for long.

"Oh, I've no doubt we'll be *very* friendly." With that, he scooped her up in his arms and carried her into the bathroom.

They played and dallied in the water, soaping each other with slow, sensual strokes and coming together once more against the tile wall. If she experienced any soreness later, she thought as Jared toweled her dry, she had only herself to blame. But she couldn't remember ever feeling so supremely satisfied or blissfully content.

They were in the kitchen supposedly making BLT sandwiches, but mostly getting in each other's way and grinning like teenagers, when Alex walked in. His eyes were bloodshot and his gait unsteady. He lowered himself into a chair with a wince.

Jared stopped buttering toast. "Did you get my text?"

"Yeah, thanks. Huge relief. I was at a bar, trying to forget what I saw at the ravine, when the message came through."

"And you stayed to celebrate," Jared guessed.

"Bought rounds for the whole damn place." He stifled a yawn. "Then I downed about a gallon of coffee so I could drive back here."

Brooke cringed at the thought of Alex behind the wheel of his truck. Then she cringed for a different reason as his gaze moved from her to Jared, lingering on their still-damp hair and their close proximity at the counter. The knowing look in his eyes showed he was a lot more sober than she'd given him credit for.

"I take it you two preferred a private celebration."

She felt heat in her face and knew she was blushing.

Thankfully, Jared didn't respond to the other man's comment except to ask, "How did it go with the cops?"

"They were impressed by my security consulting experience and accepted my version of events at face value. While I was there, I overheard them discussing a vehicle neighbors noticed on the street Sunday. A tow truck hauled it away on Monday."

"Did you get a description of it? It might belong to the vic."

"It's a white Ford F-150." He held up his left palm, which bore pen marks. "I jotted down the license number."

A cell phone rang in the other room. Excusing himself, Jared went to answer it.

Brooke finished slicing tomatoes and assembled sandwiches, conscious of Alex staring at her. After a long, awkward moment during which she felt the color in her cheeks continue to deepen, she finally lifted her head and asked, "Is there something you want to say to me?"

He smiled, hopefully. "Is there any chance you could make me a sandwich, too? I'm starving."

"Sure. I can do that."

By the time she'd put together another sandwich and carried it to the table, Jared was back. "According to Brent, the guy in the ravine has been identified as Anton Chernov. The Bureau believes he's responsible for torch jobs and hits for the Russian mafia, but they've never found enough evidence to convict him. A year ago, he left Brighton Beach suddenly. Rumor has it he was told to get lost until the heat was off him."

"What's he been doing since then?" Alex bit into

his BLT, then closed his eyes and sighed as if it were the best meal he'd ever tasted.

"Take a guess."

Alex's mouth was full, so Brooke answered for him. "Working for Sidorov. Latschenko mentioned his name on the tape."

Jared's smile of approval sent a surge of warmth through her body. "So how's he end up dead in the ravine? And where's his vehicle? The police say the white Ford truck isn't his."

She was silent for a moment, mulling over various scenarios. "Maybe an old enemy tracked him down, murdered him out of revenge and disposed of his vehicle. The location of Chernov's body—behind his employer's property—is a warning to Sidorov that his business interests could suffer if he goes after Chernov's killer."

Alex wiped his lips with a napkin. "I have a simpler explanation. Sidorov sent Chernov to kill Steve, but Steve killed him instead. Then he panicked, dumped the body in the ravine and took off in Chernov's wheels."

Jared shoved his half-eaten sandwich away abruptly. "That's crazy talk, Alex."

"Not so crazy when you consider the COD—suffocation by a plastic sheet—points to a less-than-professional killer."

"You think my brother's capable of taking out a trained assassin?"

Alex took a moment to consider his answer. "Under the right circumstances, with a lot of luck, I think it's possible."

Jared shook his head in exasperation. "You're giving Steve way too much credit."

"And you're not giving him enough." Pushing back

from the table, Alex crossed his massive arms over his chest. "But that's hardly a surprise, isn't it? You always expect him to screw up."

"Hey, I'm the one doubting my brother killed a man."

"If Steve killed Chernov, he was only doing what he had to do to stay alive. And afterward, he would have been scared and confused and wanting to ask his FBI agent brother for advice. So why didn't he?"

"How should I know?" Jared said.

"You know," Alex shot back. "And so do I."

Brooke looked from one to the other, not understanding Alex's belligerence or Jared's tension.

"Steve didn't call you," Alex continued, "because he knew you wouldn't speak to him. He told me you'd cut him out of your life like a cancer, even though he'd apologized a thousand times for what he did."

"He crossed the line," Jared said tightly. "He knew there'd be consequences, but he did it anyway."

The other man slammed his fist on the table. "Has it occurred to you, without that bad blood between you, Steve would've asked for your help and been safe now instead of on the run? That is, if he *is* on the run and not lying dead somewhere."

With a sinking feeling in her stomach, Brooke waited for Jared to answer, but he just stared at Alex, stubbornly silent. Her earlier contentment slipped away like water down a drain. Jared had allowed her to believe he was as close to Steve as she was to Savannah. That obviously wasn't true. The two brothers hadn't spoken for some time, all because of something Steve regretted and Jared couldn't get past.

Most relationships relied on some degree of forgiveness. It was the mortar that sealed the fissures caused by differing opinions and habits. But given enough pressure, even a close relationship could become brittle, fragile.

What had broken the bond between Jared and his brother?

The fact that she couldn't even hazard a guess proved she didn't really know the man she'd slept with. And judging by his closed expression, he was in no mood to confide in her. Not now, probably never. After the intimacy they'd shared and the feelings he'd awakened in her, his silence on family matters hurt like a stab to the heart. She wanted him to trust her. Was that naive, wishful thinking on her part?

Finally, Alex spoke. "If Sidorov doesn't already know his hit man is dead, he will soon, and then he'll go after your brother with everything he's got."

"We have to find Steve first," Jared said.

Chapter 14

A few keystrokes in the right database turned up an owner for the vehicle. Jared glanced up from his laptop. "It's registered to Martin Wilson."

"Wilson?" Brooke repeated. "Ed Keesing said he hired Steve on Wilson's recommendation."

"Why would Wilson drive over to see Steve, then leave without his truck?" Alex asked.

"Because it broke down?" Jared suggested.

"Or Chernov showed up," Brooke said, "and upset Wilson so badly he fled without it."

Jared's heart beat faster at the possibility of a new witness. "I have to talk to him."

But the successful contractor proved elusive. According to his neighbors—and confirmed by the stack of mail on his doorstep—he hadn't been home since Sunday afternoon. And his foreman had only received a text message that he was unavailable until further notice due to an allergic reaction to medicine. Current projects were to proceed as scheduled except for two that were on hold pending the delivery of materials.

Jared called Wilson's cell phone, but no one answered. The message he left was brief and urgent, but he deliberately omitted any mention of Steve or Chernov in case someone other than Wilson had gained access to his phone.

Further investigation determined the contractor had a son, Sam, who owned an art gallery on the other side of town. It made sense to question him in person about his father's whereabouts, so Jared, Brooke and Alex piled into Alex's truck.

As they cruised up the street, Jared scanned the vehicles parked at the curb. "I don't like how Latschenko seems to show up wherever we go."

"You want me to stay back and watch for him?" Alex asked. His voice held no trace of his earlier animosity, and Jared remembered Steve saying his friend wasn't one to hold a grudge. Or maybe Alex had realized he'd heard only Steve's side of the story, and it wasn't fair to heap all the blame on Jared. Whatever the reason, he appreciated the security consultant's offer.

"Thanks," he said. "If you see anything suspicious, don't engage. Call my cell, and we'll figure out what to do."

Alex nodded, his bloodshot eyes hidden behind sunglasses. He dropped Jared and Brooke across the street from the studio, then drove off to find a parking space.

It was the first time Jared had been alone with Brooke since Alex's arrival at the house. As she watched for the traffic signal to change, he gazed at the curve of her neck and remembered nuzzling her there, her skin slick with water from the shower. After their lusty, unrestrained lovemaking, he'd sensed the sweet, tender gesture had surprised her. It had surprised him, too. He usually felt restless after sex and needed to move away from his partner. With Brooke, he'd wanted to stay close. He'd coaxed her into the tiny shower stall not because he'd been angling for a repeat performance, but because he hadn't been ready to let her go. The fact that their shower play had led to another richly satisfying encounter had been a bonus.

It occurred to him that she hadn't looked at him at all during the drive to the studio. Maybe Alex's crack about their "private celebration" had made her self-conscious. Or maybe she didn't want to appear emotionally clingy. Whatever her reasons, he wanted her eyes on him again.

"Hey, pretty lady," he murmured, settling his hand on the small of her back.

The light changed. Brooke set off as if a starting pistol had sounded, her showgirl legs speed-walking across the street. He practically had to jog to catch up to her. When she slowed on the sidewalk to avoid mowing down a woman with a stroller, he gripped her arm and guided her off to the side. Then he turned her to face him.

"Is there a fire I don't know about?" He smiled, but she didn't smile back.

"Why weren't you honest with me?"

His confusion must have shown because she continued, "Why didn't you tell me about the trouble between you and Steve?"

His first reaction was a knee-jerk, defensive one. "It wasn't relevant."

"It was relevant to me. I believed you and Steve were close."

"You *assumed* we were close."

"You had plenty of opportunity to set me straight, but you didn't. I think I know why. Because you wanted me to believe you and I share the same values about the importance of family."

He felt a guilty twinge, but irritation overrode it, possibly because their argument was attracting the attention of passersby. "I'm close with Kristin."

"But not your brother. Why not?"

"This is hardly the time or place to sort this out."

Her only concession was to lower her voice. "You misled me, so I'd stop resisting and get *friendly.*" She uttered the last word like a curse.

"That's not true." Damn, he didn't want to fight with her. Not when the image of her naked body moving against his was still fresh in his mind.

"Then prove it."

He studied her flushed face and stormy eyes. "How?"

"Tell me what happened between you and your brother."

He could shut her down in a heartbeat, but he sensed if he did, they were finished. No more intoxicating kisses, no more magic back rubs, no more explosive releases. And no more tender moments. He didn't want to end what had only begun—but neither was he a pushover. She had to be willing to expose something deeply private, too.

"Are you ready to talk about getting shot?"

"That's not a fair exchange," she protested. "What happened to me was work-related. It didn't cause me to reject a member of my family."

He propped his shoulder against the brick wall. "If you want to check out my skeletons, you have to be willing to open up your closet door, too."

"I could ask Alex."

And Steve's friend probably wouldn't think twice about enlightening her. "So why don't you?"

She was silent, her thoughts impossible to fathom. Finally, she answered. "Because I want to hear it from you."

"No matter how sordid the tale?" he challenged.

Her eyes held his. "Trust me to understand."

He cupped her face in his hands. "I will, if you will."

Tires screeched on the road next to them, and a car horn blared in response. She jumped at the sound, then gave a rueful shrug. "You're right. This is a lousy place to have this conversation."

"We'll find a better one and finish it. But first, let's talk to Wilson's son."

The studio, aptly named Edgy Art, featured canvases with explosive bursts of color and compelling designs, as well as photos that had been digitally altered into surreal, fantastical images. After Jared strode past the displays to the back, he realized Brooke was moving at a slower pace, her eyes lingering on the artwork. Too bad they didn't have time to browse. Maybe after his brother was found and Sidorov arrested, they could come back. Shop a little. Eat at an outside café. Stroll hand in hand in the park. Then find a comfortable hotel…

His thoughts were interrupted by the sound of footsteps. A guy with spiked blond hair, multiple piercings and elaborate sleeve tattoos on both arms sauntered toward them. A weird sense of familiarity struck Jared, which he dismissed immediately. He'd have remembered this character if they'd crossed paths before.

"If you like *Betrayal*," the guy said to Brooke, who had been studying a nearby canvas, "you might enjoy the one called *Fury* hanging on the next wall."

"Are you the artist?" She leaned closer, reading off the signature in the lower corner. "Sam Wilson?"

"Yes, but only the acrylics are mine. The photo creations are my girlfriend's. Jasmine and I opened this place together six months ago and also sell our work through our website." His pride and enthusiasm were at odds with his tough looks.

"You're both very talented," she said sincerely.

He beamed. "Thanks. Feel free to wander around. I'll be at the back if you think of any questions."

"I have one," Jared said, figuring it was time to reveal the purpose of their visit. "Do you know where your father is? He hasn't been at work or home for a few days, and he isn't answering his cell phone."

Wilson was no longer smiling. "I'm the last person you should ask. We've barely spoken since I told him I wanted to make my living with a paintbrush instead of a hammer."

Another estranged family. Different issues, same sad outcome.

Disconcerted by his musings, Jared told Wilson, "He could be in serious trouble."

"What kind of trouble?"

That the artist had asked the question was a hopeful sign he cared more than he wanted to let on. "Your father was last seen at the same address as a Russian hit man." No need to mention Chernov was dead and his murderer remained unidentified.

"How do you know that? Who are you?"

He showed his FBI credentials. "A man is missing, and there's a good chance your father knows what happened. Can you think of anywhere he'd go?"

Wilson crossed his tattooed arms, the colorful patterns blending together like a kaleidoscope. "I only know where I wish he'd go. Straight to hell."

"Try again," Jared said. "And this time, limit your suggestions to places on Earth."

Resentment and stubbornness radiated from the man. He wasn't going to cooperate. Jared knew it even before he heard Wilson say, "I have no idea where he is and I don't care."

Jared wanted to continue to press the artist, but his instincts told him the guy wasn't lying.

Brooke, who had been a silent observer up to now, addressed Wilson. "Just because you have issues with your father, is it fair to deprive your child of the chance to know him?"

"What are you talking about?"

"Your girlfriend's expecting."

"How do you know Jasmine's pregnant?" Wilson demanded. "We've only told a few close friends."

"Your piece called *Creation*, dated last month, looks as if it were inspired by a sonogram."

Brooke's keen interest in the artwork hadn't been for enjoyment, Jared realized. She'd been searching for clues. His respect for her, which was already considerable, ratcheted up another notch.

"If your father knew he was going to be a grandfather," Brooke continued, "maybe he'd try to make peace with you."

"You don't understand," he muttered.

"I understand better than you think," she insisted. "My old man was a first-class jerk. He undercut my confidence with unfair criticism, and his opinions were often narrow-minded and chauvinistic. So I eventually went about my life as though he didn't exist."

"Sounds like you made the right choice."

"I thought so—until the day he had a heart attack."

She paused, her eyes bleak, before continuing in a subdued voice. "While I waited to find out if he'd live or die, I remembered times when he hadn't been a jerk. Like the many skating lessons he drove me to and the hot chocolate he bought after I came off the ice so cold my teeth chattered. Like the self-defense techniques he taught me after a date turned scary." Her lips curved in a wry smile. "I realized, although he sometimes hurt me, I had hurt myself more by not seeing him. And I decided if he lived, I'd make him part of my life again."

Jared wondered whether Brooke's message of reconciliation was meant solely for Wilson or for him, as well. It certainly hit home. Only now did he realize how much he'd missed his brother's companionship. He and Steve had had many good times together.

"My father is a fitness freak," Wilson told Brooke. "I don't need to worry about him having a heart attack for a long time."

"Forget clogged arteries," Jared interjected. "Think gunshot wounds. Your father's actions appear to be those of a man on the run."

"If you say so."

"You may have had a falling-out with him," Brooke added, "but do you really want him dead?"

Wilson stared at her intently but couldn't quite manage a dismissive comeback. Finally he shook his head.

"You must be able to suggest a few places he could be."

"We haven't spoken in years. I don't have a clue."

Jared felt disappointment descend on him like a suffocating cloak. What supreme bad luck that his only promising lead to Steve was involved in family conflict and couldn't help him. Or was that poetic justice? Ironically, his anger toward his brother, which had once blazed like wildfire, had faded to glowing embers over the past few days.

"Call his cell phone," Brooke urged Wilson. "If he sees it's you, he might pick up."

It was a long shot, but Jared's muscles tensed as the guy placed the call.

Answer, damn you.

A moment later, Sam Wilson said, "Uh...hi, Dad."

Jared couldn't hear the other side of the conversation, but the older Wilson's surprise and concern were evident by his son's next words. "Nothing's wrong with me—except for the FBI agent who's breathing down my neck. You gotta talk to him."

The artist shoved the phone at Jared as if he couldn't get rid of it fast enough.

Jared didn't mince words. "I'm investigating the disappearance of Steve Nash. I know you saw him on Sunday. I also know a professional killer named Chernov showed up and you abandoned your truck at the scene. The man who hired him is almost certainly looking for you. I can offer you protection, but you have to tell me what happened."

A long silence followed, and he half expected to hear the click of a disconnected phone. Instead a deep voice said, "I want more than protection."

Jared swallowed. "What do you want?" If it was

money, he'd borrow whatever was necessary to meet Wilson's demand.

"Go to my house. I've hidden something there. We'll talk again when you can tell me the color of my front door."

"Where are you?"

"A place you'll never find unless you follow my instructions."

"You have to give me something in return."

"Like what?"

"Tell me if Nash is still alive." Whatever the answer, regardless of the pain it might cause him, he had to know.

The contractor replied without hesitation. "I'll do better than that. If you do what I say, I'll take you to him."

"Can we trust him?" Alex asked, after he'd met them at the gallery and learned of Wilson's promise.

Brooke couldn't blame him for being suspicious. Wilson Sr. had every reason to say whatever he figured the FBI wanted to hear. She glanced at Jared, interested to know if he shared her misgivings.

"This isn't about trust," he said. "We'll meet his demand because he's our only lead."

"I'll stand on my head and sing karaoke," Alex said, "if it means I can see Steve again."

Jared grimaced. "Fortunately, he didn't ask for that."

Alex rubbed at the stubble on his jaw. "I don't like the way he dodged your question about Steve. What if 'I'll take you to him' means 'I'll take you to where his body's buried'?"

Brooke was appalled by Alex's speculation, and her

first instinct was to object. Then she realized she had no basis for ruling out the possibility—other than her fervent hope that it wasn't true.

"At least Kristin and I could finally stop wondering," Jared said softly.

"Let's head over to Wilson's house," Alex said, already pivoting on his heel.

Jared stepped into his path, forcing him to stop. "I have something else in mind for you."

"What?"

Jared called out to Sam who was rearranging artwork on a display board. "The people who are after your father might try to get to him through you. Alex can make sure you and your girlfriend leave town without being followed."

"What about our gallery?"

"Lock it up and put a 'gone painting' note on the door. Your safety's more important than a few lost sales."

Wilson nodded slowly. "Yeah, okay. Jasmine's been bugging me to take some time off before the baby's born, so it might as well be now."

"I'll take care of them," Alex told Jared, "but I want to go with you to meet Wilson."

"Okay. Call when you're done."

After Wilson wrote out his father's cell-phone number, he turned to Brooke. "I'll think about what you said. My gramps took me canoeing most summers, and I loved hanging out with him, even though he and my old man weren't close. When my kid's old enough, I'll let him—or her—decide what to do."

Shortly afterward, they split up. Within minutes, Jared and Brooke arrived at a two-story residence with an impressive portico and a royal blue front door. They drove around the block checking parked cars. One was occupied by a guy smoking a cigarette. On their second pass, he tossed the cigarette butt out the window but didn't start his car.

"He's watching Wilson's house," Jared said, voicing the same conclusion Brooke had reached.

"I have an idea how to get rid of him," she replied, "but I need your phone."

With a quizzical look, he passed it over. She dialed 911 immediately and reported seeing a man masturbating in his car while she was walking with her young daughter. She gave the location of the parked car and its license plate, but when asked to identify herself, she claimed her cell was dying and hung up.

A few minutes later, she watched with satisfaction as the guy was hustled into a squad car and taken away. Hopefully, he had a record and the police would hold him for a while.

"Remind me never to get on your bad side," Jared murmured.

They set off for the house. Wilson had said to call again, and Jared was punching numbers into the phone when she grabbed on to his arm.

"What's wrong?" he said, looking up.

She pointed to a broken window that had been hidden by a lush mulberry tree. Glass shards littered the garden underneath it. Quickly trading his phone for his gun, Jared positioned himself next to the window, his body stiff, listening intently. Brooke's stomach knotted, remembering the lone surveillance guy. Were more of Sidorov's men lying in wait inside the house?

Several long minutes passed. Jared darted a look

inside the home, then crawled carefully through the broken window. After what seemed like an eternity, the front door swung open, and he gestured for Brooke to enter.

The chaos in the living room took her breath away. The coffee table had been overturned. Papers and magazines lay strewn across the Persian rug. The leather couch cushions had been sliced open at intervals and stuffing protruded from the gashes. In the kitchen, every cupboard, every drawer had been emptied onto the floor. The fridge door hung open, and the smell of rotting food nearly made her gag.

She glanced at Jared, whose tight jaw and clenched fists communicated his alarm clearer than any words. If the intruders had discovered what he'd been sent to retrieve, he'd be unable to fulfill his part of the deal with the contractor.

While he dialed Wilson's number, Brooke noticed a broken picture frame containing a photo of a younger Sam Wilson. Amazing how different he looked without tattoos and piercings. She must have spoken aloud because Jared muttered, "You're not kidding."

A moment later, he was speaking to the contractor. "Your front door is blue. I've got you on speaker mode so I can search with both hands. What did you hide?"

"Proof that Chernov injured, and probably killed, my friend Danny MacAteer."

"What kind of proof?"

"Surveillance video from his auto parts supply business. Danny had the equipment installed because he suspected one of his employees had been stealing from him, but instead it recorded Chernov threatening him. The bastard tied him up and held a lighter against his chest until he agreed to allow his business to be used to launder money. Then he was told not to speak of what had happened or his place would be torched."

"Obviously, he confided in you."

"We've been friends for years. He gave me a copy of the surveillance video for safekeeping. I wanted him to involve the police, and he said he'd think about it. He was scared for his business, but he should have been scared for himself. The next day, his body was found in an alley. He'd been shot twice in the head."

"Have you told any of this to the police?"

"No. I can only assume Danny took my advice and somehow Chernov found out and decided to shut him up."

A shiver went up Brooke's spine. It sounded as if Sidorov's man within the police department had intercepted Danny MacAteer and learned about the incriminating surveillance tapes. That would explain why MacAteer had been killed and Wilson's place tossed.

Brooke spoke in a low voice intended for only Jared's ears. "Ask him if Chernov was alone when he visited MacAteer."

Jared repeated the question to Wilson.

"No, another guy was there. He was the one in charge, issuing orders and smiling while Chernov burned Danny."

Jared's gaze met hers, and she knew what he was thinking. The video could be enough to arrest Sidorov for extortion and possibly for ordering the murder of Danny MacAteer.

"Where did you hide the copy?" he asked the contractor.

"In the basement."

Jared and Brooke raced down the stairs, while Wilson called out further directions.

"Go into the room on the right."

Jared entered first, then halted abruptly. Peering over his shoulder, Brooke took in the damage that had been wrought on what appeared to be a guest room. The mattress, stripped of its bedding and subjected to deep slashes, sprawled on top of a knocked-over dresser. Debris crunched underfoot with every step. "The room has a floating ceiling," Wilson said. "The tiles are removable."

Broken chunks of the white tiles littered the floor, making it look like an Arctic wasteland. Whoever had searched the house had been very, very thorough.

"Check the tile in the corner by the window."

Brooke gazed upward. Where the tile was supposed to be was an empty space and several exposed two-by-fours.

Chapter 15

Jared couldn't believe his eyes. The ceiling had undergone an orgy of destruction that was chilling in its intensity. Sidorov knew a prison sentence awaited him if Danny MacAteer's video surfaced and must have given explicit orders to his men. *Do whatever it takes to find it. Don't stop until you've torn the whole damn place apart.*

Jared hated the idea that their efforts had been rewarded, but the video's hiding place had been completely gutted. He looked at the mess on the floor. How could anything as fragile as a DVD have survived?

"Do you see it?" Wilson asked.

He hesitated. If the evidence to punish Danny MacAteer's killers had vanished, then so might the contractor's interest in the deal he'd made with Jared. To buy time, he said, "I need to get a chair to reach it."

He glanced at Brooke. When they'd first met, he'd told her that she asked too many questions, but now he looked forward to any ideas or insights she might have to offer.

"Ask if the DVD was left loose or attached to the tile," she whispered.

She hadn't given up on finding it. And while he appreciated her positive attitude, it was hard to share it.

"Well? Is it there or not?" Wilson was losing patience, which increased the risk that he'd assume the worst and disconnect. If that happened, it was unlikely they'd ever be able to find him—or Steve.

Jared repeated Brooke's question.

The contractor's response was enlightening. "I didn't hide a DVD. I hid a micro SD card. It's taped to the underside of the tile."

Jared felt the first glimmer of hope. Wafer-thin and small as a thumbnail, the object could be somewhere in the jumble at his feet.

Setting down the phone, he began rooting through the debris in the corner. Brooke hunkered down on her heels to help. It was slow going due to the miniature size of the object they were searching for and the quantity of material to sift through. Everything was coated with a fine white grit from the smashed tiles. Wilson demanded frequent updates, which further grated on Jared's nerves.

After ten disappointing minutes, his fingers encountered a small raised section on the broken tile he was handling. His pulse sped up as the white powder gave way to reveal a tiny card.

"I've got it," he called out.

"Thank God."

"It's time for you to fulfill your side of our deal. I want to see Steve Nash."

"Will you go after Chernov's boss for Danny's murder?"

"If the video contains what you say it does, there shouldn't be any problem getting a warrant for his arrest. I'll arrange it after I see Nash."

"I'll call you in two hours. That should give you enough time to watch the video."

Jared agreed and pocketed his phone. He had trouble separating the card from the chunk of ceiling tile, either because his nails were too short or because his hands weren't entirely steady. Things were winding down fast. Soon he would find out if Steve was alive or dead.

"Let me try," Brooke said.

He glanced over at her. White powder smeared her right cheek, perspiration beaded her upper lip and clumps of hair stuck to her neck. A vision of stunning beauty she certainly wasn't at the moment. So how did she manage to make his heart beat faster?

She extended her hand, waggled her fingers. "Admit it, Jared. You need my help."

He needed more than her help, he realized. He needed her.

Whoa. Where had that crazy notion come from?

Anxiety over Steve must be throwing him off kilter. Obviously, he was grateful to Brooke. She was the reason the gallery owner had called his father, and Jared was now in the possession of evidence that could put away Sidorov. And there was no denying he was drawn to her. She was smart and sexy and spectacular in bed. But that didn't mean he needed her. Or did he?

Unwilling to pursue that line of thinking, he placed

the tile in Brooke's palm. Her lips curved as her long thumbnail sliced through the tape, and the card popped off.

"Thanks," he said.

"Anytime." Her smile faded. "It's sickening to think what's on it."

"It'll be worth watching if it means Sidorov finally goes to prison."

The return trip was uneventful, and they were soon sitting on the couch viewing the surveillance footage on his laptop. Wilson hadn't misrepresented its importance or ugliness. Acting on Sidorov's orders, Chernov had inflicted excruciating pain on Danny MacAteer until he had agreed to everything they wanted and begged for mercy.

As the disturbing video concluded, Brooke rubbed her arms as if she were chilled. "That was horrible. MacAteer didn't stand a chance against those two brutes."

Jared nodded as his fingers flew over the laptop keyboard. "I'm sending the file to Brent right away so he can start working on the warrant. The sooner Sidorov's picked up, the safer everyone will be."

"What about the dirty cop? If he told Sidorov about MacAteer's visit to the police, he's an accessory to his murder."

"When Sidorov's in FBI custody, I'll make sure he's questioned about that." Jared breathed in the distinctive scent of her hair and rested his hand on her toned thigh. "Right now I'm more interested in finishing the conversation we started outside the gallery."

Her expression turned wary. "So much has happened since then, I'm not sure I remember where we left off."

Although he doubted her claim, he gave a quick

recap. "We agreed to swap sordid tales. You tell me about getting shot, and I dish up the dirt about Steve and me."

"Or we forget the whole thing," she suggested.

"Do you really want to do that?" If she wasn't ready to open up to him now, then she might never be, and the need was all on his side.

She hesitated, then shook her head.

He cupped her face in his hands. "If you do it fast, it won't be as bad. Think Band-Aid removal."

Her lips curved in a faint smile. "I always have to psych myself up before ripping those suckers off."

"How about I go first, so you can prepare yourself?"

"You trust me not to chicken out?"

"I trust you." Settling back on the couch, he got straight to the point. "Steve and I fought because he slept with my long-term girlfriend. There were extenuating circumstances—Ashley and I had split up, and she came on to him—but he knew I wasn't over her, and he took her to bed anyway."

"Do you know why?" Brooke asked.

"Spite. I had no patience for his BS when he was a rebellious, unmotivated teenager, and he never forgot that. So when he saw the chance to get back at me, he made it count."

"Does your sister know about this?"

He nodded.

"What's her take on it?"

That was an easy question to answer as Kristin had made no secret of her opinion. "Her view is Steve didn't intentionally try to hurt me. He was flattered by Ashley's attention and acted without thinking, like he often does. Afterward, he was sorry, but I was too angry to believe him."

Brooke's next question made him realize she was more attuned to him than the woman he'd thought he might marry. "What aren't you telling me?"

He shrugged. "Kristin says little brother did me a favor. Without his interference, I might have gone after Ashley, and our getting back together would have been a huge mistake." He added, "I resisted the idea for a long time, but she's probably right."

"About Steve or Ashley?"

"Both," he admitted. Steve was an impulsive person, not a vindictive one. And Jared knew he would never have been truly happy with Ashley. Spending time with Brooke had made him realize that. His gorgeous, intuitive PI got his brain clicking, his blood pumping and his emotions stirring. He didn't want her to disappear from his life after Sidorov's arrest. He wanted to keep seeing her. But before he spent more time thinking about the future, he had to deal with the past. "I'm sorry I misled you about my relationship with Steve. I liked the caring, big-brother-to-the-rescue image you seemed to have of me, and I didn't want to wreck it."

"You shouldn't have worried about that. Families are complicated. I know better than anyone. The important thing is you came looking for him."

His next words slipped out before he could stop them. "I just hope he's alive."

"He is," she insisted. "Wilson believes you won't arrange for the arrest warrant until you see Steve."

He shook his head. "Wilson knows that if Steve's dead, I'd have even more reason to go after Sidorov."

Her upset expression made him regret his candor.

Although he needed to prepare himself for the worst, he shouldn't have unloaded his worries onto Brooke. He reached for her hand and gave it a reassuring squeeze. "Forget what I said. I'm on edge, that's all."

"I believe Wilson will take us to Steve, and he'll be okay," she said solemnly.

He nodded, hoping she was right.

The silence stretched between them. It was her turn to talk about her scars, but he wasn't going to rush her. Let her take a few moments to organize her thoughts, figure out where to start. He didn't care about the details. He cared only that she trusted him enough to share the experience that had changed her life.

Stop procrastinating, Brooke told herself. *Suck it up and spit it out.* It didn't matter how she described it. The events of that awful night couldn't be altered by her choice of words or tone of voice. Nothing could change what had happened or the truth she'd had to live with.

Jared's advice drifted into her mind. *If you do it fast...*

So she did, blurting out, "I killed my partner."

His shocked expression gave her a morbid sense of satisfaction. He'd probably assumed she'd been reluctant to share her memories because they brought her pain and fear. He had no way of knowing it was the guilt and regrets she found unbearable. The knowledge that she was responsible for the death of a good cop, a husband and a father, had scarred her more deeply than the bullets that had riddled her body.

"Help me understand this," he said. "You pointed a gun at your partner and pulled the trigger?"

"Not exactly," she muttered, though the result had been essentially the same.

He brushed a strand of hair away from her face. "Why don't you tell me *exactly* what happened?"

She lowered her gaze to her tightly clasped hands. "We got a call one night. B and E at a private residence, the home owner threatened with a knife. When we arrived at the scene, we saw someone who matched the description of the intruder fleeing, so we gave chase. Cliff Danes, my partner, was fifty-two and forty pounds overweight, so he fell behind after a few minutes."

"But you kept going," Jared supplied.

"I didn't want the suspect to get away. But even more than that, I wanted to prove I could do the job, even if I was a rookie and a woman."

"A lot of new cops, particularly female ones, fight an uphill battle for acceptance," he acknowledged.

She shook her head. "It was more than that. I was furious because we'd argued at the beginning of our shift. Danes told me that my go-it-alone attitude was going to put me in harm's way, and then he'd be stuck saving my ass." Her partner's words had turned out to be eerily prophetic, yet at the time she'd focused only on how much they'd stung, how much they'd reminded her of her father's repeated criticisms.

Her face burned with shame. "I didn't listen to him. I thought I knew what I was doing. I didn't respect his expertise or experience." She shook her head, her throat tight. "I wish I'd shown him the respect he deserved. I wish I could go back to that night and stop it all from going so horribly wrong."

Jared rubbed her shoulder. "Tell me about it."

This was the hardest part, the reason for her nightmares. Inhaling deeply, she forced out the words. "When the suspect ran to the next street, I drew my gun and followed. I should have waited for backup, but I was confident I could handle some short, skinny guy with a knife. The next thing I knew I was flat on my back with my ears ringing and blood gushing out of me. Then he came at me again, and I saw the shotgun in his hands. I would have been killed, but Danes showed up and drew his attention, taking the shot intended for me.

"I watched him take the hit, saw his body fall and waited for the next shot that would finish me off. But Danes was wiser than me. Before he followed me, he'd called for backup. The shooter heard the sirens closing in on him and hauled ass out of there."

"Did they catch him?"

She shook her head. "No, he got away. I found out later his MO matched that of a cop killer in Nevada. The B and E was his favorite ruse to lure police to the scene."

"You couldn't have known that," Jared pointed out.

"I don't blame myself for what I didn't *know.* I blame myself for what I didn't *do.*" Swallowing the bitter taste of guilt, she continued, "If I'd waited for Danes, if we'd gone into that street together, a good cop wouldn't have ended up on a slab in the morgue."

"Or your partner might have died anyway."

"Look, I appreciate you making excuses for me, but Danes was right. I don't play well with others, and I never should have become a cop. It took his death to make me face that truth, and it's the reason I got my PI license. So I can go it alone—without relying on anyone else and with no one else relying on me."

"I don't want to argue with you," Jared said, "but hindsight is always twenty-twenty. I told you I was once beaten and locked in a shed. What I didn't tell you was my partner had wanted to pull out that morning, walk away from our assignment. I refused. I told him it was too dangerous, that we'd probably be killed if we tried to leave, and he agreed to sit tight until the bust went down."

She felt sick as she remembered the rest. Their covers had been blown, Jared's partner had been murdered, and Jared had barely escaped with his life. "Your partner's death wasn't your fault. If you had acted differently, the outcome might have been the same or worse."

"It took me a long time to accept that truth," he said in a husky voice. "How long is it going to take you?"

She stared at him, jolted by his question and the similarities between their experiences. They had both made choices they regretted. They had both lost partners and struggled to deal with the aftermath of the loss. Deep down, she was convinced Jared hadn't been responsible for his partner's murder. So why couldn't she believe the same about herself?

Her eyes stung as she considered the possibility that she wasn't at fault—at least not entirely. That maybe she'd taken on more than her fair share of blame. And maybe she'd been wrong to punish herself with crippling guilt and terrifying nightmares. She might finally be ready to reevaluate the past—but only because an FBI agent with painful memories had coaxed her into revealing hers.

It was hard to believe she'd known Jared for such a short time. They'd been through so much over the past few days, and she wasn't ready for their time together to end.

But of course, it would. As soon as he knew his brother was fine and Sidorov was arrested, he'd return to his job and his life. And she'd go back to being a PI, working alone, living alone.

What she'd once considered the ideal arrangement had now lost its appeal. She didn't want to be on her own anymore. She wanted to be with someone who understood her demons and accepted her anyway. Someone who made her smile, made her burn. Only one person was capable of all that. Jared. A future with him by her side would be—

Her brain wouldn't finish the thought. Instead it offered up her partner's damning character assessment of her. As much as she wished otherwise, those words hadn't been the griping of a cranky colleague. They had been objective and all too accurate. She was a solo act, not a team player. That was why none of her romantic relationships had lasted beyond a few months. Because her bed partners eventually caught on to the fact that, except for sex, she didn't need them.

Her thoughts were interrupted by the ring of Jared's cell phone. He glanced at the caller ID. "Alex," he said, flipping it open. "Where are you? Wilson will be calling soon to arrange the meet."

She turned away so he couldn't see her disappointment. She should have been relieved the final countdown was about to start, thrilled that Jared would soon be reunited with his brother and Sidorov would be locked up. Except that then her time with Jared would also be over. And she would go home alone.

Chapter 16

An hour later, Jared and Brooke arrived at the rendezvous point Wilson had chosen. Alex pulled up beside them in his truck. Ahead of them, nestled among mature oak and beech trees, sprawled a massive stone house. The garage was a separate three-car affair set at an angle to the main driveway. At the back corner of the property stood a separate white building that looked as if it might be a workshop.

Standing in the fading evening light, Jared saw a man in his fifties emerge from the building. He possessed the tanned skin and strong physique of a laborer, and he crossed the yard, pushing a wheelbarrow loaded with cement bags.

The contractor jerked his chin at Jared. "I thought you were coming alone."

"Alex and Brooke helped me find you."

After acknowledging them with a curt nod, Wilson said, "Show me the card."

Jared held up the slim square between his thumb and forefinger. "There's definitely enough evidence on it to get an arrest warrant for Sidorov. Where's Nash?"

"Inside."

"I want to see him."

The man set down the wheelbarrow and dusted off his hands. "First, I should tell you what happened."

"Steve can do that," Jared said, already turning toward the house.

"Unfortunately, he can't."

Every muscle in Jared's body squeezed tight, including his heart, which struggled to keep beating. *Please, let my brother be okay.* He turned back, his expression grim. "Why not?"

"Because he doesn't remember what happened."

"I don't understand. He's lost his memory?"

Wilson wiped his sweaty brow with his forearm. "The only way to explain it is to go back a little. When I learned about Danny's murder, I was sure Sidorov had been responsible. That got me worried about a young workman I'd been mentoring."

"My brother."

"Yes. The last time we'd met, Steve had told me he was crazy about a girl named Marisa Sidorov. I figured, with that last name, she had to be related, and Steve needed to know one of her family members was dangerous."

"So you went to the house where Steve was working."

Wilson nodded. "We talked for a while upstairs. Then I headed into the washroom. When I came out, I heard voices. Steve sounded really scared. I crept along the hall and saw Chernov with a gun, saying he was there to make sure Steve didn't touch Sidorov's daughter ever again. There was a hammer at my feet. I didn't think, just picked it up and threw it. I nailed him good, but as he went down, the gun went off."

Jared's mouth was so dry he could barely speak. "Steve was shot?"

"A bullet nicked him. He didn't cry out or fall down. I didn't even realize at first that he was injured."

Wilson's story was out of whack with what Jared knew. "I searched those bedrooms thoroughly. There were no bullet holes in any of the walls."

"I know a shot was fired," Wilson insisted. "Wait a minute. There was a window open because of the paint fumes. The bullet must have gone outside."

"What happened after the shot?"

"Chernov tried to get up. He still had the gun, so I fought with him. I screamed at Steve to help me disarm the guy, but he was holding his head, stunned. That's when I realized the bullet had grazed him. Finally, my shouts must have got through to him because he dropped to his knees to help me. Together, we worked to subdue Chernov and keep his weapon pointed away from us. While I held him down, Steve trussed him up in drop sheets."

"You smothered him?"

"We weren't intending for him to die—but he *was* trying to kill us. That's why I wanted you to see the video. It proves the guy would have maimed or killed Steve if I hadn't intervened."

"What happened next?"

"Steve barely made it downstairs before he passed

out. I carried him to Chernov's truck, then went back for Chernov. I thought about contacting the police, but after what happened to Danny, there was no way in hell I could trust them to keep us safe from Sidorov. Instead, I sent him a text from Chernov's phone, saying the job was done."

"Was fear for your safety the real reason for not involving the police?" Jared asked. "Maybe you were afraid the police wouldn't believe you that Chernov was killed in self-defense."

"Especially if Steve wasn't in any shape to back you up," Brooke added.

Wilson looked away. "After the adrenaline wore off, I was shaken by what we'd done," he admitted. "I knew our actions were justified, but I wasn't willing to risk that we'd be arrested. The ravine behind the house seemed like a lucky break. So I pocketed the gun, wrapped the body in plastic and dragged it down to the ravine. I figured the body wouldn't be found for a long time, if ever."

Alex stabbed an accusatory finger at Wilson. "I get why you didn't go to the cops, but you should've taken Steve to a hospital."

"I wanted to, but I couldn't take the chance that the doctor would figure out his injury was caused by a bullet. He'd have had to report it to the police."

"Concussions, left untreated, can kill people," Alex countered. "I saw that happen in the army."

"I saved his life and brought him to a safe place to recover," Wilson shot back defiantly.

Wilson had a point, Jared realized. Without the contractor's help, Steve would be dead. Instead, it was the hit man sent to kill him who was lying in the morgue.

"How is Steve now?" Jared asked.

Wilson took a moment to answer. "At first, he suffered from terrible headaches, disorientation, nausea, but he's on the mend, just weak. He doesn't remember what happened, and I haven't been able to bring myself to tell him. Hell, I wish I could forget as completely as he has."

"So, what does he think happened?"

"He thinks I hired him for a job, but he tripped and hit his head, so he has to take it easy for a while. He's been mostly out of it. He hasn't mentioned Marisa or her father. I'm not sure he's even aware of what day it is."

That explained why he hadn't called Kristin, Brooke thought. "You've done an awful lot for a guy who isn't your employee," she said.

Wilson shrugged. "He's hardworking and resourceful. I liked him from the moment we met."

Jared crossed his arms over his chest. "The fact that he looks remarkably like your son—minus the ink and piercings—didn't influence you at all, right?"

"Steve and Sam may have the same coloring," Wilson said tightly, "but that's where their similarities end. Sam only ever worked hard at looking like a freak and defying me."

"Your son isn't a headstrong teenager anymore," Brooke said. "He's a successful artist and businessman. And I suspect you haven't given up on him completely or you wouldn't have answered your phone so fast when he called."

Wilson stared at the ground. "Yeah, you're right. I miss him."

"You might want to tell him that."

"You can do that later," Jared said. "Right now I want to see Steve."

Wilson motioned for them to follow him and resumed pushing the wheelbarrow across the yard. He set it down next to an eight-foot trench that circled the house. "Watch your step," he advised. "My company was hired to fix the foundation along with other maintenance work."

The only way across the trench was to walk single file over a narrow board that led to the front door. Brooke went last, her breathing accelerating as she realized any misstep could result in a painful fall.

The interior of the house also showed evidence of the contractor's presence. New windows, still bearing their stickers, and sheets of drywall lined the perimeter of the spacious living room. Wilson led them past a curved staircase to a darkened room. Following a soft click, the glow of a lamp illuminated a light-haired man lying facedown on a pull-out couch made up with sheets and a blanket.

Brooke had expected Jared to head straight for the makeshift bed, but he surprised her by hanging back and letting Alex go first.

"You've got company," Wilson said, shaking the man's shoulder before moving aside.

The young man rolled onto his back, and Brooke caught her breath. Jared's brother did look a lot like a younger Sam Wilson. A small square of gauze was taped to his temple. He squinted against the glare of the lamp at the person nearest him.

"Alex?"

"Damn, I'm happy to see you," Alex said, his voice

thick with emotion. He clasped his friend's hand between both of his and held on for a long moment.

Steve gave him a tired grin. "I'm happy to see you, too, despite the fact that you look like you've been partying hard while I've been flat on my ass. What're you doing here?"

"When you didn't call your sis on Sunday, she hit the panic button and sent out a search party."

"What?"

"You've been MIA for maybe a week, man. We all thought something bad had happened to you."

"For real?" He struggled into a sitting position. "Things have been kind of foggy since I banged my head." He frowned. "How did you find me? Did Martin contact you?"

Alex shook his head. "We pieced together he was the last person to see you and called him."

"We?" Steve interrupted, frowning. "Who is *we*?"

"Jared, of course, and—"

Steve's whole body stiffened. "What do you mean, *Jared, of course*? He wouldn't care if I fell off a cliff and broke my neck."

The resentment that infused his words was so different from his easy banter with Alex that Brooke felt sick. The happy family reunion she had envisioned was unlikely to take place. Because while Jared's attitude toward his brother may have undergone a huge change in the past few days, Steve was still harboring a whole lot of hurt.

"You're wrong," Jared said, moving forward into the light so Steve could see him.

The younger Nash brother curled his lip. "Familiar words coming from you, big brother."

Alex cleared his throat. "I think you two could use some time alone to catch up."

Brooke agreed wholeheartedly. Although she'd been looking forward to meeting Steve, the introduction could come later. The brothers needed privacy to patch things up, assuming Jared could find the right words to show he'd let go of the past. Ideally, Steve could be convinced to do the same.

After giving Jared a look of support, she followed Wilson and Alex out of the room and closed the door. It would be wonderful if Jared could fix his relationship with his brother. The fact that he was even willing to try gave her hope he might be willing to work on their relationship. Because if not, she had to face up to a tough, irrefutable truth: leaving Jared was going to tear her heart out.

Jared barely noticed the door closing because his attention was focused on Steve. His brother's face looked thinner than he remembered, and there were dark shadows under his eyes. Nothing a few meals and some extra sleep couldn't remedy, he hoped. Steve was one lucky guy, considering he had been the target of a hit man. Only Wilson's fast action with the hammer had spared his life. A life Jared had been slow in realizing he valued very much. But how was he supposed to get that message across when Steve's defiant eyes promised to misinterpret every word he uttered?

"I've thought a lot about us over the past few days," he said, pulling up a chair so he was on the same level as Steve.

"I find that hard to believe since I've been persona non grata with you for months."

"I won't deny I was angry, and I had every right to be. But now I wish I'd accepted your apology when you offered it."

Steve shrugged. "You missed your chance. I'm done apologizing."

His brother wasn't making this easy, but Jared forced himself to continue. "I was wrong to lay all the blame on you for what happened between you and Ashley. She was hardly an innocent party."

In fact, though he'd denied it at first, he'd come to believe she was the one primarily responsible for the chain of events that had led to the estrangement between Steve and him. After all, she could have picked any man to sleep with after their breakup. She didn't have to come on to Steve—if Jared was to believe his brother's story.

Steve kicked off the sheet but remained sitting, his back resting against the upper section of the couch. "Wow, I never expected those words to come out of your mouth. *Saint* Ashley's halo seems to have picked up some tarnish."

He ignored the mocking remark. "Why did you do it? I have my suspicions, but I want to hear the truth from you."

His brother looked away.

"Talk to me, Steve."

A few more moments passed before his sibling spoke. "The truth is I've always felt like a screwup next to you. So when your old girlfriend grabbed my hand and started dirty dancing with me at that bar, I thought, *Steve, my man, you've just hit the jackpot*. It was only afterward, when I sobered up, that I knew I hadn't won. I'd lost big-time."

"Ashley wanted to kill any chance of me and her getting back together," Jared mused aloud, "and sleeping with my brother was a surefire way to accomplish that."

"Hold up," Steve interjected. "Have you ever considered she genuinely liked me? That she got fed up with your zealous dedication to your job and wanted to be with a more fun-loving guy like me?"

It was tempting to dismiss his brother's insinuations as brazen ego, but a voice inside him pointed out there could be some truth to them. Ashley *had* resented the extra hours he'd worked, and she'd spent the time they weren't together partying with her friends. So Steve might not be so far off the mark as he'd originally believed. "Maybe she really did want to be with you," Jared conceded.

His brother did an obvious double take. "Hey, what happened to you? Alien abduction?"

He smiled reluctantly. "Not that I remember."

"Then what?"

"You disappeared, and I had reason to believe you were dead."

Steve came as close to sputtering as Jared had ever heard him. "You believed I was dead because I was *late calling Kristin*? Holy melodrama, bro."

Of course, Steve would think he'd overreacted. But his brother hadn't spent hours, his stomach churning with agonizing fear, his mind reeling with horrific possibilities, while he waited for the official ID of a corpse he suspected was his own flesh and blood. Jared could still feel the sweet rush of relief that had hit when he'd learned it was Chernov, not Steve, lying in the morgue. His brother had no idea how plausible his death had seemed—and Jared was in no hurry to enlighten him. First, he wanted a doctor to examine Steve. Then he wanted to understand more about memory loss, if it could be reversed and how. At this point, he wasn't even sure he wanted Steve to regain those lost memories, since they included him helping to kill a man.

Instead of justifying his concern, he said merely, "Some wires got crossed."

Steve snorted. "I'll say."

"Mistake or not, it shook me up good. And that's when I realized I wanted to put an end to the bad feelings between us."

Steve was silent for a moment. "I don't know if that's even possible."

Jared swallowed, his mouth suddenly dry. "What do you mean?"

"We were at loggerheads long before Ashley. We'd argue, cool off and then argue some more. It's a vicious cycle."

"We're very different people, but that doesn't mean we stop talking or stop caring."

"If you say so." Steve sounded less than convinced.

Jared racked his brain for another compelling reason to salvage their relationship. "It would mean a lot to Kristin if we could get past this."

Steve's eyebrow kicked up. "Is that emotional blackmail I hear?"

"Maybe."

"And that's the best you can do?"

Knowing that his next words had to be spoken from the heart, if he was ever to break through Steve's reserve, he said solemnly, "I love you, brother. And I want you to be in my life always."

Several long seconds ticked by. Jared tried to read Steve's expression but couldn't. More than likely, Steve didn't believe him. Or if he did, he didn't reciprocate Jared's feelings.

It had been a long shot. The idea that his brother might want to start over as much as he did. But obviously too much damage had been inflicted in the past. As the last of hope drained away, he braced himself for another of Steve's sharp-edged remarks. However, he'd forgotten his brother's most exasperating—and endearing—trait was unpredictability.

Without warning, Steve rose from the couch and grabbed hold of him in a hug that felt so solid and so good his eyes began to sting. He couldn't remember the last time they'd embraced, but he knew he was going to make sure they did it more often. A few backslaps later, the two men separated, exchanging sheepish smiles.

Steve wobbled, as if his legs were too weak to keep him upright. With a curse, he sank back down on the couch. "Where do we go from here?"

"How about we head over to Kristin's place? I know she'll want to see you with her own eyes. Then a trip to the doctor to check out your banged head."

"Sounds good."

"But first, there's someone I want you to meet." Jared went to the door and opened it. "Brooke?"

She appeared at the end of the hallway. As she came toward him, he saw uncertainty and concern in her expression, and he remembered the tense exchange she'd witnessed earlier between him and his brother. Fortunately, the reunion had been everything he could have wished for. He smiled because it was the fastest way to reassure her and also because he felt so damn happy.

Brooke's answering smile had him tugging her into his arms and kissing her. Passion flared instantly, but acting on it would have to wait for a more opportune time. He nudged her through the doorway and spoke to Steve. "I want you to meet Brooke Rogers, the PI who helped me find you."

"A PI, huh? The surprises just keep coming."

"Glad to meet you," Brooke said. "Your family's been so worried about you."

"I'm beginning to get that."

"Brooke convinced Wilson's son to contact him so I could ask about you," Jared supplied. "If she hadn't, we'd still be in the dark."

Steve stared at her. "Martin told me his son and he never talk."

Jared smiled. "Trust me. Brooke can talk anybody into anything."

"No, I can't," she said indignantly.

"I have evidence to the contrary." He cupped his hand over her shoulder. "You talked me into involving you in my search for Steve. You talked Keesing into allowing us into the house on Middleview. And you talked Sam Wilson into calling his dad."

"Okay, I guess I can be persuasive at times," she conceded.

"One of your many exceptional skills." He gave her an affectionate squeeze and was rewarded by the relaxing of her body against his. Her hair brushed against his neck. Her scent wafted into his nostrils. His happiness grew to fill every part of him.

"When do you want to leave?"

Steve's question broke through his musing. And he was suddenly conscious of his brother's gaze alternating between him and Brooke, as if trying to work out the exact nature of their relationship. "The sooner the better," he answered.

"I'd like to thank Martin before I go. And Alex, of course." He grinned mischievously. "If I'd known being out of touch for a few days would make my loved ones rally together, I'd have disappeared months ago."

Jared treated him to a stern look. "Believe me when I say, little brother, if you'd faked your disappearance, I'd have slugged you, not hugged you."

Brooke spoke up. "I overheard Wilson say he had to move some lumber from the storage building to the house before it got dark, and Alex offered to help him."

Jared pulled out his cell phone and pressed Alex's number. "He's not answering."

"Probably left his phone in his truck," Steve said. "He does that all the time."

"Do you know Wilson's number?"

"Not offhand."

"I'll try Alex again." Jared fiddled with his phone, then frowned. "My battery's dead. I'll have to go get them."

"I need to change," Steve said, glancing down at his torso. "This shirt belongs to Martin."

"Do you need any help?" Brooke asked.

"Nah, I can manage."

"I'll wait in the kitchen," she murmured, heading for the door.

Jared started to follow her but stopped when he heard Steve say, "I see why you're suddenly willing to forgive me."

He turned back. "What do you mean?"

"You don't care about Ashley or my mistake anymore. You've fallen hard for the PI."

"Her name is Brooke," Jared said tightly.

"You love her."

Jared stared at him, the word *love* ringing in his ears. Yeah, he felt more for her than lust or caring for her. He respected her loyalty, her resourcefulness and her courage. And being with her made him happy. But did all that add up to love?

Steve laughed softly. "If I were you, I'd stay away from cards for a while. Your usual poker face has been seriously compromised."

His brother's smirk was more annoying than he remembered. "A guy with a head injury shouldn't be so quick to offer opinions about others based on a few minutes' observation."

"Her eyes went supersoft when you put your arm around her, bro."

"They did?" The question popped out of his mouth before he could prevent it.

"Uh-huh. Methinks she's smitten with you, too."

He wondered if his brother was being honest or pulling his leg. A tough call, given Steve's love of practical jokes. Then again, the guy could be surprisingly perceptive. But what if he was wrong? What if Brooke's feelings were something other than love? "You know all those times I called you a pain in the ass?"

"Yeah."

"I was right."

"Oh."

"Except for today. Thanks for telling me about Brooke."

"You're welcome. If she's the reason for the changes in you, then she's worth hanging on to." Steve pointed to a laundry basket near the door. "Pass me that blue T-shirt, will you?"

He tossed the shirt to his brother, then headed outside to find Martin and Alex. Partway across the yard, he realized he was whistling. Hadn't done that in ages. And Brooke was the reason.

Brooke stood at the kitchen window, sipping water and mulling over her feelings for Jared. She definitely wanted to keep seeing him, and his actions today seemed to convey he was in no hurry to end their relationship. He'd complimented her to his brother and tucked her against his side as though she belonged there. Or was she reading too much into the gesture?

The uncertainty was killing her. She needed to know his future intentions toward her, even if it was only the assurance that he would call her after they parted. She could already imagine herself staring at the phone, willing it to ring.

Ridiculous. Pathetic.

She used to scoff at women who did that. She wasn't scoffing now. She was…in love. So why did she feel so unsettled? Falling in love was supposed to be a joyous experience, but that was only true when you weren't worried you'd taken the plunge solo.

As she tipped the glass to her lips, she saw Jared striding toward the workshop. Her eyes hungrily roamed over his muscled body, lean arms and long legs. She remembered the ecstasy of making love with him as well as the comfort of talking with him in the dark. Warmth spread throughout her body, filling her heart. No other man had made her feel both strong and vulnerable. No other man had made her yearn for a connection beyond a transitory, physical one. Without a doubt, Jared was the man she wanted in her life. Did he feel the same way about her?

While she feasted on the sight of the man she'd come to love, three figures emerged from the woods. One of them motioned to the others to split up, a bandage on his raised hand. *Latschenko.* The glass slipped from her hand and shattered in the sink.

Jared kept on walking, oblivious to the danger he couldn't see.

Her mouth dry with fear, she ran to the sliding door. A series of gunshots rang out, and Jared pitched face-first into a truck-sized stack of chopped wood.

Chapter 17

Brooke's breath whooshed out as if she'd been kicked in the stomach. Her heart raced faster and faster as her eyes failed to detect any signs of movement near the woodpile. Had he dived for cover? Or fallen? Was he intentionally hiding out or too injured to move? Was he dead?

Her mind screamed an anguished denial. She had finally found a man to love. She couldn't lose him now.

The urge to go to him was strong, but if she did that, she'd be leaving Steve unprotected. Jared's brother was still recovering from his injury and too weak to fend for himself. She knew what Jared would want as clearly as if he were there to tell her. He would want her to remain with Steve.

With numb fingers, she reached for the phone on the wall. The absence of a dial tone chilled her to the bone.

The men outside must have cut the line at the road. Like Jared's phone, her cell phone's battery was dead. They'd both delayed recharging, a stupid mistake. Help wasn't coming. She had only herself to rely on.

Grabbing a wicked-looking knife from the butcher block on the counter, she retraced her steps to Steve's room and knocked on the closed door. As an afterthought, she shoved the knife behind her back. No point scaring him before she had a chance to explain.

"Were those gunshots?" He shuffled into the hall, his steps slow and awkward. "I can't remember if Martin said hunting was allowed around these parts." He paused. "Speaking of Martin, I thought my brother was going to get him."

Brooke didn't know how to respond. Should she tell him about Jared? What if he insisted on going to Jared's side and was shot, as well? Steve didn't remember a hit man had been sent to kill him, and there was no time to update him on Sidorov's recent activities, but she needed to warn him about the danger outside.

"Those shots weren't fired by hunters," she said.

Steve's eyes widened in alarm. "What aren't you telling me?"

"Your brother's been investigating a former member of the Russian mafia," she admitted.

Steve responded in a surprisingly calm voice. "Jared's trained to handle situations like this. He's probably already called for backup and is holed up somewhere safe."

She thought about Jared's dead cell phone. He wouldn't have been able to call anyone, but he might have found a hiding place. "I think we should head for the attic. It'll take them a while to search the basement and other floors."

More shots rang out, underscoring the urgency of the situation. She sent up a silent prayer none of the bullets had hit their intended targets.

Steve moved to the staircase, but stopped when he realized she wasn't following him.

"I need to do something first," she said.

"I don't think Jared would want me leaving you alone."

Evidently, Steve had picked up on the fact that she and his brother had become close while working together to find him. "Don't worry about me," she said. "I'm an ex-cop." For the first time since her injury, she could refer to her former profession without feeling shame or guilt. She had Jared to thank for her changed perspective.

"Go," she urged him. "I'll only be a minute."

Steve didn't argue, either because he sensed he wouldn't be able to change her mind or because he figured she could take care of herself. Grabbing on to the handrail, he started to climb, pulling himself up one step at a time.

Brooke's thoughts turned back to the second volley of shots. Who had fired them? Sidorov's men? Or Jared? The kitchen was the best vantage point from which to see the woodpile.

She had barely set foot in the room when she spied an unfamiliar figure beyond the glass and ducked back into the hall. Her hand tightened on the knife while her heart thudded with dread at what would happen next. The man had only to fire a single shot to shatter the patio door and gain entry to the kitchen.

But the sound of breaking glass didn't come. *Why?*

Because of the wide trench around the house, she

realized. The guy outside couldn't enter through the patio door, meaning he'd have to look for another point of access. The only one she knew of was at the front of the house.

A noise overhead indicated Steve was still on the stairs. It would take him another few minutes to find the trapdoor to the attic and haul himself to safety. She had to give him those extra minutes.

Her mouth dry, her palms damp, she headed to the front door and opened it ever so softly. The board stretching over the trench looked narrower than she remembered, but she forced herself to cross it without hesitation. The figure had been moving along the west side of the house, so she sprinted in the same direction, determined to come up behind him. She needed the element of surprise on her side. Otherwise, her knife would be useless against the gun he surely carried. The thought made her stomach churn.

She circled the house. On the final leg of her trip, the detached three-car garage blocked her view of the woodpile and carriage house, which was just as well. She couldn't afford the temptation of looking for signs of Jared. Not when all her attention had to be focused on the man she was following. Turning the corner of the house, she finally spied him. He was just about to step onto the board leading to the front door. The hand closest to her held a gun. He had only to notice her presence and lift his arm to kill her, but she felt no fear, only calm certainty. *You can do this.* She ran straight at him, her knife positioned to stab.

At the last moment, he glanced in her direction. His face registered disbelief, and instinctively, he jerked away. Her blade sliced through empty space, but her upper body made contact, a hard slam that jerked him off balance. She heard an angry shout accompanied by a clanging sound. Arms windmilling, he plunged downward followed by the overturned wheelbarrow. His foot must have jarred the front wheel loose, she realized. Gravity had done the rest, tugging them both into the trench.

She stepped to the edge and peered down. He lay on his back, the wheelbarrow and two cement bags pinning his legs. His eyes remained closed, but his chest rose and fell in a quick yet steady rhythm. When he regained consciousness, he'd likely have a few broken bones to contend with. The thought didn't bother her in the least.

"You are one aggravating bitch," someone said behind her.

She whirled around with a sickening sense of déjà vu. Latschenko was pointing a gun at her.

Jared felt wood shavings tickle his nose and a stinging sensation in his right hand. His instincts had screamed to get low, so he'd obeyed, dropping in the midst of the woodpile. A second later, a spray of bullets punched holes in the split logs near him. Sweat broke out on his brow as he listened for clues of activity around him. He didn't dare move; the shooter could be watching. Sidorov must have decided he wanted the owner of the incriminating micro card killed and sent someone after Wilson. If others got in the way, they were to be disposed of, as well.

Several long moments passed. Jared continued to lie motionless, resisting the urge to sneeze, resisting the urge to check his throbbing hand. Maybe the shooter would assume he was dead.

"Hey," a gruff voice called out.

He'd been expecting either Sidorov or Latschenko, but the voice belonged to one of the men who had followed Brooke and him into the ravine.

"I know there are two of you in the white building," Sidorov's man continued. "Come outside."

The guy must have been watching the property long enough to see Wilson and later Alex enter the structure. The sound of rustling clothing suggested he was in motion. Jared lifted his head for a quick look. Wearing jeans and a black T-shirt with a Megadeth logo, the shooter was crossing from the woods to the open door of the workshop with his gun drawn.

"I'm not going to hurt you. My boss has some questions for you," the guy continued.

I'll just bet he does, Jared thought. Like *where's the micro card?* And *why was Wilson's truck parked on Middleview the same night Chernov went missing?* A bastard like Sidorov wouldn't be satisfied with mere answers. He'd want blood. Wilson had caused him too much trouble, and Alex couldn't be left behind as a witness. Neither could Steve nor Brooke…

The angle was all wrong, but Jared knew he had to take the shot anyway. He reached for his gun. As his hand brushed his jeans, he nearly passed out from the pain. When his vision cleared, he saw a raw, oozing wound in his palm. A jagged shard of wood, stained red from his blood, lay on the ground nearby.

He tried to curl his shaking fingers into a fist. Couldn't do it. Which meant there was no chance of holding a gun steady or squeezing off a round. And at this distance, his left hand couldn't be trusted to hit a moving target.

Forget the gun. Find something else.

Scanning the surrounding area, he glimpsed an ax stuck in a chopping block. A lethal weapon if he could get in close, but the stretch of grass separating him from the shooter made that scenario impossible. He'd be riddled with bullets long before he reached the guy.

"This is your last chance," came Megadeth's gruff warning. "I won't ask nice again."

Jared grabbed the ax with his uninjured hand. Between the woodpile and the back of the white building, bushes grew in sparse clumps. If the shooter's attention strayed at all, he'd be visible, but it was his only option. Dropping to the ground, he army-crawled on forearms and belly toward the workshop. After five very long minutes, he had reached his destination and risen to his feet.

The workshop was constructed of vertical wooden boards. Holding the ax in his left hand, he slammed it into the first board and yanked. A second later, the night air exploded in the staccato sounds of gunfire. Bullets thudded against wood. A shriek of excruciating pain ended in a choked sob. Someone had been hit.

Jared swung the ax again, the blow vibrating up the muscles and tendons of his arm to his shoulder. A board let go, then another. The gap allowed him to see inside. Wilson lay on the ground, moaning, while Alex worked feverishly to stanch an outpouring of blood from his leg. The severity of the contractor's injury meant he couldn't escape out the back, no matter how many boards Jared removed.

Only one chance remained—and he took it, knowing it would leave him vulnerable. "Alex," he hollered to the security consultant. Then he sent his gun flying across the workshop floor.

"Drop the knife."

Brooke didn't want to yield to Latschenko's demand, but she had no choice, given his Glock was aimed at her chest. Releasing the knife, she watched it fall to the ground, furious with herself for having been caught off guard.

"Kick it into the trench," Latschenko said.

She did so, her anger fueling its flight. The handle of the knife bounced off the dirt wall and plummeted straight down.

"We'll wait inside." He motioned for her to step onto the board ahead of him.

She thought of Steve and didn't move. "Why are you doing this?"

"I do what my boss tells me to do."

His response was totally predictable and totally unacceptable. "Your boss is like a puppet master, jerking people's strings to make them do his dirty work. You don't have to. Just get in your car and drive away."

Latschenko regarded her with contempt. "If I did that, I'd lose my job."

"Get another job."

"Not so easy," he muttered.

He had a point, she realized. The employment prospects for a guy with a criminal record couldn't be good. Which was probably how he'd wound up working as muscle for Sidorov. A guy had to eat and so did his family.

His family.

"Does your son know?" she asked, remembering Jared had mentioned the boy lived with his mother, Latschenko's estranged wife. "Does he know your new job involves killing people?"

"I haven't killed anyone."

He was so adamant she believed him, and relief swept through her. But that relief was short-lived when she considered his employer's ruthlessness. "That could change tonight. If Sidorov orders you to shoot me and you do it, you'll have blood on your hands. The same hands you hug your little boy with."

"You talk too much."

She kept her eyes on his face and away from the gun he held. "Think how horrified and ashamed your son would be if you were arrested for murder."

Latschenko's lips twisted into a sneer. "You don't care about him. You're only trying to save yourself."

"My motives don't matter. It's your actions that count. You're his father. His protector. His hero. Is anything worth destroying his faith in you?"

Uncertainty flickered in his eyes.

She pressed harder. "Where should your loyalty be? With a guy who orders others to kill for him? Or with your child?"

He didn't answer her right away. She hoped that was an encouraging sign as she'd made her most compelling argument. While she waited for his response, the sky was growing darker and the temperature was dropping. The ground under Jared would be getting colder, too. Could he feel the chill? Could he feel anything at all?

She wanted to scream at Latschenko to choose his son over Sidorov and let her go, so she could find and help the man she loved—if it wasn't already too late. Instead, she bit the inside of her cheek and waited.

"Even if I wanted to walk away from this," her captor said, "Sidorov would never let me. He'd kill me for sure."

"He wouldn't be able to do that if he were in prison."

"Like that's going to happen."

"You could put him there by telling the police what you know."

"It would be my word against his. And he'd hire a high-priced shark to twist everything I say."

"His lawyer would have a tough time arguing against your testimony *and* the evidence we have on a micro card. It proves Sidorov ordered Chernov to injure Danny MacAteer and threatened to kill him."

"So *that's* why Sidorov's so desperate to get his hands on it." Latschenko's eyes narrowed speculatively. "Where is it?"

She hesitated, unsure of his intentions. Would he use it to get his boss arrested or score points with the man? Before she could make up her mind, Latschenko's cell phone buzzed like an agitated bee.

"Don't answer," she urged, afraid to lose momentum when he finally seemed to be questioning his loyalty to Sidorov.

Ignoring her, he lifted the phone to his ear. "Nice of you to finally check in."

His tone was too sarcastic for him to be speaking to his boss. She remembered the third man near the woods. What had he been up to while she'd been arguing with his compadre?

A moment later, Latschenko's face flushed deep crimson as he yelled into his cell phone, "You are one stupid bastard, Petroff. You were told to find and hold the contractor. Not kill him and shoot whoever happened to be nearby."

Brooke recoiled in horror at the news Wilson was dead. And who else had been shot? Alex? *Jared?*

Latschenko continued to rant. "The boss has questions. How's he supposed to get answers out of corpses?"

Corpses? Sickened by his words, she could barely keep from crying out. Only a short time ago, she had been filled with optimism, believing Wilson would reconcile with his son, Alex would once again enjoy the company of his best friend, and she would talk to Jared about a future together. Now violence had blown away all of those possibilities, and her heart ached for what would never be.

"It's your mess, Petroff," Latschenko was saying. "You can clean it up. Find a shovel and start digging. I'll come when I'm finished with the PI." He flipped his phone shut with a curse.

A distant part of her noted his forehead was beaded with sweat. He wasn't the one who had screwed up. Why was he so stressed? His reaction only made sense if Sidorov had put him in charge and would blame him for whatever went wrong today.

She would use his fear. Use it to convince him to betray Sidorov and Petroff. And if that proved impossible, at least she would have given Jared's brother the time he needed to hide. It was the least she could do for the man she had loved and lost. "Your problems are only beginning," she said to Latschenko. "When Sidorov gets wind of the carnage here, he'll make you kill your trigger-happy buddy."

"No, he won't."

"It'll be the perfect way to rid himself of a loose cannon and own you."

"Nobody owns me," Latschenko said through gritted teeth.

"If you commit murder for him, you'll be like a dog with a master, for as long as he wants you to be."

"If he wants somebody dead, he can do it himself."

"Tough talk, but if he orders you to kill, do you really think you can refuse him?"

"Shut your mouth." He raised his gun level with her face, but she was committed to finish what she'd started.

"You've seen firsthand how ruthless your boss can be. If you defy him, he'll kill you or threaten your loved ones to force your hand. For your son to be truly safe, Sidorov has to be arrested and locked up."

Latschenko's eyes took on a haunted expression, as if he finally comprehended his choices. Kill for Sidorov and be trapped in his employ indefinitely. Disobey orders and put his family at risk. Or betray him and trust the legal system to deliver justice.

"If I gave evidence against him, he'd hurt my family for sure."

"You could make a deal with the prosecution. Witness protection for you and your family in exchange for your testimony."

Latschenko wiped sweat off his brow with his free hand.

"It's a lot to consider," she said. "Maybe you need to get away from here to decide."

He looked tempted by her proposal, and the gun slowly lowered. She waited to feel a rush of relief, but all she felt was numb. If Jared was dead, her own life held far less meaning.

Suddenly Latschenko's body went rigid. "Too late."

Detecting the low rumble of a car engine, she swung around. A sleek black Mercedes glided down the driveway past the huge detached garage and parked diagonally, blocking in Jared's car and Alex's truck. The driver's tinted window slid down several inches but did not reveal its occupant.

"I expected your call twenty minutes ago." The heavy accent and imperious tone matched the voice Brooke had heard on the recording. Sidorov had come to check up on his men.

"I wanted to make sure the place was secure," Latschenko answered, his gun once again trained on Brooke.

"Is it?" the other man demanded.

"Oh yeah," came the muttered reply.

The car door opened, and Sidorov stepped out, dressed in dark, expensive-looking clothes. Brooke noticed a slight bulge under his jacket, indicating he was armed. "Where are the others? Do they have Wilson?"

Latschenko motioned to the back of the property. "Petroff is with him in the white building."

No mention of the fact that Wilson was dead, Brooke noted. Latschenko was leaving that surprise for his buddy to explain to Sidorov.

"Where's Koponov?"

Latschenko jerked his thumb at the trench. "He's down there, out cold."

"How clumsy of him."

"He didn't fall on his own. The PI shoved him."

The dark eyes Sidorov trained on Brooke were rife

with displeasure. "You seem to cause trouble wherever you go. I assure you that will end tonight."

His threatening words broke through her numbness, making her heart beat faster. Not so long ago, it would have been fear revving her system. Now it was the desire for revenge. This man may not have pulled the trigger himself, but he was responsible for tonight's bloodshed. She couldn't stand the thought that he would get away with it.

He turned to Latschenko. "Call Petroff. Tell him to bring the contractor to me."

"That isn't possible. Wilson's hurt."

Sidorov shrugged. "Then I will go to him."

"What do you want me to do?"

"Wake up Koponov. He needs to climb out of that hole."

Latschenko shot a quick look into the trench. "I doubt he can. His leg looks like it's broken. If I had some rope and your help, we could maybe pull him out."

"Don't bother. He is of no use to me injured. When I'm finished with Wilson, we leave without him."

Sidorov's callousness to his employee's plight rendered Latschenko momentarily speechless. Then he licked his lips and pointed out the obvious. "It could be days before someone comes across him. In this heat, without water, he could die."

"Or he could live and talk too much. That's unacceptable." Sidorov's gaze traveled to the gun in the other man's hand. "You will keep that from happening."

Latschenko's left eye twitched. "You want me to shoot him?"

"No need to waste a bullet, just fill the hole with dirt. To anybody coming by later, it will look like the work is finished."

And no one would suspect a body was buried there, Brooke thought.

"It is good he is unconscious," Sidorov continued. "He will not feel a thing."

"And the PI? What happens to her?"

Brooke held her breath, certain her fate would be the same as the injured thug's, but the order to bury her alive did not come. Instead Sidorov said, "She might be useful when I question Wilson about the micro card. Some men are squeamish about seeing a woman in pain."

She recoiled instinctively. Torture. That was how Sidorov intended to get information out of Wilson. Except Wilson was already dead, so her usefulness would last only until he discovered that fact. Her only chance at survival lay with Latschenko. "Wilson is no fool. He'll know as soon as he gives up the micro card, you'll kill him and me."

Sidorov's lips curved in a sinister smile. "*I* don't kill people. I pay others to do it for me."

"Nice company you keep, Latschenko," she said. "Your family would be so proud."

"Do not speak of my family," the man hissed.

"Your boss has already told you to bury a man alive tonight. Later you'll be disposing of me...and Wilson." She saw a flicker of revulsion pass over Latschenko's face and pressed harder. "You don't have to do this. You could end it now."

Sidorov made a scoffing sound. "Why would he want to end this? I haven't paid him yet."

"There isn't enough money in the world to justify killing three people."

"Sure there is," Sidorov said confidently. "I think tonight's work is worth a twenty-five-thousand-dollar bonus. How's that sound, Latschenko?"

The other man gave a stiff nod. "Sounds good."

"Get to work. But first, tie her hands."

At Sidorov's direction, Latschenko fetched rope from the trunk of his car and bound Brooke's wrists in front of her. She didn't speak to him again. What was the point? He'd made his choice, and she hoped he choked on it. He headed back toward the house.

"Come along," Sidorov said, shoving her ahead of him.

The three-car garage blocked the view of their destination. The workshop lay on the crest of the hill, its white walls hiding the misery Petroff had caused. Once they reached it, Sidorov would take the micro card off Wilson's dead body, then have her executed to guarantee her silence. She had to escape before entering that building.

But how?

As she walked, she searched the ground for something to cut through the rope on her wrists. She saw nothing promising, no sharp-edged rocks, no broken glass, just a vast stretch of vegetation and dirt. The only thing working in her favor was Sidorov hadn't drawn his weapon. He must have been confident in his ability to control her without it.

Wrong. Conceited.

Locking her elbows, she extended her arms in front of her, then swung them like a bat and slammed her bound hands into Sidorov's shocked face. Blood spurted from his nose, and he staggered backward. She went after him, stiff fingers going for his eyes, but at the last second, he jerked his head away. Her foot snaked behind his. One hard shove and down he went, his mouth spewing what she assumed were Russian obscenities. She straddled him, her hands tunneling under his jacket, sliding over his shirt toward the holster and his gun… almost got it…

Something slammed into her temple. Intense pain rocketed through her, and she brought her hands up to protect her head while she struggled to keep Sidorov pinned on the ground. When he couldn't land a second punch to her head, he retaliated by punching her in the stomach. Winded, she gasped for air, then drove her fists into his mouth, earning an enraged bellow. His body bucked like a bee-stung bronco underneath her, and he rammed her shoulders repeatedly. The element of surprise and sheer determination had got her this far, but his extra eighty pounds of body weight and the full use of his hands gave him a distinct advantage. Within minutes, she lay sprawled on her side with the barrel of his gun pressing against her cheek.

"Lie still," he ground out.

In her peripheral vision, she could see his face was streaked with blood. The sight cheered her, but she didn't dare smile.

Moving slowly, as if his every muscle were aching, he got to his feet. Then he motioned with his gun for her to do the same. When she was upright, he told her to turn around. The hard metal of the gun nudged her back. Her breath caught as she wondered if he was angry enough to abandon his "no kill" policy and make an exception for her. If he squeezed the trigger, the bullet would hit her heart…a heart that had been so reluctant to love. A whimsical thought, but true. It had taken a very special FBI agent to show her what she'd been missing. The connection between them was precious and extraordinary, and she should have been brave enough to share her feelings of love with Jared sooner. Now it was too late.

Sidorov put his hand on her right shoulder. The gun dug into her spine. "Walk or die."

Chapter 18

She chose to walk, even though it would only delay the inevitable. At the end of the walk she would be murdered. In the meantime, she felt the breeze slipping through her hair and smelled the earthy tang of the grass and trees. The sky was a beautiful inky blue above her.

While she savored the last few minutes of life, her legs trudged mechanically up the hill. She could hear Sidorov huffing behind her. The steep incline was taking its toll, but his hand remained firmly on her shoulder, claiming her as his prisoner. As they approached the carriage house, she saw the door lay ajar. To the right, a man wearing a loose black T-shirt and baseball cap was digging awkwardly with a shovel, his back to the hill.

"Hey, Petroff," Sidorov called out.

The man didn't turn or acknowledge their presence in any way. Instead, his head began to bob rhythmically. That was when Brooke noticed white wires sprouting from underneath the baseball cap. An iPod. He was listening to music while he worked.

"Petroff!" Sidorov shouted this time.

"He can't hear you," she said irritably. "He's got earbuds in."

"Idiot," Sidorov muttered, his hand leaving her shoulder. "Sit."

"What?"

"Sit down and don't move."

She did as he ordered, her movements awkward due to her bound wrists, the ground hard under her butt.

Sidorov strode ahead, gesturing with his arms, trying to draw Petroff's attention. The man continued digging, head bobbing, until Sidorov was less than an arm's length away. Suddenly he whirled around and slammed the shovel into Sidorov, whose gun went flying. Screaming in fury, Sidorov launched himself at his employee-turned-enemy, but Petroff twisted away so fast Sidorov met with empty space and crashed to the ground. Unwilling to admit defeat, Sidorov levered himself up on his hands and knees, but his attacker was waiting for him. The shovel swung again, catching him in the leg. He toppled over and lay groaning. Petroff stood above him, brandishing the shovel.

"Stay down."

Brooke jolted at the familiar voice. It was Jared wearing a black rock-band T-shirt, his face partially hidden by the baseball cap. With his free hand, he tugged out the earbuds and knocked the cap to the ground. Then he looked at her, his gray eyes filled with relief and concern and an intense emotion she'd never seen before. Later, she would ask him about it. For now, she was overcome with joy he was alive.

"Nice disguise," she managed. She remained sitting on the grass in no hurry to move because her head and stomach were sore from Sidorov's fists.

Jared gazed down at her. "The shirt and cap are Petroff's, but Alex's iPod was the pièce de résistance. I knew it would force Sidorov to come in close."

She thought about Latschenko's phone conversation with Petroff and his rant about dead bodies. "Where is Alex? Is he okay?"

"He's fine. Watching over Wilson, who took a bullet."

"So all that stuff Petroff told Latschenko?"

"Let's just say my gun pointed at his head encouraged him to lie convincingly. I knew I couldn't come to you, so I'd hoped to lure Latschenko here and give you time to hide in the house with Steve."

"That bastard!" Sidorov spit. "This is all his fault."

Jared's lips twisted as he looked at the Russian. "You should have left my brother alone."

"I couldn't do that. I had to protect my daughter."

"Your daughter is old enough to live her own life, make her own choices. Because of *your* choices, she'll have to visit you in prison."

Sidorov's eyes turned crafty. "Let me go. I will give you money, a lot of money."

"I'm an FBI agent, and in case you don't know, if you repeat that offer, you'll be charged with attempting to bribe a law-enforcement professional. Do you really want to add any more time to the sentence you'll be serving for the murder of Danny MacAteer and conspiracy to murder Steve Nash?"

The older man didn't have a comeback for that, but his body, which had been tense as a rabbit confronted by a dog, suddenly relaxed and his scowl transformed into a self-satisfied smirk. What did he have to feel good about? Brooke wondered. And why was his gaze trained studiously on the ground?

The hairs on the back of her neck stood up. "Jared, where's Sidorov's gun?"

He pointed with the shovel. "It fell into the hole."

With the weapon out of Sidorov's reach, there had to be a different reason for the man's changed demeanor. She scooted around on her butt until she could see back down the hill. *"Oh no."*

Her alarmed voice got Jared's attention, and he turned to look, as well. Latschenko had Steve in a headlock and was marching him up the hill at gunpoint.

"Come over and stand behind me," Jared said quietly.

Brooke did as he'd asked, appreciating the protective gesture but not convinced it would do any good. That was when she noticed his free hand—his right one—was covered in blood. That explained the awkward digging with the shovel. She wanted to ask about his injury, but realized it would be best not to draw attention to it.

Jared leaned forward. The movement rucked up his shirt, exposing a gun shoved in the back waistband of his jeans. That was what he'd been trying to tell her. With his injured hand, he couldn't make use of it, but she could, if the opportunity arose. And his body would act as a shield between her and Latschenko.

It was an incredible responsibility and one that terrified her. If she misjudged Latschenko's intentions, if she hesitated a second too long to fire, Steve or Jared would die. Jared must trust her an awful lot to reveal that gun to her.

Latschenko stopped a few yards away. Steve looked pale and scared, and his legs appeared unsteady, probably due to exhaustion from the steep climb. "I'm sorry," he said to Brooke. "I know you told me to hide, but it didn't seem right. I was so worried about you. And I thought I could get to Alex's phone in his truck."

His intentions had been good, but his getting caught was a bad thing for the very people he had wanted to save.

"Drop the shovel, FBI agent," Sidorov said, clearly gloating, "or Latschenko will shoot him."

Jared glanced back at Brooke. She had the impression he was trying to tell her something, but she couldn't understand what it was. Uncertainty and anguish passed over his face briefly before he reluctantly complied with Sidorov's demand. Sidorov got to his feet, grimacing in pain and favoring one leg.

"I warned you," he spit at Steve. "You should have taken me seriously."

Steve's expression was puzzled. "Who are you? Have we met before?"

"Do not play dumb. You know very well we have met and what we discussed."

"He doesn't remember," Jared interjected. "He hurt his head and has no memories of the past few weeks. Let him go. He's no longer a threat to anyone you know."

"It doesn't matter. He must pay for his past sins."

"His sins are nothing compared to yours."

Sidorov had the gall to laugh. "He does not have the upper hand. I do. And I will use it to crush him and you."

"I called the police with Petroff's phone." Jared's voice held conviction and a complete lack of fear. "They should be arriving any minute."

Sidorov's eyes narrowed. "You're lying."

"I'm not, but feel free to wait around and see for yourself."

The former mob boss stiffened, then glanced uneasily toward the road.

"You can go," Latschenko said. "I have the situation under control."

As he was the only one holding a gun, he had a point, Brooke thought. It would take only a matter of seconds for him to kill Jared, Steve and herself. She wondered why he was holding off. His next words explained his delay.

"It's better if you don't witness what happens next. You can say they were all alive when you left."

Sidorov nodded approvingly. "I will add another ten thousand dollars to your bonus. And the services of my attorney if you need them."

He limped down the hill, got into his Mercedes and floored it so fast on the curvy driveway that the vehicle fishtailed on the final stretch. The black car turned left onto the adjoining road and soon disappeared from view.

Jared turned his attention to Latschenko. "No matter how smart Sidorov's attorney is, he can't get you off for multiple murders."

"That assumes I get caught."

"If you somehow manage to escape today, it would only be temporary. I'm not bluffing when I tell you my colleagues at the FBI would hunt you for the rest of your life."

The thug stared at Jared for a long moment. "What happens if I don't kill you?"

"What?" Brooke blurted out. Jared and Steve exchanged wide-eyed looks. The man's question had caught them all by surprise.

Latschenko motioned to Brooke. "She said earlier if I gave up Sidorov, me and my family would get witness protection. Is that true?"

Absolutely, Brooke wanted to scream.

Jared took his time answering. "I would certainly recommend the DA cut a deal with you."

"You *would* say that. Why should I trust you?"

"Because I promise I'm not lying. If you testify against Sidorov, you and yours will be taken care of."

Latschenko seemed to accept that, because he released Steve, then passed his gun over, handle first. Jared took it with his left hand and gave it to Brooke.

Steve approached her sheepishly. "I'm really sorry I didn't hide as you suggested. Are you ready to lose that rope?"

She nodded gratefully.

He pulled a pocketknife from his jeans and proceeded to cut her wrists free.

The guy waved a hand in the direction of the house. "Sidorov told me to kill Koponov, but I couldn't do it. The guy didn't deserve to die for getting pushed into that trench. How could I explain to my boy I killed someone just because he made a mistake?"

"You did the right thing," Brooke said. "Your son can be proud of you for that."

"Yeah, he can." Latschenko smiled sheepishly. "You had me convinced, but then Sidorov showed up and I was afraid to bail."

"Why did you let him go?" Jared asked.

"I knew I'd be able to think clearer without him here, arguing and threatening. Besides, if the police are really on their way, he won't get far."

Jared turned to his brother. "Why don't you go check on Wilson? And ask Alex if the police can give us an ETA."

Steve had taken only a few steps when the wails of several sirens cut through the night, approaching fast. Two cruisers shot down the driveway, followed by an ambulance.

"Finally," Brooke said, smiling with relief at Jared.

"Better put the gun down, sweetheart," he murmured. "We don't want them to get the wrong idea."

No, there had been enough confusion today without adding to it. She placed the gun on the ground and walked alongside Jared as he led Latschenko to the police officers spilling out of the cruisers. Jared identified himself as an FBI agent and gave them a phone number to call to verify his claim. Latschenko grudgingly allowed himself to be handcuffed after Jared explained it was a short-term measure until the DA was contacted. Next, the emergency-services team was told about Wilson. "A stretcher is needed at that white building," Jared said. "Gunshot wound." He turned to the police officers. "There's also another suspect being detained by a security consultant."

"Don't forget Koponov," Brooke added. "He's unconscious at the bottom of the trench by the house. His leg looks broken."

One of the officers began issuing orders, dividing the rescue group between the workshop and the house. A moment later, he approached Jared and Brooke and identified himself as Lieutenant Travis. "Sorry we didn't get here sooner. We were en route when we came across a black Mercedes, its tires flat, a few miles from here."

"Did you see the owner?" Jared asked. "He has short brown hair, a hooked nose and heavy jaw, and he speaks with a Russian accent."

"I wouldn't know about the last part, but the rest of your description fits the guy we found in the car. Or should I say, half in the car and half out of the car."

"What do you mean?"

"We only stopped because the driver's door was open, and we could see legs sticking out onto the road."

"What happened?"

"As far as we can tell, somebody forced him to the side of the road by shooting out his tires. When he tried to exit the vehicle, he took bullets to the head and chest."

As Jared's gaze met hers, Brooke knew they had reached the same conclusion. An execution-style killing. But who had ordered Sidorov's murder and why?

It was past midnight by the time Jared, Brooke and the others had given their statements to the police and visited the hospital where Wilson had undergone emergency surgery. The bullet in his leg had been removed, and his prognosis was good, but the contractor needed to remain hospitalized for at least a week. Brooke left a message for his son, Sam, giving all the pertinent details. It was up to him to decide if he wanted to move past the troubled history with his father or not, but Sam's presence seemed like a promising start. Steve had been examined, determined to be in good physical condition, but urged to make an appointment with a doctor in Cincinnati who specialized in head injuries and memory loss. Jared had had the wound on his hand stitched and bandaged. Brooke's own injuries had been mostly bruises and aching muscles. Alex had offered to drive Steve to his sister's place, and Jared had agreed, which surprised Brooke. She'd assumed the Nash family would want to be all together for Steve's homecoming. When she questioned Jared about it, he said he would visit soon, but first he had an important matter to attend to: taking her home.

She drove his Mustang so he could rest his hand. She was on pins and needles the whole way to Columbus, wondering what Jared was thinking. He was silent for most of the trip, which only increased her tension. Usually, the conversation between them was easy and natural. Then again, most of their conversations had revolved around locating Steve and finding Sidorov's connection to his disappearance. Now that Steve was safe and Sidorov was dead, it seemed as though they had run out of words. The feelings she'd planned to confess if they survived the night were stuck in her throat. She wanted to express what was in her heart but…maybe she should hold off for a better time. As for when that better time might be, she didn't know. She wasn't even certain she would see him again. He had to get back to his job in Cincinnati, and she had to start drumming up more work for her business.

In retrospect, the past few days seemed unreal. Running from Sidorov's men, finding a dead body, nearly being killed several times. What a crazy time to fall in love. Or was she confused about what she felt? With all that adrenaline surging through her body, it only made sense that her every emotion had been amplified to an extreme. Logic dictated she question her sentiments, subject her feelings to scrutiny. However, deep down, she didn't believe the intensity of her response to her FBI protector could be explained by hormones. With Jared, she'd felt real passion, real love for the very first time. Her life would be returning to normal soon, but if he weren't willing to be a part of it, she would be heartbroken. She had to risk it all and tell him how she felt.

"So…who do you think killed Sidorov?" Not what she'd planned to say, but it was probably a good idea to get Jared talking before she sprang a "let's discuss our future" chat on him.

He turned toward her, his long legs shifting in the confined space in front of the passenger seat. "I've been giving that a lot of thought. I even texted Brent Young to see if he had any ideas."

"And did he?"

"He told me there was lots of chatter on the wiretapped phones of several former associates of Sidorov's. They said Sidorov had violated the agreement under which he was allowed to leave Brighton Beach. He was supposed to be out of the business. Instead, he was doing deals and lining his own pockets. Also, Chernov was on temporary loan from the Bratva—the Russian mafia's 'brotherhood'—to protect him from old enemies. Instead, Sidorov used him for personal reasons and wasted a valuable asset. The hit on Sidorov sends a clear message to past and present brotherhood members. *If you screw with us, you die.* They also said the bloodshed ends with Sidorov."

Brooke was thankful to hear the mafia would not carry on with more violence and murder, and she was relieved Sidorov was at the morgue, not holed up somewhere, plotting his revenge. There was only one person who might mourn his passing. "I can't help thinking about his daughter. Does she know he tried to have Steve killed? Is she sad or relieved her father's gone?"

"I wouldn't be surprised if her feelings are mixed. Despite his being a tyrant, he was still her family."

"Will you tell Steve about her?"

"I think he deserves to know. He cared about her enough to defy her father, and that's probably why Chernov was sent to kill him."

"What's going to happen to him and Wilson? Do you think the DA will believe it was self-defense?"

"I sure hope so. Chernov's criminal record substantiates he was a dangerous felon, with a history of murdering people. But if the DA decides to press charges, I'll hire the best attorney money can buy for Steve."

"I know you will."

"The things we do for family, right?" She could almost hear the smile in his voice.

Soon afterward, she saw the sign for Highway 270, which circled Columbus. She made the turn, drove for a few more minutes, then exited into the city. Traffic at this time of night was minimal, so it wasn't long before she had turned the Mustang onto her street, then pulled into her driveway.

Time to stop procrastinating and ask him straightout. Was their time together over?

She shut off the engine, gripped her hands in her lap and took a deep breath. But before she could speak, Jared had opened the passenger door.

"I'm seeing you inside. I want to make sure Latschenko's cousin isn't still lurking around."

She'd forgotten Latschenko had arranged surveillance on her house. The idea of someone watching, or worse—waiting inside—gave her the creeps. She was only renting the small redbrick two-story house, but it contained all her possessions and had come to feel like home.

She and Jared checked the interiors of the cars parked on the street, then did a full circuit of the house, passing through both front and back yards. Thankfully, there were no signs of forced entry on the doors or windows. Brooke unlocked the front door, and Jared went inside ahead of her. In less than ten minutes, they had searched the lower and upper floors and found no unwanted company. The last room they checked was the master bedroom.

As Jared headed for the walk-in closet, Brooke's gaze settled on her queen-size bed, a welcome sight with its lush pillows and cozy gold-and-blue patterned duvet. On the night table, the message light was blinking on her phone. She was in no mood to check messages tonight, but it did remind her that she needed to contact her sister. She plugged her cell-phone charger into the wall socket, then attached the cord to her cell phone. Savannah didn't answer her call, which wasn't surprising given the late hour. She left a quick message saying Sidorov was dead, everyone was safe, and Savannah could call her in the morning if she wanted more details.

"It's all good," Jared said, emerging from the closet. He started to cross the bedroom, his eyes studiously avoiding her bed.

Brooke moved toward him. "It's not *all good*."

He stopped midstride. "What do you mean?"

"You're about to leave and I don't want you to go."

"Is that so?" He rocked back on his heels, a half smile on his lips.

Was he thinking he was about to get lucky on her big bed? The idea had its appeal, given what a wonderful lover he was, but first she needed to know where they stood. If they did make use of the bed, would it be the last time and her poignant goodbye to a man whom she would never forget? "I want to talk about what happens next. With you and me."

"It's late. Wouldn't you rather have that conversation after a good night's sleep?"

It wasn't like him to procrastinate. He was the one who believed in ripping off Band-Aids fast, not slow. How much was this going to hurt? "I'm pretty sure I won't be able to sleep until we've talked." Her mouth was so dry from nerves she could barely speak. "Do you want this…thing between us to continue?"

"This 'thing'?" he said, frowning. "That's not a very flattering way to describe our relationship."

"Is that what we have?" she asked. "A relationship?"

"What would you call it?" He crossed his arms over his chest, his stance showing his growing annoyance. "And you'd better not say 'one-night stand,' because we both know that would be a lie."

"No, it's more than that."

"Damn right it is." He approached her, the tension in his face slowly easing. "Look, I know our relationship started out unconventionally, but that's not important. I don't want us to end. We can do candlelight dinners, movie nights, hikes in the woods or whatever you want. We're good together."

"Very good." So this wasn't goodbye after all. The intensity of her relief relaxed every muscle in her body, and she had to brace her legs to keep upright.

He cupped her shoulder gently with his uninjured hand. "Bottom line is I want more than a few dates. I want a committed relationship. I'm in love with you."

His confession unleashed joy in her heart. But, although his words were the ones she'd longed to hear, she couldn't resist asking, "Since when?"

He smoothed some wayward strands of hair away from her face. "I'd been trying to sort through my feelings for you for a while, but when Sidorov pulled a gun on you, I knew absolutely without a doubt I loved you. Your being in danger terrified me, and although I wanted to rush to your rescue, I knew I had to stick to my plan to disarm him or he'd have killed you."

She pressed her lips to his fingers, grateful for his discipline and resourcefulness. They could've so easily died tonight. Instead, they were alive with a bright future ahead of them.

Jared's gray eyes, which had once seemed so secretive, so enigmatic, were open wide, shining with happiness. "You're an amazing woman, and I want you in my life."

"I want that, too," she said. "I love you very much."

When he put his arms around her, she felt enveloped by the strength of his love. "I have a plan," he said, his voice low and sexy in her ear.

"Tell me," she breathed.

"How about I show you?" He moved back a little, and his left hand trailed suggestively down the buttons of her shirt.

Her lips curved. "Yes, a demo would be helpful."

His fingers zeroed in on the top button and went to work on it. It slipped from its hole without much effort, but the second resisted stubbornly. He brought his bandaged right hand up to lend assistance, but it was of no help, and he let it drop back to his side. She could sense his frustration building as he tried unsuccessfully to manage the button with one hand. "These things are too damn small," he grumbled.

"Let me do it." She gave him a little push. The backs of his legs bumped the bed, and he didn't fight the momentum, just went with it until he was sitting on the mattress. Her fingers began releasing buttons from holes.

"Okay, I'm happy to watch," he said, smiling back at her. "For a while."

She'd never done a striptease before, not even in the days when her skin had been unmarred. A sense of awkwardness assailed her. She was still wearing a cheap discount-store outfit, not to mention she hadn't had a chance to shower off the dirt from her encounter with Sidorov. Then again, neither had Jared. What would he find sexy? A bump and grind? Some swivel action? Why hadn't she thought to put on some damn music?

She undid the last button, then stalled out, the halves of her shirt hanging open with only an inch-wide strip of flesh visible.

"You're not chickening out, are you, Blondie?" Jared asked, the corner of his mouth kicking up.

His eyes dared her to keep going and bare it all. She thought about everything she had endured these past few days, up to and including fighting a former Russian mob boss with her bare hands. Getting naked for the man she loved didn't merit even a second's hesitation. "My chickening-out days are *over*," she announced. Then she shrugged out of her shirt, flung off her pants and underwear and launched herself into space, bringing him down onto his back on the mattress.

Her mouth searched out his, kissing him again and again, loving his eager response. He laughed deep in his throat and rolled her over. Then he began a very slow, very thorough exploration of her body that left her wrung out and begging for more. Every inch of her breasts tingled, and her core sizzled. She was on fire for him. Only him. If she combusted now, what a way to go.

He managed to pull off his T-shirt, but she took care—very special care—with removing his jeans and briefs and rolling on a condom. The feel of his masculinity between her hands, the hoarse sounds of his excitement, gave her a wicked thrill, one she knew she'd never tire of. As she took him deep into her body…as their thrusts grew stronger and more urgent…as they rocketed toward the ultimate pleasure, she experienced a profound sense of well-being and gratitude.

This man belonged to her, and she belonged to him. They shared a special connection, forged in danger, tempered in love. An unbreakable union of hearts, bodies and minds.

* * * * *

COMING NEXT MONTH FROM

HARLEQUIN®

ROMANTIC suspense

Available January 5, 2016

#1879 Colton Copycat Killer

The Coltons of Texas • by Marie Ferrarella

Zoe Robison has always loved Sam Colton, even though her sister almost tricked him into marriage. But when Celia is murdered—with a serial killer's mark left on her forehead—it's up to the librarian and the lawman to find justice...and true love.

#1880 Cowboy Under Fire

Cowboys of Holiday Ranch • by Carla Cassidy

When Dr. Patience Forbes is sent to Holiday Ranch to identify bones of murder victims, the romance-averse forensic anthropologist isn't looking for danger...until it finds her! Enter Forest Stevens, a cowboy who will put his own life—and heart—at risk to save hers.

#1881 Justice Hunter

Cold Case Detectives • by Jennifer Morey

Ex-cop turned rancher Lucas Curran always thought his sister's husband got away with murder. Now he's got a fresh lead in this investigation, and Rachel Delany is the key to his search. But the one woman to help Lucas crack this cold case may be the only one who can warm his heart...

#1882 Guarding His Royal Bride

Conspiracy Against the Crown • by C.J. Miller

Politician Demetrius DeSante has an ulterior motive in convincing Iliana Kracos, cousin to the Queen of Acacia, to be his wife. The bride doesn't exactly trust her new husband. But as threats to the royal family mount, the president must protect the princess he's come to love.

Finding love and buried family secrets in the Lone Star state...

Read on for a sneak preview of COLTON COPYCAT KILLER, by USA TODAY *bestselling and RITA® Award-winning author* Marie Ferrarella, *the first book in the new Harlequin® Romantic Suspense continuity* ***THE COLTONS OF TEXAS.***

Zoe didn't remember screaming.

Didn't remember pursing her lips or emitting the loud, piercing sound less than a heartbeat after she'd opened the door.

Didn't remember crossing over the threshold into the room, or bending over Celia, who was lying faceup on the floor.

The exquisite wedding dress her sister had taken such all-consuming delight in finding was now ruined. There were two glaring gunshot holes in her chest and her blood had soaked into the delicate white appliqué, all but drenching it. The pattern beneath it was completely obliterated.

The whole scene, which was whizzing by and moving in painfully slow motion at the same time, seemed totally surreal to Zoe, like some sort of an ill-conceived, macabre scene being played out from an old-fashioned grade B horror movie about a rampaging slasher.

And if the dreadfulness of all this wasn't enough, someone—the killer?—had gone on to draw a bizarre red bull's-eye on Celia's forehead. There was a single dot inside the circle, just off-center, and whoever had drawn it had used some sort of a laundry marker, so the bull's-eye stood out even more than it normally might have.

This can't be real, it just can't be real.

The desperate thought throbbed over and over again in Zoe's head. She'd just left Celia, what, a couple of minutes ago? Five minutes, tops?

How could all this have happened in such a short period of time?

Who could have done this to her sister?

Why hadn't she heard the gunshots when they were fired?

And for God's sake, what was that awful noise she was hearing now?

Zoe tried to see where it was coming from, but for some reason, she just couldn't seem to turn her head.

She couldn't even move.

The noise was surrounding her. It sounded like wailing, or, more specifically, like keening. It approximated the sound that was heard when someone's heart was breaking.

Zoe had no idea the noise she was attempting to place was coming from her.

Don't miss COLTON COPYCAT KILLER
by USA TODAY *bestselling and RITA® Award-winning author Marie Ferrarella, available January 2016 wherever Harlequin® Romantic Suspense books and ebooks are sold.*

www.Harlequin.com

HRSEXP1215

Love the Harlequin book you just read?

Your opinion matters.

Review this book on your favorite book site, review site, blog or your own social media properties and share your opinion with other readers!

Be sure to connect with us at:
Harlequin.com/Newsletters
Facebook.com/HarlequinBooks
Twitter.com/HarlequinBooks